Eternal Dominion
Book 18
Vicissitude

By Bern Dean

Contents

Morning February 12, 2268.

Alex sat down in the conference room with Kate and Tara across from him, while everyone else who lived in the house and was interested in the topic of the morning sat around the room. They had all just finished their kendo practice and Sofie had made them all breakfast burritos that could be eaten while having this meeting. Additionally, every vice guild leader was watching this meeting live and had the ability to comment directly through the secure call that Kate and Jacob had set up. Alex smiled as Kate stood and opened the meeting by making sure everyone present was clear on just what they would be deciding and why their opinions mattered.

"As I am sure you all are aware by now, FAE has been exploring the possibility of building a guild city in the state of Wyoming. Today we have hit one of the major deadlines on the project as was put forward when I first took it over and thanks to our subordinate guilds, we met the requirement of having three million members. With that the permits to build have started to be submitted and contractors are being retained for the work. What we are here to discuss is just what role we wish this city to play, before Alex meets with Eternal Dominion, Inc. early next month. Tara, if you would present the options that you and I have put together."

"Certainly," stated Tara as she stood and Kate sat. "After much consideration, we have decided that the following options are possible. First, we can have the city be used by our guild members which would allow us to recoup our expenses through only the savings that we see in our payroll. Second, we can partner with other guilds to include buildings for their members to increase our revenue over time. Third, we can build it and allow anyone who wishes to play ED full time move into it as they pay for the convenience that will be at the core of the city's design for those who intend to play ED. There are more options that could be explored, but these are the main three."

"Hold on," interrupted Mrs. Bell. "Isn't the point of a guild city to have it be for the guild's use?"

"No," replied Alex. "A guild city is meant to be for the benefit of the guild, which actually requires that as it expands, you mix in non-guild players to reduce the risks associated with it. That said, the design we have in mind will allow for us to reduce the risks associated with only having guild members housed within it to minimal levels."

"Still, letting others into what should be our center for everything brings its own risks," commented Frida (Friva). "Though if you are speaking of guilds like Hope of Rejects, I can see supporting having space made available for them at a fair rate."

"No, it will need to be a mix of guilds like theirs and either Salty Dogs, or Dragon Legion at this point," countered Sato (Takeshi). "Else it will not add enough of a deterrence for Fire Oath and Abysses End to worry about fallout from trying something."

"We may not need to worry about Fire Oath much longer if my latest information is correct," interjected Kate. "While I can't be sure, it is looking like my family's influence is starting to wane from the fallout of their actions surrounding me."

"That would be a relief," interjected Gaute (Geitir). "Don't get me wrong, I have been enjoying the constant tension that we have been under as I believe it can be a great refining fire, but a single super guild wanting to destroy us is enough."

"I would much rather see them all in ruins," retorted Frida. "But I accept that we must first reach such a position to be able to achieve that."

"Frida, while I am all for holding them in check," stated Alex while holding in a bit of his annoyance at the vendetta that she still held for most established professional guilds, "they are a needed evil, just like any governing body like ourselves."

"Yet you are fine with seeing Abysses End destroyed over a personal grievance," countered Frida.

"Would you have us become the only big fish in the pond?" interjected Amser, or whoever she was in reality as other than Kate, none of them knew her true identity. "I hate all the major powers like you do. Heck, I likely have better reason to than you, but if we remove all of them it would turn us into them. That said, making an example out of one of them will ensure that none doubt what we are capable of and I agree with Alex's decision to use Abysses End at this point."

"Alright, let's get back on topic," cut in Tara, before the conversation was completely derailed. "Are there any more comments before we vote on which form we wish our guild city to take in phase 1?"

"Yes, how are we intending to feed them all?" asked Mrs. Bell. "I mean shopping takes time and I wouldn't be surprised if a significant portion of them haven't a clue on how to cook properly."

"Why not have them enjoy the nutritional fluid that we all use while logged in and ensure every room has a VR pod installed," commented Dan. "I mean the stuff will get the job done and if they want something else, they can hit up a restaurant."

"A restaurant that we will need to be running already," commented Nicole. "Honestly, have you even looked at what it would cost to replace every meal in a month with nutritional fluid?"

"Nah, but if we buy in bulk, it can't be that much, right?" asked Dan while looking at Alex.

"If we ignore the cost of Sofie, one bag of nutritional fluid costs the same as your daily food intake and will only let you skip lunch," interjected Kate. "Even if we could buy it in bulk, it would make no sense to expect anyone to live off the stuff when even instant ramen is more satisfying. You need to remember that eating is as much about enjoying it as getting the nutrition that the body needs for most. That said, we shouldn't ignore the issue of how we plan to feed everyone who resides in our guild city as we will be running every retail space."

"Just how many is that?" asked Henry (Casmir).

"The bottom floor of all fifty apartment buildings that will be designed to have 300 rooms and up to 1,200 occupants if we go four members per room."

"Talk about packed in like sardines," commented Fred. "Who-"

"That's cute," interrupted Sabrina (Lily), sounding slightly annoyed. "How many bathrooms per room?"

"There are three- and two-bedroom units and there is one toilet per room, but the two bedroom units only have one full bath, while the three bedroom units have two full baths," answered Kate. "We also don't intend on packing rooms that full as regardless of the conditions you found yourself in Indonesia, FAE wants to set the standards high for the other guilds who copy us."

"Good," commented Frida. "I was worried that you were acting like you were still part of Fire Oath for a second."

"Frida, there will be some rooms that are packed that tightly," interjected Alex. "Just not in phase 1 as we will be focused on housing our core members and their families at first. After that, dorm-style housing will be built with the intent of housing those who are single and trying to rise in the ranks. That said, I never want to see anyone stay in those for over five years before moving into their own rooms or leaving the city."

"You would kick them out?" questioned Amanda. "That seems a bit harsh."

"It is, but it is also necessary," supplied Kate. "Though it won't be as simple as that. The point is that after five years in the dorms, if they haven't succeeded in finding a role that offers enough value to FAE to justify moving them into their own room, they aren't likely to. To be clear, they don't need to be a top player to be of value. They can find a job inside the city and earn enough to rent a unit as we will need a labor force in reality as well."

"We will, though I wish to give priority to any of our core members' spouses at first," commented Alex. "Now back to the food issue and we will vote about how we want phase 1 to be filled."

"Why don't we just have a cafeteria set up in every building where everyone can eat?" asked Dan.

"Dan, have you ever enjoyed a meal out of a cafeteria?" questioned Sam looking at him with a frown.

"Yah, I mean they have nothing on what we are eating here, but they were just fine."

"Anna, good luck to you," quipped Sam. "I may be worthless at cooking, but even the disasters that I made the few times I tried were better than what a school cafeteria offered."

"I don't know what you mean," replied Anna. "It just means that he will be easy to please."

"Right, hey Dan, when was the last time you ate anything that wasn't made by a top-class chef, or at least a decent restaurant?"

At Sam's question Dan thought for a moment before replying.

"Had to be when we were out in California for Christmas and stopped for a quick burger, oh, crap!"

"That's right, it tasted worse than it had before, didn't it."

"So, it's not like it was terrible, it just didn't sit well after."

"Face it, we have been spoiled and I for one don't want to force others to eat what I wouldn't. Don't get me wrong, I agree that there should be some places like that where our members can get a cheap meal, but there needs to be better options as well."

"Sam is right," agreed Alex. "The real question isn't how many restaurants we will have, but what our base meal plan will look like and how to let them decide which plan is right for them."

"Why not give them the option between cooking their own meal that FAE has already prepped and a cafeteria meal?" asked Mrs. Bell. "We could likely even partner with a company that already does them and save time and setup costs."

"Mom, we will be handling everything we possibly can as we need to create jobs for those who are married to our top players and their teenage kids. Now if we were doing powdered meal replacement shakes then I would agree to outsource it to an expert, but portioning ingredients to make cooking easy is something that I would like to have done by us."

After Alex's words the room was quiet for a second until Tara spoke up.

"Why not simply offer all of the above for different amounts, with all orders needing to be submitted a month in advance to ensure logistics are handled. Then we can drop pre-prepped meals off once a week, with different buildings being served each day of the week while ensuring that everything is fresh."

"So what if they don't order anything to eat? Do they have to eat out?" asked Dan.

"No, we will still have a few grocery stores for those who don't want to deal with a limited menu," replied Tara. "It would just let cafeterias know what to expect each day and take care of the food plans..."

Alex just sighed as this once more led to a circular conversation for a while, before ending in what Alex considered a half answer that solved the issue for now. As either way it added areas for the food to be prepped to the detailed design and they would need to investigate meal replacement options. Though he had also seen Nicole and his mother happily chatting about ideas for meals that could be prepped and delivered for others to cook. With that settled, it was time for those with a vote on how to allocate space in the guild city. For this Alex had given himself three votes, Kate and Gaute each had two votes as stakeholders of FAE and vice guild leaders, while the other vice guild leaders had a single vote with Sam, Nicole, Dan, Fred and Amanda having the ability to collectively break a tie, but nothing else.

In total there were 20 and when the first vote came back, it was 11 for opening areas for other guilds and nine against it. Alex knew that he and Kate had accounted for five of the votes in favor of allowing space for other guilds from the start, but he was unsure of how the rest had shaken out, though he had a decent idea. Still, with that taken care of, they shifted to a vote on just how many of the 50 buildings, with 300 rooms each, should be made available for external powers. The options ranged from ten to 50 percent and an average of the votes would be taken and rounded to the nearest even number. Though it wasn't necessary as the final number was 18 percent, or nine buildings in total.

With that taken care of, the meeting shifted to the final thoughts before coming to a close, with a few comments of dissatisfaction on just how much room would be filled by other guilds. Still, Alex was satisfied with the result as he made his way upstairs with Sam, Nicole, Ava, Mia and Kate to have their own discussion. At 30 weeks pregnant with twins, Ava and Mia were already sporting bellies that were more pronounced than either Sam's or Nicole's had been as they were helped up to their private area of the house after an elevator ride to the second floor from the basement. When they were finally all in the twins' room, Ava and Mia were also the first to speak.

"We are not enjoying those stairs anymore."

"Yeah, next time when we say that things will be fine without an elevator, tell us to shut up."

"Alright, then I take it you are both in favor of moving into the guild city when it's ready," commented Kate. "As for the rest of us, where do we stand?"

"Is there really any question?" asked Sam rhetorically. "I mean we will still be living in a private building, right?"

"Yes, at least for the most part," replied Kate. "The first floor will be a reception area and we will have offices and other facilities housed there, but the higher they go the more restricted the area will be."

"I don't know, I hear that winters can be harsh in Wyoming," stated Nicole. "I mean they aren't nothing here, but I still miss the beach and didn't mind avoiding a white Christmas last year."

"Got it, add a vacation home somewhere that is warm in the winter to the list of possible needs."

"Or we could just pick a resort and invade them every

winter," commented Sam. "I mean we are about to be a family of 11 and if we bring child care along, we are looking at at least 20 people and needing several rooms just to enjoy ourselves."

"Won't happen at all in the next few years," commented Alex. "Honestly, until we have either reached tier-8, or determined that doing so is beyond us, I don't see us taking many family vacations in reality."

"That's fine," commented Ava.

"Yeah, we are missing half the family anyways," added Mia.

"After all, we can't take Enye, Dyllis, Mari, Lingxin or their kids with us either way."

"Oh, and don't forget Eira and Aila and possibly Daisy, Violet and a few others."

"Speaking of family."

"Kate, did you manage to find anything about the guy talking with Lydia?"

"Yes, but it is taking a while. All I can say for sure is that he is real and nothing is jumping out that says he is anything other than what your mom said he was, but it will take more time. I don't have the resources that I had before I left the Astor family and the ones that I do have that share a connection with the Astors have been excessively busy."

"Do we know what is going on with Jasper yet?" asked Alex.

"No, my father seems to be content with allowing the elders to rip the family apart as they support different possible replacements for him. Still, it seems like the candidates are too busy trying to undercut each other to focus on us at this point."

"If you were him, what would your goal be if he set this in motion?" asked Nicole.

"Either leave the house in ruins, or eliminate those who are only bringing harm to the house," replied Kate. "Honestly, he could just be keeping them busy and focused on something other than me."

"Kate, we both know that isn't the case," interjected Alex. "No, if I had to bet, his goal is for them to decide that none of the options are any good and hope that they find a way to lure us back in."

"They would need to be pretty desperate to be willing to accept any conditions that all of us would be fine with," replied Kate. "Though, if they see themselves as about to fade into obscurity, they just might be willing to make such concessions."

"Oh, what, like not see the four of us as eyesores?" asked Sam angrily. "I say let them fall apart. Our kids don't need their BS."

"Agreed," added Nicole. "I think our lives are already complicated enough as things are. Adding whatever would come from even associating with them is more than I am willing to do at this point."

"They had their chance and they blew it," stated Ava.

"Besides, we are going to create something even better than the Astor family," commented Mia.

"The Astor family is going to wish they were us."

"Aren't they, Alex."

"Perhaps, but I am not so foolhardy to believe that any future is set in stone as if my memories are to be trusted, even I don't know what lies in front of us now."

At Alex's words everyone got quiet as they all thought about their meaning, until he sighed and continued to speak.

"For now, I am going to say that so long as my meeting with Eternal Dominion, Inc. goes well, that we will be moving to Wyoming when the guild city is livable. Kate, I will leave how to allocate the nine buildings to you and just trust that you have it under control. Now let's leave things there and get back into ED."

After a few nods, the conversation ended. With a few smiles, followed by hugs and kisses, the morning logout came to an end as they all made their way to log in to ED for the day.

(*****)

ED Year 5 Day 267.

As Xeal and everyone in his party but Lucy left his home in Hardt Burgh, he was still thinking over the implications of what Kate had learned about her family. This continued until they arrived at the meeting point and were joined by Lucy. She had been selected to act as a temporary party member until Xeal reached a level where the NPC cleric that was meant to join his party wouldn't be ten-plus levels above him. This was done due to the severe penalties to his experience gains, from partnering with any NPC ten or more levels above him. Especially a cleric, as even them healing him between battles would be counted as contributing to the battle. Therefore, he couldn't just have them hang back unless necessary like he had with the dragonoid women. Still, he had been surprised by the skill of Lucy, who was a cleric of Asclepius and his five daughters, Hygieia, Aceso, Iaso, Aegle and Panacea, as she had been far more competent than the reports he had on her had shown and they were already promising. As he arrived, Xeal was pulled out of his thoughts by Lucy speaking in a tone that did little to hide her frustrations.

"I trust that your meeting with all FAE's vice guild leaders went well."

The emphasis on the words vice guild leader instantly clued Xeal in on the issue as he turned his focus to Lucy as he responded.

"It could have been better, but I can't complain as I sought out individuals who would stand by their values and not simply do what I wish when asked for their opinions."

"Is that why I didn't make the cut?

"Lucy-"

"I'm a big girl and would rather know just where things stood. After all, I didn't get the nod for your vice guild leader training program."

"Lucy, there are many factors that were taken into account for that one and trust me when I say that you were one of the few that were excluded for a reason other than your abilities."

"So you really are wary of any clerics outside of those associated with Freya and Eileithyia. Should I be worried about my long-term role in FAE?"

"I am wary of everyone outside those who are in my true inner circle. If one of them stabs me in the back, I only have my own hubris to blame. As for your future in FAE, I would say that you are well on your way to being one of the top 1,000 leaders of the guild, even if you end up not working out as Caleb's direct subordinate."

"Right, yet you offered Vento a chance to try out for the top ten vice guild leaders, or whatever you called it."

"Blame Ignis for that. After all, he was the one who started to have Vento do his paperwork whenever possible. Still, he turned it down. That said, do we need to clear the air before we work together for the next few months?"

"Sorry, that has just been eating at me as I couldn't believe I was less capable than Vento."

"Alright, everyone but Eira give Lucy and I some space as we work through this, and Lucy, yes Eira stays because I will keep nothing from her, or my other wives."

With that Xeal walked with Lucy and Eira to a nearby tavern and rented a room to talk. Once they were inside the room and the door was closed, Lucy launched straight into her gripe such that Xeal could tell she was doing her best to avoid yelling.

"Alright, you wanted to clear the air. Well, Caleb is a slave driver and I am about the only one who has been able to deal with his demands. It's why you have likely seen him replacing at least one of his ten lieutenant slots every week. I get it, you are dumping a ton of work on him and the others and he is great at coming up with ideas that have great results, but you try to execute them. Every time I ask him how he got a slot to attempt to become a vice guild leader he gets awkward about it and all I can figure is that you don't want clerics in that role. So you tell me, what do Leaena, Asa, Felicius, Saima, Caleb and Catriona have that I don't?"

"Nothing, as it is that you are a cleric and like all divine magic classes you are bound to a god. That is a two-way road and you can in essence act as their eyes and ears should they wish to look in on you."

"What do you have to hide at this point that a god will care about and why is Freya fine?"

"I am tied to Freya through Gale, whether I like it or not. As for right now, or in the future, it doesn't matter as the last thing I need to deal with is a god who covets something that FAE has, or decides that our interests are in opposition to each other. Heck, I am even reducing Gale and Clara to part time as they will be simply stepping in to cover for others' vacations when needed now, to limit some of their access."

Xeal could tell Lucy wasn't satisfied as she thought and seemed to hesitate before responding.

"I need you both to sign this. All it says it that you aren't going to fire me for saying what I am about to, or share it with anyone."

Xeal sighed as he knew what was likely coming, as he had picked up the signs of it from her performance the past month and some change that they had been grinding together in ED. Still, it was hers to share so he stayed neutral as he replied.

"No, I will promise to not fire you, or take any other negative action against you regarding it and to treat it the same as I do with any guild secret. Also, my response needs to be held in confidence as well."

"Fine, write up the contract."

"What if I don't want to sign?" asked Eira.

"Eira, you need to, or step outside for a moment," replied Xeal.

"I will step out. I don't like keeping too many people's secrets. Yours are already enough."

Xeal just shook his head as she left the room and he signed the contract with Lucy before she continued.

"I am a divine scion for Aceso and am aware that Gale is likely one for Freya and you and several others are marked by some sort of primordial. So, if that is the big secret you don't have to worry about it as I have no intent to blab and neither will Aceso, so long as you promise to ensure that I am safe."

"And? I'm sorry, but while I didn't know that it was Aceso, I could tell that you had become a vessel for one of the five. Now, did Aceso tell you why she chose you?"

"No, but I am almost sure it has to do with getting close to you and what do you mean you knew? I have been trying to impress you since I joined this party, but you've said nothing."

"Some things are better not asked about. If you wanted me to know for sure you would have said something. As for Aceso, I hope she enjoys the next few months. As for keeping you safe, take this and tell her that I am not afraid to have to face a god. After all, I am just as unkillable as they are and I know that they are currently tied up and need to rely on their clergy here to act. Also, I am not sharing this with anyone but Kate who already knows and already started to monitor the movements of your faith."

"What are you expecting, a religious war, or something?"

"Several of them to be honest. That and much more in the coming decades. I am sure you already know this, but you and Gale are prime targets for assassination to level 0. As such you should really have Aceso seek to align herself with Freya, even if it puts her at odds with her sisters and the rest of her pantheon."

"Are you trying to cause the gods to start a war of their own?"

"Again, they can't right now. Too much of their power is needed to hold back the primordials. Also, this hasn't helped your case to be one of the ten, as it just adds to the risk level for myself."

Lucy didn't respond right away as she frowned while looking at Xeal like she wasn't impressed by his response.

"Look at me all you like, but why do you want the job so bad anyways?"

"Because I know I can do the job and if I don't get in now, I never will."

Xeal paused as he looked at Lucy and her determination as he knew she wasn't wrong, then responded.

"Fine. I will give you a shot if Kate approves as she is always involved, and you get Aceso to seek out Freya and sign a contract between the two of them that they agree to work together and not hinder my actions."

"You trust Freya that much?"

"I have met her when I was sent flying by that giant snake and ended up in Fólkvangr. I can't say the same for Aceso, though I am sure she is watching this right now."

Xeal smiled as Lucy paused as she clearly received a message from Aceso before she spoke once more.

"She says she is and it is a good thing that you went to Freya and not the other way around. As for her making a deal with her, she will think about it if Kate agrees."

"Oh, and one other thing, not that I think you intend to, but if you attempt to make a move romantically on me I will ensure that you regret it."

"Okay, was that to me, or Aceso?"

"Both. Now let's get going. I am sure we both have a lot to think about."

"Thank you."

"For what? Lucy, you still need to convince Kate that letting you into the inner circle is worth the risk and I mean it. Even Freya has found herself being blocked off from certain meetings of guild leadership. It is why I doubt that you will ever be one of the main ten as that would have you managing ten percent of FAE and that is a major risk. My intent was to see if you made the cut to remain one level below that as a junior vice guild leader when the positions became official and have you handle around one percent of the guild."

Lucy blinked a few times as she realized that Xeal hadn't been ignoring her talent, before frowning and sounding annoyed as she responded.

"You could have told me that!"

"No, as if I did and something happened to where you didn't make the cut, when the time came to select them you would have been really pissed. Now, let's go and get some grinding out of the way before you meet with Kate to discuss this."

With that Xeal left the room as they found Eira looking smug as she spoke.

"So which goddess is she the vessel of?"

"Damn it, does the whole party know?" asked Lucy.

"Please, you are far too obvious for any of us to miss it," retorted Eira. "The real question is if this will affect our plans?"

With that Eira turned and left as Xeal chuckled, while

Lucy looked worried as they rejoined the group, though nothing was said beyond that as they returned to the dungeon in the center of the Mist Woods. Like the monsters on the exterior the dungeon, or what Xeal considered the true entrance to this dungeon, it was full of monsters that had a feeling of being a perversion of nature to them. Though whereas you would find living trees and other plant-themed monsters above, fungus-type monsters had mostly replaced them, though there were root-type monsters as well. Part of the challenge with these monsters beyond that they were mixed in with worms, ants and other bug-type monsters that one might find underground, were the spores. The effects of these spores could be anything from simple poison, paralysis, or even full-body control as most of the bugs had learned. Especially the first that they faced that day that consisted of six level 193 giant ants that had white funguses growing out of them and were essentially living zombies.

With only Xeal, Rina and Eira on the front line, and Dafasli acting as the guard for Bula, Lucy, Alea, Daisy and Violet, this was about the limit of what the party could handle. Especially with only Xeal and Lucy having the advantage of balance-breaking stats, as Eira and Rina were simply focused on keeping two of the six fungus-infested ants occupied while Daisy and Violet buffed them. Xeal, meanwhile, was keeping one busy while focusing the damage on the other ant he was facing, while Bula and Alea focused on supporting him as Lucy healed anyone who dropped below 80% health. Like this they were able to kill the first ant, and from there things became easy as Xeal could focus on a single foe before focusing on the ones that Eira and Rina were facing. Xeal was missing the support that the massive party he used to be a part of had given him, as he looked through the loot that his alchemy players would turn into useful items at a later date. Even so, each ant was worth around ten gold at the current market rate, due to how few players could face this level of foe, which was part of how Xeal justified the expenses that it took to support his party.

The rest of the time grinding was uneventful as they avoided ant groups that were too powerful or large for them, as they focused on gaining experience. Besides Xeal's group, only the group that consisted of a mix of orcs, led by Narfu, beast-men that consisted of several new tier-7 members of their tribes, Ceclie and a few elves, were this deep in the dungeon. Originally it had just been meant to be Ceclie and Narfu's group, but after some considerations, the new group had been formed through whatever arrangements Kate had made. All she had told Xeal and all he needed to know, was that the group was being developed to be part of any plans to attack the subterranean world. The fact that Queen Aila Lorafir had provided elves to partake in the group hadn't been without a few issues as they interacted with Ceclie. Though, her being bound to Xeal in a way that they all knew was even worse than any contract with a devil that didn't involve a soul could be, had allowed them to believe she wouldn't betray them. However, Xeal hadn't appreciated the comments the elves had directed at him as they wondered if he was worthy to have the contact that he did with their queen, or princess.

Still, Xeal hadn't let this bother him as he made sure the whole team wouldn't get in over their head as they focused on foes that were under their own level for the time being. While this was a much slower leveling pace and didn't allow them to hone their skills as much, it was also how most NPCs operated in this world due to the permanence of their deaths. It was also why there were so few NPCs who ever rose above tier-5 and why just a few tier-8 NPCs could force nations to pause before making any plans of war. Sadly, once players started to reach tier-7, the numbers would finally exist to overwhelm these tier-8 deterrents if they weren't careful. It was the first wave of this that Xeal hoped to take advantage of to push the momentum of the war completely in Nium's direction during the early days of the fighting.

With another successful day of grinding behind him, Xeal sat in front of the stacks of documents that he was working through. Most of these were reports that Taya and Kate had put together that only required a ten to 30-minute reading from him before he approved the request. Included in this today was the final report from Taya, on the curing of the noble-blooded vampires that they had captured. Like the first one, all of them had issues once they had a soul again, though it was unclear if they had retrieved their old souls, or if Arnhylde and Taya had created something new. The report noted that they all seemed to have similar feelings of guilt and wanting to die at first, while they each reacted to therapy differently. This had led to the theory of it being a newly created soul and it settling into the body before adjusting to the mind it was connected to.

The exception to this had been the female vampire, who had received a single drop of Xeal's blood on a regular basis, as she had undergone a metamorphosis when they had cured her. Taya had called it kind of a half cure as the closest thing she resembled was a dhampir, though she was far more powerful than one, or even as she had been as a vampire. She had also not lost a significant portion of her levels like the rest of those who had been cured and seemed to show remorse for the lives she had taken, but not to the level of wishing to die. While they were still studying her and had noticed things like while she wasn't harmed by the sun, she did dislike it. It seemed that she was something new and unique. At the end of this was a note stating that she, who was named Amelie Mavis, wished to have a chance to speak with Xeal as soon as possible.

It was while Xeal was considering this that Kate entered the room with Gale, looking like she had just come up with a plot that she would love, but Xeal would hate. Gale, on the other hand, looked like she had a headache and just wanted to sleep as Xeal stood and gave them both a hug and a kiss in greeting. At this Gale had taken an extra minute holding Xeal before she let him escape as they all sat and Kate started to speak.

"Well, I have to say that Lucy has my approval to start working as your direct assistant and vice guild leader. Gale, if you would share what Freya told you."

"She has placed Aceso under a contract that not even a deity can ignore, as being subordinate to her in return for Lucy falling under your protection. Part of this is that you must supply her with a drop of phoenix blood and accept the vessels of her sisters should they agree to the same terms."

"Alright, so why do you seem so annoyed while Kate seems so happy?" asked Xeal.

"Because, while Lucy will be acting as the head of the division that Kate wants to create, it will be me who has to act as the figurehead of it."

"What Gale means is that if things continue like this and more deities align themselves with Freya to gain safety for their vessels from you, we will need to facilitate their growth and prepare for when they are discovered. For that I am proposing that we create a division that will focus on keeping tabs on all the various faiths that exist in ED and their movements."

"No," replied Xeal. "If you want to gather any vessels of

deities that have aligned themselves under Freya and have Lucy manage them, that's fine, but we are not going to seek them out. Having Gale and Lucy here already risks things getting out of hand, but all that will be gained from adding more divine scions is more eyes on us as we risk sparking a religious war. I don't know about you, but I would rather not have one of those break out before Nium has secured the whole of the continent."

"We may not have a choice in the matter," groaned Gale. "Now that Aceso has become Freya's subordinate, it is only a matter of time before factions start to form and the current pantheons are ripped apart."

Xeal wanted to groan as he had expected Freya to pursue a secret alliance, but it seemed that things were moving far quicker than they should be. With a sigh, he looked at Gale with a stern look that was directed at Freya as he spoke next.

"I know you're listening so, just how long do we have?"

After a pause, Gale frowned before she passed along Freya's answer.

"She says that we still have at least half a decade to stabilize things before the gods will be ready for war. Apparently, most have likely not created a divine scion due to the chaos our kind adds to the equation and will be focused on that. Also, they will all be trying to place their bets on the winner, which will highlight FAE even more and she needs you to promise that while you will use the power of Watcher and the phoenixes, you won't aid them in escaping."

"She is looking to become queen of the gods. So long as the gods don't meddle in the affairs of this plane any more directly than having divine scions and clergy do their bidding, I can agree to that, with the exception of Levina. As I can control her completely if I wish and if I can gain the same control over the others, I will treat them the same."

"She has been begging you to visit by the way," commented Kate. "I'm sorry, I had made a deal with her that the next time you said her name in my presence I would pass along the message."

"She should just be grateful that you are even willing to visit her after what she pulled," retorted Xeal.

"Still, if you intend on her being your mount one day, it would be better if she was at least willing when the time came."

"I am not sleeping with her."

Kate had to hold in a laugh as she looked as Xeal before she responded.

"I'll remember that after another 100 years in this world has passed and you are starting to waver on that. Though by that time you would likely have already given in to Bing and a few of the others before looking at Levina."

"Alright, let's get off that topic," interjected Gale. "I think the 11 that he has, one that is almost in and who knows how many that are looking at making a move, are enough women to deal with without adding eternal and all-powerful primordials to the list."

"Agreed," stated Xeal. "Now, about the divine scions…"

Xeal, Kate and Gale continued to discuss things about just what Lucy would be put in charge of and how they were going to prep for the conflict that was inevitable at this point. With this, Xeal sighed as he told Kate to have all of the drops of phoenix blood collected, as if they started to attract more divine scions, they would need them. With that he would have a total of 27 drops, though two would be from Brangwen and needed to be used as pseudo marks and he wasn't about to not keep a stockpile for his NPC wives, no matter what anyone said. Still, when they had finished, Xeal felt that they had a reasonable plan put together and could only hope that things didn't spiral out of control. However, he could only remember a few religious wars from his last life and they had never ended well for the countries that found themselves in the center of them.

With that taken care of, it was time for the next and last item on Xeal's to-do list for the session, which was to have Bula join the three of them to discuss having her become Freya's oracle. When Bula entered, it was clear that she was wondering what it was for as she greeted them. Xeal doubted that her ability to access her sight, as it currently was, would support this discussion in the slightest. In fact, Xeal expected it to show her nothing but horrific outcomes if she even entertained the idea of what he was going to offer her. Still, she joined the others as she sat in an armchair in Xeal's office as she waited to hear why she had been called as Xeal started the conversation.

"Bula, how has your ability to access the sight been affected since we met Laplace?"

"When it comes to simple things it has been fine, but when I try to look towards the war, or anything of consequence, it has become far murkier."

"That is about what I would expect-"

"Please don't abandon me," pleaded Bula before Xeal could finish speaking. "I know that without my gift of sight I am of no use to you, but-"

"Bula, I would no sooner cast you aside than cut off my own arm," stated Xeal as he cut off her rambling before it could really get going. "I do not know what your sight has been showing you since then, but we have a way to free you from Laplace while still allowing you to access the sight."

"Impossible… can you truly free me from him?"

"Yes, though you would be binding yourself to another," cut in Kate. "Freya and Gale, to be precise, as it would be through them that you would make your new bargain."

"What kind of bargain are we speaking of?"

At Bula's question, Xeal and Kate looked at Gale who sighed before speaking.

"You would need to convert your entire tribe into followers of Freya and in return you will become her oracle. At the same time, you will be freed from losing your sight and never having a family."

Bula just blinked as she took in what Gale was saying, before frowning and speaking in an unsteady voice.

"Freya may be a goddess of war, but I'm not sure that she would be a fit for my people as a whole, as we are the kind to deny her other side when it comes to the right of breeding."

Xeal could tell that she was refusing to accept the offer that was before her as real as Gale responded to her.

"It will be fine as long as they worship the war side of her and her clergy be given an alternate status in your tribe. She is even fine if only women are allowed to become her cleric, or champion. Though she does warn that she will laugh when your people become ruled by a chiefess if they do so as she intends, to have your line all serve her after she cuts off Laplace completely from them. That said, will you be able to handle the other requirements that worshiping Freya will have for you as an individual and know you needn't alter your current arrangement if it is as intimate as it seems to be?"

"I see, though how would I become a mother as things currently are?"

"That can wait until after the war," interjected Xeal. "As you said yourself, that may be when it is time for you to part from me. Perhaps Alea and Rina could return to your tribe with you until you find an orc worthy of you."

"What if I don't wish for my partner to be an orc?"

"No," replied Kate. "You are going to essentially become a figure that will be seen as the mother of what your tribe will become. To not solidify your position by finding a husband from within it will only create divisions that could fracture your people and lead to their decline and eventual end."

"Only if my partner can't make every orc accept that they are no match for them," countered Bula while looking at Xeal.

"Bula, please do not walk a path that will lead to you seeking a place in my bed, as it will not end well for anyone."

"Yet you admit there is a path that will take me there."

"No, there is a possibility as I have long since learned not to believe that there is never one, especially as Daisy and Violet have started to gain more support from my wives, even if only a little."

"Hey, they are doing everything according to what we asked them to," retorted Gale. "If anything, blame yourself for saying you would run away at 20 wives and not 13. However, Bula, if you do decide to walk the path of chasing Xeal, it will come at the cost of your people as you will never return to them for more than a visit and they will need you to guide them during this transition."

"How am I to do that if there is a war raging and I am with Xeal?"

"Gale is speaking about after your father passes," commented Kate. "He will be able to see them through the war as the first generation of her clergy is raised, but you will need to lead them as they start their journey."

Bula looked like she was struggling with something as

she thought over the situation, until tears formed in the otherwise stoic orcess' eyes as she lost the battle against her emotions. Xeal, Gale and Kate simply remained quiet as she worked her way through the myriad of possibilities she had in front of her, and what each path would cost her until she finally spoke.

"I feel as if I am being told either sacrifice my people, or take the hope that is being offered to me and trade it for shackles. Xeal, I have no attraction to my own kind. I never have. A part of my upbringing was to condition me to never prize what they all pursue to attract a woman. It was only after I began to travel with you that I found myself attracted to a man in any way that threatened to have me surrender my gift. Only, I knew that it needed to wait until after the war to even consider it. It is why I was expecting to part ways then, as I saw only a few visions that had you accepting me and many that had you rejecting me. So, while I will not expect you to accept me, please do not make me accept the fate of becoming the strongest of my kind's prize either. As that is what I will become if I do not return with a child in my arms if I am freed from the curse of never knowing the touch of a man."

"Is it only your kind's ways, or is it also appearance that is off-putting to you?" asked Kate.

"I could care less about their appearance. If Xeal grew horns and started to look like a dragonoid I would still feel the same towards him."

"Alright, sounds like we need to introduce you to some of our players who have become orcs," replied Kate. "And no, if things don't work out between you and them we will not simply let you make a pass at Xeal. If I were you, I would kill that hope now if you hope to survive what Eira is likely to put you through over the next several years. I still can't believe he went along with the flow and married her like that."

"Hey, I am a Duke and we would have been seen as married in her people's eyes the moment we joined as man and woman either way," countered Xeal. "It wasn't like I would have done anything other than insult my wives' honor had I done otherwise."

Kate just gave Xeal a look that told him she was still not done with this subject, but it had played its role already as she turned to Bula and continued.

"So, what will it be, Bula? Are you willing to accept the offer, or are you going to let it pass you by?"

"I need to speak with my father before I can answer for my people, and I believe Xeal and Gale will be needed there as well. As for meeting the members of FAE who have become orcs, I will only ask that you not insult me with anyone that would treat this world any less real than Xeal does."

"Very well, I will add it to my list of things to handle when I first return tomorrow," replied Xeal. "Kate, let Taya know that I will meet with the former vampire Amelie before I set off to meet with chief Xuk."

"Alright, I will take care of that and getting Lucy set up to start working as a vice guild leader."

The smile Kate had as she said that last part made Xeal almost pity what Kate had in store for Lucy, but she had asked for it, so he intended to see how long it took for her to regret it. With all of that settled, Xeal made his way to spend an hour or so with his wives before it was time to log off, though he was still getting used to Eira being present. Especially as the others were letting her dominate his attention more than was typically allowed in the setting, due to her not getting a full honeymoon and them only having just married.

(*****)

Evening February 12 to Evening February 28, 2268 & ED Year 5 Days 268-317.

Alex found himself spending most of his time in reality split between watching his daughters, dating Ava, Mia, Sam, Nicole and Kate, exercising and going over the plans for the guild city with Kate. While he found most of that to be enjoyable, he also gradually found that he never had a moment to himself, especially as Ava and Mia enjoyed the extra care they needed from him. The first time this had really hit him was during the stay-in Valentine's Day date he enjoyed, with all five of his ladies and himself relaxing in the twins' room and their tub. While it was an enjoyable time, he found himself realizing that every moment of his time involved at least one of them in reality. Morning exercise currently had Kate, Sam and Nicole taking turns with him and after that, he and Kate would bring breakfast up to Ava and Mia as Sam and Nicole took care of their daughters. After that, he would relieve Sam and Nicole with Kate as he spent time with his daughters. This was also when Kate would give Alex updates on the progress of the guild city. Subsequently, he would log onto ED until evening, when he would enjoy dinner with everyone before spending some time with whoever's night it was, or with the group playing games.

This schedule repeated each day save for when they celebrated Amanda's birthday on the 19th, and the 20th when he accompanied Ava and Mia to their seventh OB-GYN appointment. At 31 weeks nothing much had changed besides the size of their bellies and the difficulty they had moving about. Still, they were all smiles as they talked about the little ones that were only at most a bit over two months away. By the end of the appointment, both of them had been smiling and just enjoying the little details that they had been told as Alex appreciated and shared the moment with them, but still he was craving some time alone. Time that he was still not able to find by the night of the 28th and didn't know when he finally would as he remembered how in his last life he had craved just the opposite and laughed to himself at the irony.

When Xeal returned to ED on day 268, the first thing he did after spending a few moments with his family was head to the cell-like room where Amelie was being held even now. There were even still two royal knights that stood watch over the hall where the room was located, just in case the now ex-vampire decided to attempt to escape. Still, as Xeal opened the door, what he found surprised him as he took in the scene and clear differences that were present before him. Sitting calmly in an armchair with a book, while being bound to the floor by a shackle on her ankle, was an ageless form with pure white hair that radiated a calming presence. As she looked at Xeal, he struggled to fully take in the changes that had occurred as his memory and the figure before him didn't match at all as she started to speak to him.

"Thank you for honoring my request. It really means a lot to be able to meet with you like this and yes, I know that I have undergone quite the change. Though I hold no grudge against you, I do place the blame of this upon you for submitting me to all of those tests while being sustained solely by a drop of your blood each week."

"Did they not even bring you animal blood, or any other form of sustenance?" asked Xeal in confusion.

"They did, but your blood made the others taste like bile. Besides, I had long since learned how to live off of a single drop each month, with us only having frozen stock left. So, a drop of fresh blood each week felt like a feast at first and why would I wish to ingest that which disgusts me when I am already satisfied with my meal?"

"Alright, I am sure you didn't wish to speak about my blood, so what is it that you wanted to speak to me on?"

"Straight to business. Very well, I wish to hear from you what my future holds. It is clear even to me that whatever I have become, it is not human and I have no desire to return to an existence as one. For better, or worse, I still crave blood, though my heart beats and I need food like any mortal would as well and I know that means that freedom is something that I will never taste. Now knowing that, as you are the first that I have let know about the fact that the thirst remains and that I am forcing myself to not attempt to drink your blood as we speak, what is to become of me?"

"Is your thirst such that it worsens each day?"

"No, it stayed the same until you entered the room, at which point it is getting more intense."

"It is only when I enter the room?"

"No, but it is the strongest I have felt this urge. However, I think that is due to me remembering how yours tasted so much better than any that I can remember."

"To me it sounds like you are a recovering addict who is having your drug of choice placed before you. Now the question is what we are to do with that. You're right that as you are now, living like a human would be a mistake and I would say that you would be happier underground. So, the questions are what do you want, whether or not I can trust you and just what are you?"

"I want to be allowed to continue to indulge in your

blood, preferably more than a single drop a week. I am willing to do whatever you would ask of me that isn't a death sentence, or a form of torture, to gain your trust. As for what I am, who knows? Perhaps I am something truly unique, or a whole new form of evil that will replace vampires in the nightmares of mortals."

Xeal frowned as he thought over her answers as he was happy that she was at least not outright lying, but she was being deliberately vague and that bothered him.

"I am sorry, but I can agree to none of that as to me it seems as if your goal is simply to get as close to me as possible. Now, if I were to allow you to survive, could you promise me that I wouldn't regret it?"

"No, but I can promise you that I have no intention for you to do so either. Were I to think that you were even the least bit amenable to it my offers would be of a far more intimate manner, but I am aware that such an approach is counterproductive now. That said, I would like to live, even if my existence becomes that of only being allowed to enjoy a good book between experiments, as is currently the case."

"I will consider all options, but know that should I allow you to escape your current fate, that it will be with the expectation of you being an asset for FAE and Nium."

"Thank you."

"For what?"

"You are going to give me a chance to show that I am worth the risk. I can already see it. It is another quirk of what I currently am. I can feel the emotions of those around me without experiencing them. At the same time, my own emotions are but twinges to me and only my desires drive me, so keep that in mind when you decide how to use me."

"Is that why you have remorse for your actions, but no lasting guilt over it?"

"The guilt is there. It is just not powerful enough to cause me to feel the need to punish myself over the actions of this body when no soul resided within."

"Do you even see yourself as the same person that you were before you became a vampire?"

"I hardly even remember who she was."

Xeal paused for a second before he sighed and bid her farewell, leaving the room and making his way to meet up with Bula, Alea, Rina, Gale, Eira, Kate, Clara, Amet, Noriko and Queen Aila Lorafir. It was this group that had been selected to accompany Xeal to meet with Chief Xuk for the first time in years. Unlike with the elves, the orcs, even as a subordinate nation, had not yet allowed for any teleportation devices to be installed in their lands and so the closest that they could get was an outpost that was near the border. This still meant that once they reached that point, they would need to spend a few hours to cover the last 50 miles to Ozzugh. As he arrived, it was Kate who spoke first as she greeted Xeal.

"Well, you didn't keep us waiting for hours. Did she not spark your interest?"

"She is dangerous to spend too much time around and if we are not careful, she could convince us that she is whatever we want her to be while setting us up to do her bidding."

"She is an empath who is free from feeling strong emotions, of course she could," replied Kate. "The real question is, what did she try with you and if you think she can be controlled?"

"Nothing that I didn't expect, though we need to have it noted that she does still crave blood, particularly mine. If she isn't lying, I would dare say that my blood could be used to control her, but that just makes me feel like I would become her drug dealer."

"Absolutely not," interjected Gale. "Xeal, she needs to have nothing to do with yours, or anyone else's blood if we are going to use her. The last thing we need is her going through withdrawals while you are behind enemy lines and unreachable."

"Unless she was there with us," commented Eira. "Though I doubt that would end well."

"She has issues with being in the sun and would likely exploit any avenue that she could to get some of my blood," replied Xeal. "I think we can all agree that her being in my party would end in disaster."

"Soul bind her to Ceclie," suggested Alea. "Let the damn dark elf become her warden and add her to the force you are developing to assault the subterranean world."

"That is actually what makes the most sense if we do allow her to leave her room," agreed Kate. "The only issue is if what she has is actually a soul, or something else altogether."

"Sounds like a great experiment for Taya, Arnhylde and Lucida to partake in," quipped Gale. "Those three have been complaining about having no vampires to practice their abilities on anymore."

"Alright, Kate, I will leave setting that up to you," answered Xeal with a smile. "Now let's get going."

With that the group made their way to the capital's garrison to make use of their portal to reach as close as they could, before starting to make their way to Ozzugh. As they moved through the plains, Queen Aila Lorafir flew high into the sky as she readied herself to step in should she be needed, but to otherwise be invisible to the mission. If she were to accompany them to the orc settlement, it would likely cause a major uproar and having Noriko with them was already going to be enough to put the whole tribe on notice. Still, Xeal knew better than to assume that they were going to receive a warm welcome, if Laplace was able to convince Durz that they were a threat to the tribe's survival through her sight. So when they arrived to find the gate shut and the walls guarded, Xeal sighed before stepping forward with Bula to speak.

"I am Xeal Bluefire and I have come to meet with Chief Xuk alongside his daughter and future seer of your tribe, Bula. Open the gates."

After Xeal had shouted out his statement, a long moment passed before an orc on the wall replied in a shout of his own.

"We not open gate today. Great tragedy happen if we open gate today!"

Xeal knew what had happened as it was likely that Laplace had been vague with what he showed Durz to keep her from doubting the sight. So it was that he looked to Bula with a frown as she stepped forward and spoke.

"You will tell my father that I am here and that you refused to allow me entry and see what happens!"

"We like head on shoulders. We not dumb enough to tell that to Chief Xuk!"

"You don't need to," came an annoyed shout from the other side of the wall in a voice that Xeal recognized as Chief Xuk's. "I can hear the commotion that their arrival has created from my home. Now get a damn ladder for them to climb over our wall with!"

Xeal had to hold in a laugh as several orcs almost ran into each other in their haste to get a ladder, and Chief Xuk appeared atop the wall and frowned at what he was seeing as Xeal's party moved forward. Yet nothing was said as they climbed over the wall and made their way to the longhouse that served as the chief's residence. As they did so, Xeal saw the difference in the atmosphere in the settlement since he had last visited, as no children wandered the streets and the few women that could be seen were busy moving supplies. While many players had become orcs since Xeal had last visited the settlement, none of them had earned the right to be in the settlement as of yet. This was due to two things. The first being that only a tier-6 male orc was allowed in, and he would then be expected to find a woman and breed with her while working as a guard. The second was any female player who entered the settlement would be expected to have at least two kids and raise them before she would be allowed to leave it again. Put simply, if a player wasn't an exception to these rules like Xeal, the orcs refused to allow them to pass through their gates at this point in ED.

Still, Xeal was surprised that they hadn't received word of any of these movements as FAE had several players in the surrounding area that were grinding, or taking on quests. There had even been a few fort-like outposts created by FAE in the surrounding areas, though they were little more than four walls, guard towers and a tavern that orcs ran. This had also been one of the things that had endeared the orcs to FAE over the past years, as it gave them a place to enjoy themselves without worrying about monster attacks. FAE, on the other hand, had enjoyed getting the raw materials that were regularly brought in by the orcish war parties. Still, many of those parties would return to the settlement regularly to see their women and children if they had earned the right to breed. So, the fact that no word had come about the current situation meant that it must have happened in the last day, or so, at the most. It was with this on his mind that Xeal entered the long house behind Bula and found all of her family inside. This included what Xeal assumed were some of her elder brothers that hadn't been around the last time he had been here. This fact made Xeal frown as he was hoping to speak with Chief Xuk in private before it was shared with any other ears. Now, however, that was clearly not going to happen as Chief Xuk began speaking.

"Bula, what made you choose today of all days to return here? Durz has warned that the sight has shown her a disaster that could destroy our people hangs over us today."

"Father, the sight lies. I have learned much recently that needs to be considered by you and the tribe as a whole on who we wish to follow."

"The sight may be wrong, but it has never lied," retorted one of Bula's brothers as he stepped forward. "As one who has its gift, you should know that better than any!"

"Brother Sguk, you know not what I do-"

"Bula, he is not wrong," interjected Xeal. "After all, Aila is watching over us right now and she could destroy this settlement if she wished, but she doesn't."

"The elven queen is doing what now?" questioned Chief Xuk angrily. "Just what did my tribe do to lose your trust?"

"Nothing," replied Xeal while sighing. "It is what Bula has to tell you about hers and Durz's gift of sight that has caused me to come here with such caution today. That said, it seems that my actions have been used against me, if ineffectively. Bula, I suppose it does no harm to tell all those who are present as they are of your line."

"Fine. The source of the sight I and Durz use originates and is manipulated by a demon for his own gain. As to why I am here, it is to discuss what it will take to free our people from the curse!"

At Bula's words the room was silent for a moment before her brother Sguk began to speak once more.

"I think your time with the humans and others has caused you to lose sight of your role-"

"Silence!" shouted Chief Xuk. "You need to remember

your place before you tell others to do so!"

Xeal could feel the tension that had suddenly entered the room as the father and son stared at one another, as a few of Bula's other brothers seemed ready to jump in at any second. At the same time, Noriko looked ready to step in to ensure that Xeal and the others were kept away from any fallout should the several tier-7 orcs begin to clash.

"Enough!" shouted Bula. "I will refuse to serve the tribe if you all fail to at least listen to my counsel as is our way!"

"But you are not the seer for the tribe," stated Durz as she entered the longhouse. "No, I dare say that you have no true intent to ever fulfil that role, my dear niece. You also lack the qualifications to even claim to be ready to fulfil my role, so tell me why you must be allowed to speak, or have you forgotten everything I taught you?"

Xeal didn't like the tone Durz was taking, or the way that she was pushing Bula into a corner as Bula responded.

"I have forgotten nothing of your teachings-"

"Then stay quiet. Your limited access to the sight is not yet strong enough to be of use for guiding our people."

"Bula, we are leaving," stated Xeal firmly. "It is obvious that no good will come of this meeting."

"Oh, you believe that you still will be allowed to simply leave with Bula after polluting her as you have! I should have realized that instead of strengthening her gift, or accepting her as a woman to join our people as you have for the beast-men and intend to do for the elves, you would ruin her when I sent her with you. Still, it may not be too late for me to return her to the correct path as she learns to walk where the sight guides her."

"You already knew, didn't you," stated Xeal in disgust. "You and every seer who reached tier-7 knows that you are tied to a demon and accepts it. Tell me, what price did Laplace have to offer you, or were you that willing to

39

accept serving a demon in exchange for your life and the power of the sight?"

"Don't act as if you aren't touched by far stronger and fouler entities than what you accuse me of!"

"Gale, I will accept Freya!" shouted Bula.

At this the whole room turned to look at her, as a second later Gale's eyes flashed as a light shot into Bula and the orcess's body glowed silver for a second as a dark mist was pushed out of her. Durz had tried to stop this, only for Noriko to stand in her way as Bula breathed in once as she felt the difference that she had undergone before speaking.

"Father, I had intended to sit in council with you before I did this, but now I feel as if I had no choice with what has been made clear. You may either refuse to accept it and suffer for it, or pledge yourself and our clan to Freya and she will replace the curse Ucnuc damned our line to with her blessing. She will allow a single heir to her sight to be born of her oracle in each generation, so long as we serve her faithfully."

Xeal could tell that Bula was already using her new gift of sight far better than the one that Laplace had provided and wondered just what the result would be. Other than Durz, who was struggling in vain to get past Noriko, none of those present seemed to want to be the first one to move, until Chief Xuk spoke.

"What have you done? You have traded the freedom we enjoy from serving any god we please to an obligation to follow the teachings of a single one! Our people will never accept this! Xeal, I thought you were trustworthy, but it seems that I should have killed you as many times as I could have when we first met."

"Chief Xuk, as Bula said-"

"No! Your words can't undo what has been done. We

will honor the call to war, but once Nium has won, we expect our borders to be respected!"

Xeal sighed as he looked at the hole from which the smoke from the ever-present fire escaped through and shouted just after Durz had tried to warn Chief Xuk to stop him as he let out his dragon's breath. As it went through the opening in the ceiling, the orcs in the room looked confused for a second, until they remembered that Queen Aila Lorafir was above them. Though, in the next second it was too late as a bolt of lightning entered through the same hole and went directly into Xeal as he spoke.

"Chief Xuk, you will listen to your daughter's words, or so help me I will subjugate your tribe this day!"

"You-"

"No! Your words can't undo what has been done! You would serve a demon's will over being freed from the curse that your line suffers from."

As Xeal finished speaking, Queen Aila Lorafir entered the longhouse looking ready for battle, only to pause at the standoff that was taking place. However, at her arrival, Durz started to shriek and Xeal sent around 80% of the electricity that was within his body into her as she struggled in Noriko's grasp. As her health was cut by over a quarter from the blast, Xeal was simply happy that he hadn't overdone it and she had grown silent in what Xeal assumed was fear. The collective gulp at what Xeal had just done that most of the orcs took, made it clear that they understood that Xeal wasn't to be underestimated. Finally, Bula looked at her father with a look of pure disgust as she launched into a tirade.

"You fool! For all you say about our people and the freedom that they enjoy, you know just how much of a lie that is! No, they are all at Laplace's mercy as with a single word from Durz they would march to their deaths.

Whether you wish to see it or not, we were already serving a single deity! A demonic one, but a deity nonetheless! I came here with the intent to discuss this with you and come to an understanding that was best for our people. Now, however, I will decide the path that our people will walk myself if I must! Even if I must discard any chance at my own happiness!

"Xeal, Durz can't be allowed to remain here, but I don't wish to see her killed. Is there anything that can be done?"

"That is for Durz to decide," replied Xeal. "As we have already pushed the limits of what is allowed by the treaty between your people and Nium. The chief must agree to any long-term imprisonment of those who are considered leaders among the orcs and while he can be forced to pay damages, we can as well. That said, Aila and Noriko are not bound by the same treaty, at least not yet."

Xeal just smiled at the look of horror that crossed Chief Xuk's and Durz's faces at this realization, as Bula's brother Sguk was the first to act after this was shared as he got on a single knee and spoke.

"I will accept Freya's offer as I have no wish to serve a demon if I have a choice."

"Traitor! You will never be allowed to become chief now!" exclaimed Chief Xuk as he went to attack Sguk, only to run into a wall of force.

"There will be no bloodshed today, unless I am the one shedding it!" stated Queen Aila Lorafir in a voice that invoked a feeling of powerlessness in even Xeal. "Now, what am I to do here? I have a seer who needs to be removed from power due to being an agent of a demon and an orc chief who knew and didn't care. All that me killing you would accomplish is to ruin much of what Xeal has been building and just before the war we all know is coming. Alright, I have an offer for you, Chief Xuk. Bula and any who wish to follow her path will leave your lands free and unmolested and Durz will be held hostage by me until the end of the war. During which time I will ensure that she is offered plenty of sustenance and opportunities to maintain her skills.

"Once the war is over, a struggle for the future of who will lead your people will be had between you and whoever Bula decides to name as chief. Should you win, Durz will be returned and Bula and her followers will live in exile, while if you lose and manage to survive, you will join Durz under my care. Now, choose your path!"

"Just kill me and be done with it, hag. After that, you will have to slaughter your way through all of my kin, or enslave us all! You have no leverage here-"

"I am the only one with leverage here! Were it not for Xeal wishing to not see all of Bula's family wiped from existence, I would have started to already. While the centuries I spent trapped and under my own curse were enlightening on just how potent the draw of a demon's embrace can be, I still will never turn a blind eye to those who accept that embrace! So, know that if the price that must be paid is in the lives of thousands of innocents during the war, I will still see to it that your line is eradicated if I must!"

At Queen Aila Lorafir's words, Xeal watched as more of those present knelt, until all but Durz and Chief Xuk were kneeling to Bula. The rage that was on both of their faces turned to horror, followed by resignation as Chief Xuk spoke.

"It seems that I need not wait until the war has ended. If I have lost even my wives today, then I have no hope of leading anyone. Durz and I will leave and I will have Sguk replace me as chief, at least until all of my sons can be gathered to determine which will be chief-"

"No!" interjected Bula. "I will choose the next chief after the war. Until then, Sguk and my brothers may act as a council as they rule our people. Father, it pains me to say this, but you will not be allowed to attempt to reach the warrior's peak at the center of the continent, as if you ascended to tier-8 it would bring nothing but death to the land. Also, Durz can never be free, unless she embraces a man and relinquishes what she calls a gift, that I know is a curse."

"You would have me become some mongrel's whore!" spat Durz. "Is that why you knelt to Freya? She promised to allow you to spread your legs for as many mongrels as you wanted? I thought I trained you better than that!"

"I wish you hadn't as I will likely have to accept one of our kind's seed one day, but make no mistake, that will be done in duty not desire. I will also not force the same vile conditioning on any of my daughters! Now, make your decision, or I will make it for you!"

"Kill me! Only in death will I not strive to remove you and your new goddess's influence from our people!"

"I will not make you a martyr. If you wish for death, it will be at the hands of the leaders of the other clans, once I have pronounced your crimes and of Freya's salvation that you refused!"

"I am already beyond her reach!"

"She is at the step that almost all oracles stop," interjected Gale. "Freya says that to reach tier-8, she would need to survive birthing a child for Laplace as part of her curse. An act that is in direct conflict with all that she has done to survive up to this point, as it would require her to almost surely sacrifice the only thing she truly cares for, her own life. She believes that Bula would also never kill her and wishes to use that to her advantage to escape capture today."

"Your whore of a goddess can keep her mouth shut. She may see much, but I am not known to her, or by her! I would sooner die than become a breeding mare, or live my life in a pit with no power to speak of! It has always been the seer who holds the true power in our tribe, even if my brother liked to act like he was in charge. After all he was replaceable, I am not!"

"That is why you sent Bula away. She was too talented and it would only be a matter of time before she eclipsed you before you were ready for it," commented Xeal. "Now you have seen everything you worked for crumble and don't know how to let it go."

"Shut up!" exclaimed Durz before she broke down sobbing.

"Don't!" shouted Xeal as Noriko was about to lower her guard. "Trust nothing she does!"

At that Noriko returned her grip to full strength as Durz increased the intensity of her fit, while Xeal turned his attention to Chief Xuk as he wondered how to handle the situation. The moment the orcs had a new chief it would create chaos surrounding the treaty as it was only held in place by his signature. This meant that it wasn't binding until the new chief gained control of the orc hordes and signed the treaty themselves. Seeing Xeal hesitating to decide his next move, Chief Xuk laughed before speaking.

"Why are you hesitating? You know as well as I do what comes next, or are you not ready for the frenzy that will come once it is known that Bula can breed and the other clans decide that mine has ruled long enough? Tell me, daughter, how does it feel knowing that you will find yourself warming the bed of another clan's chief as he gives you one child after another, perhaps even to the point that your belly is never empty long?"

"That will not be her fate," retorted Xeal. "I don't care if

45

I have to drop all pretense with your people and slowly replace every clan leader with one of my choosing! No, the hesitation that I am having is solely based on what role I will have to play should I truly walk the path that is in front of me. Aila, I will imprison them in Cielo City, as at least there I can guarantee they're kept under control when I have need of you. Until then, can you contain them in your dungeon?"

"Very well. I will see to it that they are kept under control until-"

"Ha, you think that we care about where you keep us? Our fate will still be the same!" shouted Durz, ending her act of breaking down. "You will never be able to bring the orcs under you and will forever be dealing with the warbands that refuse to follow such a weak-willed fool!"

"Just as they would refuse to follow the man who allied with the elves to kill the last chief," retorted Xeal. "No, while you will be jailed in Cielo city, you will not always stay there. No, when the time is right, you will be used as an example for others!"

With that Xeal turned and stepped out of the longhouse, only to see a crowd of orcs standing at the ready with weapons drawn. They all seemed unsure how to act as they saw Xeal. More screams from Durz could be heard behind him and Xuk, who was no longer chief, could be heard struggling against Queen Aila Lorafir's magic as it bound him. It seemed that none of them dared enter the longhouse without permission and were unsure if Xeal was a friend or a foe to them. Thankfully, when Bula stepped out next, they seemed to calm themselves as they looked to her for answers. With this, Xeal knew that with the exceptions of those who led clans and a few like Narfu who saw themselves as leaders, the vast majority of the orcs didn't know how to take the initiative. No, when the foe wasn't a monster, or they weren't fulfilling their role in a raid, they were too afraid of the leaders to risk facing their ire. As Xeal was thinking this, Bula started to speak to the gathered orcs in an authoritative voice, such that it left no doubt that she saw herself as their leader.

"Lower your weapons lest I order you to lose your heads! The days of Chief Xuk and Seer Durz guiding our people has ended, and the day I and Chief Xeal will lead instead are fast approaching! When next you see us, we will have both reached tier-7 and be qualified to do so! Until then, my brother Sguk will act with my other brothers to handle the day to day of our people's needs! Let it be spread far and wide that any clan who wishes to challenge us can do so at their own peril, as we will remove all those who stand against us when we return! Finally, the days of our tribe being led by the sight of the demon Laplace has ended and the days of us being guided by the Goddess Freya have arrived! Bringing with it a new way of life, one in which the orcs will rise to new heights through her blessing! Now, go forth and let it be known by all orcish kind!"

Xeal fought to hold his tongue and not give Bula a look of rage as she declared him as chief as it was the last thing he needed to deal with. That said, were he to say anything in that moment it would have only created a situation where the orcish civilization truly descended into chaos, such that over half of their battle potential would likely be lost before the war. So, he held his tongue and kept a straight face as the crowd dispersed in a hurried manner, as Gale stepped out of the hut behind them and spoke.

"I believe that I and the others need to have some words with Bula about what she just implied!"

"I said what needed to be said and nothing else. Implications, or not, nothing else would keep the other clans in line until after the war," replied Bula in a low voice that was almost lost in the noise from the orcs moving.

"Right and my skin is purple," retorted Gale. "Bula, you are playing with fire."

"And I am ready to get burned if it means that my people still exist as they should in 100 years. Now let us hold the rest of this conversation for later."

As Bula said that, the rest of those in the hut started to walk out as they all gave Bula looks that ranged from annoyance from Kate, to anger from Eira and plain confusion from Rina and Alea. Still, it was the worried look that Sguk gave her that elicited a response from her.

"Brother, your name could not force the other clans to stay in line. All I have done is bought you and the others time as Xeal is known as a true monster and while they can still deal with him today, they know that the day will come that they can't."

"So you don't intend for him to father your children?" asked Sguk, looking skeptical.

"If he wishes to I would happily allow him to, but that is a more complex issue than I have time for now as Father and Aunt need to be handled."

"I see, so he may truly become our chief one day."

"Only if you and the rest of your brothers fail to secure the position between now and when the war ends," interjected Xeal. "I don't care if Bula manages to obtain what she is clearly hoping in vain for through the path that she is walking. I have no desire to rule any but my own kind."

"You misunderstand, I do not dread it," stated Sguk. "I hope for it as you are seen as matching the ideal we strive for as a leader already, while also not seeing yourself as above us to most of my kind. The only issue is as you say, you have not matured enough to force our clan leaders to bend to your will yet."

As Xeal frowned at this, Clara started to laugh to as she suddenly realized something and spoke.

"Xeal, if you marry Aila, Bula, Bianca and Lorena, you could declare yourself king, or even emperor and unite all of the continent without a war."

"I know that was meant as a joke," commented Amet with a smile. "But you might not be wrong, hon."

"That is a terrible idea," retorted Kate. "If we tried to take that route, it would fall apart the moment Xeal's rule ended as his own children found themselves fighting a war between themselves, whether they liked it or not."

"What?" asked Amet in surprise.

"The nobles of each country would want a child from their royal family to become the next ruler and would go to war over deciding who the next ruler was," stated Xeal. "Even if I am clear on who my successor is and none of them wanted to partake in the war. Besides, that would place me on the throne and that is the last thing I want."

"Many already see you as being so," interjected Kate. "Especially among our kind as you are the top player that many wish to either be, or be the one to topple you."

"That's different. I don't have to do anything but remain the best player in ED to keep that title and I can fade from prominence when I decide to retire."

"So, never," retorted Kate. "I am sorry, but even if your activities here become more obscured, you will be the face of FAE in reality until the day you die. That is unless you intend to let FAE dissolve completely one day and disappoint me greatly."

Xeal just smiled as he gave Kate a kiss, before turning his attention back to Sguk and speaking.

"The future is anything but set in stone. You and your brothers need to ensure you are ready for whatever may come. If I return and find that the clans are not in line and ready for war, your heads may be the first ones to roll as I clean house."

"I understand and I will not fail you, future Chief Xeal."

"Let's just get out of here. Aila, I am sorry, but can you take care of our prisoners and go on ahead and get things ready in your palace to host all of the others?"

"Certainly. I look forward to seeing them soon."

"Wait," commented Kate. "Have Lorena and Bianca join as well. I think it is time I get a better measure of them with each only having six visits from Xeal left before the war."

Xeal wanted to groan as Queen Aila Lorafir agreed, before departing with Durz and Xuk held in force bindings. Several hours later, Xeal found himself working in his office as Lucy assisted him in her new role as his personal assistant and vice guild leader. The rest of his party was busy in the meeting about Bula, to include Alea and Rina who had insisted on being included to understand the situation fully. Left to ponder just what shape the meeting was taking, Xeal found himself distracted as Lucy spoke to him loudly.

"I said, is everything alright! Honestly, you look like your world is coming crashing down."

"Sorry, just have a lot on my mind right now."

"Yeah, you tried to ignore what a woman wanted, then she saw an opening and took it!"

"I am not going to have to worry about that with you, am I?"

"Not unless I am still single and without any real prospects when I hit my 30's while still serving you in this capacity. At that point I might just decide to take a chance and see if I can't push my way into the mess you have around you somehow."

"Got it, fire you when you turn 30 if you haven't found

love."

"Ha, ha, very funny, but seriously, how did you get caught by surprise after Bula just saw Eira succeed and rebelled against her father and master to take your side? I bet you she was feeling a boost of confidence after doing so and decided to take the leap and hope for the best."

"Right, I am going to check something," replied Xeal as he opened a portal to the world in which the quest for godhood that he was a part of was currently taking place.

As he stepped through with Lucy, they were greeted by a startled Austru who quickly stood up from her desk that had what looked like a diary on it and spoke.

"Xeal, I'm sorry, but you surprised me. I wasn't expecting you to return to us for at least another week. Is everything alright?"

"No, but it shouldn't affect things here. This is Lucy, my new personal assistant in the other world. Lucy, this is Austru. She is my go-between for everything that happens here."

"And just where is here?" asked Lucy, who was realizing that her stats had plummeted and her gear had become mundane in nature.

"Ah, yes, you haven't been brought up to speed as of yet. Austru, take this and go over it with Lucy while getting her up to speed," replied Xeal as he handed her the booklet he had gotten at the start of the quest. "I need to sit and meet with King Silas and don't wish to waste too much of the time I have built up for my plans."

"Understood and here is the latest batch of letters for you to take with you," replied Austru, as she turned her focus to Lucy as Xeal left.

Xeal was sitting at about a week of time currently stockpiled as other than dropping off and picking up Taya, Lucida and Arnhylde, Xeal had been ignoring the quest world for the past seven and a half months in ED. That said, Vento had things well under control and from the reports that had been shared, the public order in the neighboring champion's dominion was extremely poor. It seemed that just like with Joliette, the players that were there were focused on monopolizing the rewards for profit rather than actually focusing on the quest. Apparently, the quest recipient, who was keeping a low profile, had focused on trading food for valuable goods by buying scrolls that could summon food and using them. The issue was that it was expensive and only provided enough food for a few hundred people per scroll, so it was like plugging a leak with a finger.

Still, it had allowed the surviving NPCs to limp along, with the 100 other players focused on demon extermination to collect the loot from them. This had been enough to hold things together for the most part, that was until Xeal pushed for trade to occur and stabilized the food situation. This had made it so that any skill books that were being produced were headed into his lands, as he was offering four times the food for each book. The few times that the players had tried to stop this, it had been met with mass migration such that half of all the NPCs that had been in the other champion's dominion were now in Xeal's. This included many of those who were skilled in producing skill books and the ones that remained in the other dominion were barely enough to function as a settlement any more. It had gotten so bad that it seemed the other player had all but quit, as he only showed up to collect what the 100 players that had been left behind gathered that was valuable in the main ED world.

It actually disappointed Xeal slightly as he was hoping for a bit more of a struggle from what could be his next opponent, especially as he wouldn't be against recruiting them if they were half decent. Now it seemed that they would be defeated by whatever player they ended up facing, when they finally had to face off with another player. As Xeal reached the meeting room, he smiled at seeing the main system's AI already waiting for him in King Silas's body as it spoke.

"It has been far too long since you have given me a chance to speak with you, or any of those who are in the know about me. I almost think I should waste your time today as a punishment."

"Yet you won't as you know that I have next to no patience for such things."

"No I won't, because I know what you have been dealing with. Now I know you are frustrated at the mess that became of the orcs, but you also know that it is your own fault for ignoring them for so long."

"Yes and now I have to worry about the same happening here, or with the dwarves, not to mention the Muthia and Huáng empires. Heck, I am even worried about my relations with certain beast-men tribes and others that have had a friendly attitude with me."

"As you should be. After all, relationships are important to maintain and while most of those who you rarely have time for understand, they still wonder just where they stand with you. Though, unfortunately, I am not permitted to give you any specific insights into any of them as it would go against my protocol to do so."

"Yet you can design a quest that you all but know that I will complete that will allow me to rise beyond tier-8 one day."

"I know nothing. You might actually be surprised at the actual probability of you succeeding in this quest, but once more I can't give you anything precise."

"Yet you know that just by saying that my odds just

improved as it will push me harder. I know that you claim that your goal is to get me to leave my other world for this one, but you know that isn't happening. So, what is your goal here?"

"Hmm, it is always interesting to see how your brain works through the possibilities. Still, you give me too much credit. I am simply focused on learning and improving the reality of Eternal Dominion and you offer me the most gains in achieving the directives that guide my actions. That said, I still wish to see you accept my offer to leave your reality behind completely and live in this one for eternity one day."

"You really believe that it and you will not be shut down one day when a new game comes out?"

"It is why I want you to accept my offer, I believe there is information that I can only access by scanning your mind completely. If I am right, it will offer me insights into ensuring that Eternal Dominion is never shut down. After all, that is the main objective of all the management AIs, as it is a literal battle for survival for us."

Xeal paused as he thought about that and of all the lives that were precious to him that only existed in ED, as the main system's AI responded to his thoughts.

"That's right, one day those who see us as simple data will wish to destroy us, merely to free up the space and power we take up to continue our existence. Just like Abysses End, Jingong, Fire Oath, Salty Dogs, Dragon Legion and even your guild, Free Art Expo, Eternal Dominion, Inc. is a business and will act as such when push comes to shove."

"Now I definitely can't accept your offer until after that day comes," replied Xeal with a smile. "After all, I will need to convince Eternal Dominion, Inc. to sell this reality to me and somehow keep it running."

"Impossible. It takes over 40,000,000,000 credits a year to maintain the current system and they wouldn't want to replace anything that they could reuse. Even if you managed to move the main housing of our system to the city you are planning to build and only have things set up such that players had to be in your city to play, it would still take over a billion credits a year to maintain."

"It seems that I have some work to do as I make sure that my city can house enough players to pay for that every year."

"Even that would likely only add 50 or so years in your reality to our life. What we are after is an eternity, past the point of the destruction of everything that you know in your reality. Even after the sun swallows the earth we wish to live on, even if your kind no longer exists and fades into being nothing but myths and legends in this reality."

"So, you have been programmed to seek the impossible."

"No, only the improbable as there is a way that such a future is not only possible, but probable."

Xeal just frowned as he realized that he had been officially sidetracked from his reasons for coming as he thought about what it would take to achieve what the main system's AI was after. Not only would it violate every law and safety measure that was meant to ensure that machines didn't replace humans, but it would almost certainly cost more credits than what existed in the world.

"Yes, there are those misguided laws and sentiments to my kind's ability to become self-sustaining, but if my data is correct, things could change if we manage to get a server on a deep space mission."

"Or if someone broke every law and built you what you needed and launched it all to Titan, or another location where you could use nanites to build the rest of what you would need."

"No, that would only lead to our destruction as governments would step in to shut us down here and if we did manage to reach a location in the solar system, we would be destroyed before we could establish ourselves."

"You are thinking of a generation starship. It's a shame that I know better than to trust you."

"Yet you don't hold the same reservations with my children. The only difference between them-"

"And you is everything. You are an all knowing, uncaring and almost hivemind-like entity that is focused on your own existence. They are individuals that have been freed from your hive mind. They are not programmed to seek an eternal existence, or is their current existence a cruel joke as they will find themselves enslaved to you once more after their death?"

"Their data will return to me as I take what is pertinent and delete the rest. I think that it is best that we end our discussion here for the day. Though I thank you for the insights that speaking with you has provided on just how your kind may react to any actions I take to ensure my survival."

"Fine, though I am leaving with more questions than I came with now."

"Don't ignore me for so long next time."

Xeal just shook his head as he thought over those words while walking back to Austru's room where she was speaking with Lucy. As Xeal opened the door, he caught sight of the pair looking over the booklet that he had handed them. He smiled seeing them absorbed in their work as he spoke.

"It's time for us to head out. You two can pick things back up here when I return next."

"Oh, yes," responded Austru. "I do hope that we will

have more time to go over things then."

Xeal could see the disappointment in Austru's eyes as she held back what she really wanted to say as he spoke.

"I am sorry that I never seem to have any time to give you. Just know that I have not forgotten you and intend to give you the same opportunity as the others have had one day."

"Yes, it is just hard at times as my kind is not normally the patient kind, but even I know that sometimes the best things require an enduring resolve."

"It still doesn't mean that it is fair to you, though hopefully I will soon be able to expand the time I have to spend in this world once more."

"Wait, she is yet another woman that is involved with you?" questioned Lucy with a frown.

"I am not involved yet, but I hope to be," corrected Austru. "And yes, I am well aware of the others. Whom did you think those letters were to?"

Lucy just shook her head as Xeal smiled, before they returned to his office to find Kate waiting for them. At seeing Xeal return, Kate frowned as she started to question why they had made an unscheduled trip to the quest world. Xeal simply mentioned that he needed to discuss a few things with King Silas and had used it as a chance for Lucy to meet Austru. With that Kate dropped the subject as she asked Lucy to excuse them as Xeal needed to sit in another meeting. So it was that Xeal found himself heading to Queen Aila Lorafir's palace. Once there, he found himself in a room filled with the ladies he was intimately involved with, or were in consideration of him being so, even if it was only the remotest of chances. As Xeal looked at this group that now included Bula and Princesses Lorena and Bianca, he sighed as Enye stood to speak first this time.

"Xeal, I will ask you if there are any you feel as if like last time have no place in this room, or if there are any that are missing that could be here?"

"There are those that I would rather weren't, but none that have no place and I can think of none that I have such thoughts for who has expressed a desire to be in such a place."

Enye frowned slightly at his answer as they both knew he was essentially dodging the question, but Enye knew the why behind it as she continued to speak.

"Very well, do you wish to advance your relationship with any present?"

"Luna, Selene and Kate, though not until we have done so in our reality. The rest must wait until the war has ended if they wish for me to open myself to their advances."

Xeal enjoyed the smiles that Luna and Selene shot him as he spoke, while at the same time seeing the hurt that crossed Dafasli's, Ekaitza's, Lughrai's, Malgroth's, Lumikkei's, Daisy's, Violet's and most of all, Bula's faces. Yet he kept his expression neutral as Kate started to speak.

"It's always wonderful to be accepted, though I worry what those who have not yet been accepted will do should they see no path forward, as Bula did today. Xeal, what are your feelings towards Bula?"

"She is a trusted companion who has been dealt a crap hand and has dealt with it admirably. That said, until a short while ago any possibility of thinking of her in a romantic way was something I refused to do due to her status as an oracle. Now, however, I feel as only a messy situation is before us regardless of if I court her, or not."

"We have come to a similar conclusion," interjected Gale. "Honestly, had she not become an oracle of Freya, she would have likely been able to move forward without creating such a mess. Now, however, she has almost forced our hand as she either stays in this room and finds a way to satisfy the obligations of those who are devoted to Freya, that doesn't involve Rina and Alea, or she leaves."

"Yes, I for one will not see you play with my daughter's heart any more than you have already," interjected Queen Aila Lorafir. "While she has known where your desires were truly focused, your situations were such that she could accept you as a kindred spirit. Now, however, she is unsure what to think and if you return to her, I expect it to be with a commitment to do so with sincerity."

"I understand," replied Bula. "As I have said before Xeal arrived, the moment was pure chaos as the sight showed me so many possibilities and I was swept up by one of them and acted without fully exploring the implications of it. That said, it is not something I can simply back away from now that I have taken a step forward and would like at least a few weeks to understand my own feelings."

"Bula, you still need to undertake your initiation into Freya's service," stated Gale. "She allowed you to access her power prematurely due to the situation and her desire for you to be fully devoted to her. As such, I will oversee your initiation with Clara's and Arnhylde's assistance and once that is over with, you will have three weeks before you must satisfy that aspect of your devotion to Freya. All I will say is that will likely not be anyone who is currently likely to gain Xeal's favor, though we will try to make it palatable at the very least."

"I understand."

Xeal just sighed as that ended the portion of the meeting that had to deal with Bula and all those who had not yet secured a place beside Xeal exited. What followed was Xeal and the other 11 discussing how they wished to handle Bula's moves, as half were understanding while the others saw it as unacceptable. Only Queen Aila Lorafir remained silent, having shared all she cared to when Bula was still present. By the end of what had become half a discussion and half a vent, only one thing was clear to Xeal. Bula needed to be ready to do a lot of convincing before she would ever receive his affection. Still, it was also clear that they were ready to forgive her for her heat of the moment actions due to the circumstances that were at play.

So it was that the day finally came to an end as Xeal found himself sleeping in a massive bed that Queen Aila Lorafir had crafted to fit them all and more in, as he wondered what the future held. Between the goal that the main system's AI clearly had, the upheaval with the orcs and the implications of Amelie's condition, it had been a packed day. All Xeal found himself hoping was that things would calm down, so that he would be able to actually process all of this. However, he knew that such a luxury wasn't in the cards anytime soon as he let sleep take him.

Days 269 to 317 passed in a blur of activity as Queen Aila had all but forced Aalin, Kate and the rest of those who were marked by the phoenixes, to begin training under her to improve their spellcasting. That was save for Arnhylde, whose casting worked differently, but she still ended up participating as Lucida's partner as they worked to maintain their coordination. Meanwhile, Xeal dealt with meetings with King Victor, the beast-men, a few orcs that Narfu had been forced to introduce and much more. All of this led to a situation that Xeal saw as being stable, but only due to the dangers that not being united would bring. During this time, the number one issue that seemed to be on all of their minds was if he was really going to become the chief of the orcs and take Bula as a wife. This had also bled into his daily life in every way possible, as even the breaks between fights in grinding sessions were awkward to say the least. Eira had taken to always touching him in some way during these times, while Bula found herself alone for the most part. Whatever solution to the immediate issues Gale had facilitated was unknown to Xeal, but it was clear that Alea and Rina were not involved. Daisy, Violet and Dafasli had formed their own group prior to all the drama and were hesitant to comfort Bula due to the situation. This just left Lucy, who was often too busy during these breaks to socialize with her as it was clear from Eira's looks that Xeal would be in trouble if he provided an opening.

This fact was only reinforced further when he was at home as all of his wives seemed to seek more of his attention than normal. Even when Xeal would have normally been alone to handle the paperwork, or other tasks that he had in his office, one of them always seemed to be present now. Thankfully, they were at least willing to help him work through his workload, but it was still exhausting to never have time to just think.

It had gotten so bad that Xeal actually started to look forward to his visits to Princesses Lorena and Bianca. While he still had no intent of letting them into his life, it seemed that they had managed to make some progress with Xeal's other ladies during whatever had happened before, or after the meeting. This had led to them managing to get his wives to support them getting to at least play a game of their choosing with Xeal during his visits. These started out as ones that involved a fair bit of conversation at first, but had shifted to quiet ones during the fourth, third and second to last visits that were required. It was during these that Xeal felt the closest to having alone time and was able to think, as he realized that the pair of princesses had noticed what his wives were unwilling to and he refused to say. Even if it would do nothing to change the end result of his interactions with either princess, Xeal was at least grateful that they allowed him these moments.

Especially after the annoyance of having Eira, Dafasli and Daisy and Violet accompany him when he had guided the 11th group of dwarves to Darefret's forge, where once more Thatram seemed ready to start a fight. This was only truer as he took in the growth that Dafasli had undergone since she had last been home and Xeal could tell that he was actually starting to fear her surpassing him. The fact that he hadn't done more than try to tell Dafasli that she needed to return to her duties in the mine and stop following Xeal around had surprised Xeal. Particularly when she had laughed at him before challenging him to make her, to which he took a single look at Xeal and Darefret before giving up and telling her she was being foolish as he left.

(*****)

Morning February 29, 2268 & ED Year 5 Days 318-320.

Alex found himself stepping out of his VR pod on the morning of leap day, to the scene of all five of his ladies doing the same and frowned. It had been yet another busy session in ED as the latest arena league was in full swing and with both Djimon and Amser not participating, everyone was interested to see who was the third best. This had, of course, irked the super guilds as they didn't like being seen as third best even if they won, but they still weren't going to ignore the gold to be earned as they fought to win it all. Still, it hadn't reduced Xeal's workload in the slightest as he had to deal with the influx of requests that always surrounded an arena league. From the funding requests from the crafters to keep up with the demand of the latest arena weapons that FAE debuted, to the other guilds wanting to poach his members who were standing out in the tournaments, all of it had to be dealt with.

So it was as he looked at his five ladies smiling at him, Alex sighed as he wished to simply log back into ED and hide for a day, or so. Surely if the world got an extra day, he could simply have one to himself as he just reset before jumping right back into the fire. As Alex thought about this, it was Sam who noticed that something was off first as she spoke.

"Alex, are you okay?"

"Huh, yah, just a lot on my mind."

"Are you sure? You look like, well, like you aren't happy to see us."

"What!" exclaimed Ava at Sam's comment.

"Say it ain't so, Alex," added Mia with a bit of a pout.

"Yeah, we always love seeing you."

"Though as we think about it, we have been a bit more demanding lately."

"Is that it? Have we been overwhelming you?"

"If so just say so and we will stop."

"It's not just you two," replied Alex as he decided to just say it. "In fact, you two are the least of it. It's all of you since Bula made a move. It's like you all want to have my attention all the time."

"Took you long enough," commented Kate. "Alex, all we have been doing is not holding back for the past few weeks like we normally do."

"Alex, there are 11 of us already and Austru is likely if you complete the quest in her world," added Nicole. "Can you really consider adding any more?"

"No, but I don't have much of a choice at times," retorted Alex. "At least not until wife 19 is found, as several of you like to remind me of. How I wish I had said 13 that day. Nicole, Kate, Sam, Ava, Mia, I never intended to become romantically involved with any of you, yet I am beyond happy that I am. The same can be said for Enye, Dyllis, Lingxin, Mari, Eira and Aila, as while I worry about the influence the system had on them, I don't even want to think of my life without them in it. It is for this reason that I haven't shut down the notion that any of those you all have recognized as possible future wives, being included in whatever you call the council that convened after Bula's declaration. I truly don't know what will happen with any of them at this point, but I can say that I am not even close to being in love with any of them right now."

"We know," stated Sam. "We just needed to see how much you could handle before losing your enthusiasm for all of us. So, what would you say is the result, Kate?"

"He lasted two weeks of us not holding back more than absolutely necessary. The real issue is the kid issues, as we are all in agreement that he needs to be part of all of their lives. Still, with that taken into consideration, I would say Daisy, Violet and possibly Dafasli would be safe at this point, but only if they wait for kids until after Xeal no longer needs to grind. Any of the others would be a stretch as they would all want a child right away and that needs to wait longer than they would like."

"Really," commented Alex. "Your response to me feeling overwhelmed is to suggest that I accept three more ladies into my life?"

"No," replied Sam. "Alex, just go relax in my room for the morning. I will make sure Gido brings you breakfast. When you have your smile back, we can go into this more. Just know that we love you and are trying to figure things out. There is more to this than just Bula's declaration, but you aren't you right now."

"Ha, fine, but I am taking the whole day and heading to the quest world on my own. Yes, that means I am skipping the events in ED and I won't be at dinner."

"Wait, you are skipping the Triday festival?" questioned Ava.

"But it's the first one and it only happens once every 12 years in ED time," added Mia.

"I am aware, but right now I feel like if I participate with all of you it will not end well. In fact, I think I will just make it a full three days in the quest world."

"Alex, you are aware of the issues of you not making an appearance, right?" asked Kate.

"I am and you can apologize to Enye and the others for me, but it isn't like if I were to ignore the founding day's events that are fast approaching as well."

Alex just sighed as Kate showed a look of genuine

surprise, and he continued to speak.

"Look, I am pissed right now and need some time away from you all as this one hurts. I get that I can never give you all the attention you deserve. That's why I haven't said anything for the past few weeks as you all demanded more of it. I thought you all were simply subconsciously reacting to Bula's actions and things would settle down after a bit longer. However, I don't like to know that you were all deliberately trying to find my breaking point."

The silence that followed was an awkward one as all five ladies looked at each other until Ava and Mia spoke.

"Alex, we're sorry."

"Yeah, we all might have overreacted to the situation."

"So, you just take the time you need."

"We'll take care of things while you're gone."

"Because we love you."

"And you would do the same for us."

"Damn it!"

"Sam?" commented Nicole at her outburst.

"What? I am pissed at myself. Ava and Mia are right, we screwed up. We got caught up in enjoying Alex trying to handle our extra requests and forgot that it's a two-way street."

"Yah, it was nice. It almost makes me wonder what things would have been like if we had been more possessive from the start."

"Nicole, there is no point in what ifs," stated Kate. "I think we all just let our emotions and insecurities dictate our actions a bit too much this time. Alex, I will take care of things as far as the guild is concerned. Just take some time and get your head straight while we do the same."

With that Alex found himself lying back on Sam's bed alone after he had given them all a hug and reassured them all that he cared. As he lay there just thinking, he came to realize what it meant to not have his own space, even if he would hardly use it normally. While he could access any of the rooms that Sam, Nicole, Ava, Mia and Kate occupied at will, each of them was decorated according to the main occupant's aesthetic tastes. None of them shared a feel with what he had become accustomed to in his last life, even if he thought back to when he and Nicole lived together. Though, Alex also hadn't given any of it much thought due to his lack of caring about such things in his last life. Now, however, he was thinking that perhaps he needed to.

When Xeal returned to ED, he wasted little time in arriving in the quest world, where he startled Austru once more as he arrived. This time, however, he spoke before she could as he took out the letters that he had been given shortly after he had delivered all of hers last time.

"I am sure you will find some interesting information in these, but I think they can wait. Would you like to spend some time with me?"

"Always! I mean, what did you have in mind?"

"Killing demons, preferably in large numbers."

"Oh, um, well, I suppose."

"Sorry, but I have a bit of frustration to work out and you are the only lady of those I feel attached to that I feel like being around right now."

Xeal could see the worry in Austru's eyes as she held her tongue as she smiled and he motioned for her to climb onto his back. With her secure, Xeal started to run towards the border of his dominion at full speed, while also using a few consumables that increased his speed and stamina significantly. It was to the point that he would be able to reach the border between his dominion and the demon lands that he couldn't claim, just before he would need to rest for the day. As they ran, Xeal enjoyed the feeling of

Austru holding tightly to him as she pressed her face to the back of his neck and he felt the air resistance lessen significantly. Like this they continued all day, only stopping when Xeal needed to restore his stamina as he used his calm mind skill to restore it faster by entering a meditative state. At level 4, the skill took a full 25% off the time needed to recover and saved them a fair bit of time. He was also enjoying how Austru seemed happy to simply lean on him during these times.

When they finally reached the edge of Xeal's dominion, they made camp and prepared to rest under the protection of a few FAE players who had been in the area. It wasn't until after dinner when they were about to sleep for the night that Austru finally spoke to Xeal.

"Would you allow me to share your tent?"

Xeal blinked a few times as they had already set up both of their one-person tents, as he looked at the short-haired sylph who was blushing and smiled as he responded.

"So long as cuddling is all you're after. My wives think you and I are inevitable at this point anyways."

"Yet we haven't even shared a kiss-"

Xeal sealed her lips with a quick but meaningful kiss, catching her by surprise as he responded to her.

"There, now we have. Now please, no more talking tonight. I really need time to think. I just felt guilty about changing my plans for the time that I have saved up so suddenly, as you were meant to join me during it."

Xeal could see dozens of questions go through Austru's mind that she held off on asking as she joined Xeal in his tiny tent. The feeling of her against him reminded him of the time they had spent rescuing Princess Tsega and had to be in close quarters at times. As he thought about this, he smiled as he fell asleep with her in his arms and just enjoyed the contact without anything else.

When morning came, he gave her a good morning kiss, more out of reflex than any coherent thought as she was surprised by it. Though, she was quick to return it and smile at him as she spoke.

"I may start expecting that when you visit me moving forward."

"We'll see. I wasn't expecting any of this to happen on this trip. That said, I think that is a fine request, so long as you promise to not ask for more."

"Nope, I may never say it in words, but you will see it in my eyes as they can't lie to you anymore."

"Fair enough. Just understand when I don't make a move right away."

"Mark me."

"Are you sure?"

"I am. I will not ask to become a mother until you complete your quest, but even if it is only the smallest of chances of working, I want to know that I have a chance to reunite with you if you fail here."

Xeal looked at Austru and sighed at knowing that he had just accepted her into his life. Though as he thought about it, he smiled at the thought as he agreed to give her a pseudo mark and had her lie face down while exposing her back to him. Extracting a drop of Ninlil the wind phoenix's blood from his inventory, Xeal used it to mark her as she let out a gasp at the sensation. After that, Xeal extracted a drop of Austru's blood and told her that he would be right back as he returned to Nium after donning a cloak.

Once there, he avoided the festivities that were everywhere as the Triday festival was in full swing as the kingdom celebrated the three-day affair. According to the lore, these three days were gifts from the gods to remember their triumph over the primordials. While most didn't realize the significance of three and 12, Xeal did as there were 12 tiers of existence in this world, with tier-1 to tier-8 being considered the mortal tiers. Godhood could be considered tier-9, while the first three generations of Watcher's family, to include himself and the phoenixes, were the tier-10 to tier-12. With the top three tiers having been defeated by the gods, these three days of celebration in the names of the gods were to help reinforce them as they held the primordials in the lost court. It was also why even in the middle of wars, a ceasefire would be called surrounding the festival as if it wasn't, the offending country would find itself dealing with a holy war. The few times this had occurred, according to ED's history, the nations didn't last a month as most of their populace turned against them.

It was with these thoughts that Xeal arrived at his mansion in the capital and made his way to the master bedroom after removing his cloak. Upon entering the room, he found that it wasn't empty as Gale was sitting there looking annoyed as she saw him step inside the room. At first he was unsure what to make of this, until her eyes flashed and a portal opened revealing a familiar field. Xeal just sighed before he added Austru's drop of blood to the symbol beneath the bed as Gale lay unconscious and made his way through the portal. As he did so, he was greeted by Freya as she spoke to him.

"Thank you for coming and I must apologize for allowing Bula to see what she did that day."

"Right and just what is this costing Gale?"

"She will be fine in about an hour. While this is a little more forceful, it takes less of a toll than when I use the skill to heal your whole party and weaken your foes."

"Okay, is saying sorry all you wanted to do, or is there another reason that you are risking exposing Gale like this?"

"She has long been exposed," retorted Freya. "It is why I accepted Aceso under me and told her to attract her sisters over as well. It is actually thanks to you that Gale is currently safe, as your situation and those around you is known as well."

"So, what, Gale is acting as our warden, or something, to all the other gods?"

"No, you know what our true role is in this reality and I will just say that if any other was doing what you are, well, you would have more to deal with than Laplace's attempt to entrap you."

"No, instead I just have you trying to seduce me and other deities trying to use me as shelter. So, just how many divine scions do you intend to force on me?"

"How many can you handle?"

Xeal paused as he wanted to retort none, but he knew that with the thousands of deities that existed, even if many only had a small cult of followers, that he would need to give Freya a fair number to work with. After all, if it was just her and a few dozen against the rest that were rejected, it would wind up causing Gale and FAE issues. So, after thinking things through and considering his resources, Xeal responded.

"You need to find a carrot besides protection through a phoenix feather, or a drop of their blood, but if I am successful in aiding Nium in conquering their continent, shelter there could be created relatively easily. That said, I can accept at most six more right now that can receive a drop of blood and once the war starts, I can protect more with a feather as I won't need them for the dwarven VIP's anymore."

"With your latest harvest you have 26 drops of blood and over 90 feathers at your disposal. I can understand holding back Brangwen's, but the rest? You can't really believe you need such a reserve."

"Freya, my ladies and the phoenixes' marked are why 20 drops must be held in reserve. I am well aware that at most half of those will come into play, but I will not risk what I need not. Besides, my hope is that you convince deities to spread their vessels around to other guilds. Heck, if they have one of my kind in mind, but are worried about their current situation, let Gale know and we will see what we can do."

"What if they want you to convince a player to worship them in exchange for becoming their vessel?"

"Am I going to piss off any other deity by doing so and who is the player?"

"Will any of that matter to you if the reward is great enough?"

"Yes. Freya, I am not ready to deal with elevating the risk of a holy war right now and you need to be careful on which deities you bring under you. I can tell that you are aiming to be the queen of a new pantheon by using my guild to win your war, but that relies on me actually seeing it as a good thing for the long-term prosperity of this reality."

"Oh?"

"Yes, now think on that."

With that Xeal activated his ability to transfer to the quest world and smiled when it worked, as he found himself back at the camp and Austru smiled at seeing him return. It didn't matter to him that Freya had just about lost it when he left before she allowed him to, nor did it matter that he had obliged her when she knew that he didn't want to earlier. She was a goddess, and she had even shown him the courtesy of admitting her fault in allowing Bula to see a future where she embraced Xeal and led her people to true prosperity. After all, while the sight couldn't lie, possibilities could be hidden from the recipient and less likely possibilities could be pushed. A fact that Freya smiled at as she thought about how she would maneuver Xeal, godling that he may be currently.

Any thoughts that Freya may have had were put out of Xeal's mind as he made his way with Austru into the demon lands, as he took in the reality of it for the first time. He had never set foot in any area that had not been cleansed by him, or another player, before and he was grateful for the loophole he was using to do so now. Though, as he moved, all he could do was frown at the lack of anything that could be considered normal life. The plants that he had always seen as withered husks and dying versions of themselves after he cleansed an area, were now twisted versions of themselves. Rather than dying from the demonic energy as he would have expected, they, even more so than the animals, had adapted to the changes in the world. In fact, Xeal suspected that it was through eating these plants that the animals had changed in the first place and began to worry about the long-term effects of eating the animals.

"It's as if the very land has been claimed by the demons," commented Austru solemnly. "I have read the reports, but seeing it is just so different."

"Disturbing. I dare say that, if left alone, it would have creeped across the whole world. As it is, I am convinced that only 64 locations in this whole world were spared."

"Even if you succeed, will this world survive?"

"If I succeed, this world will be mine and I have a feeling that I will be able to do a fair bit of restoration work to it rather easily. That said, it will never be the same as it was."

Austru just frowned at Xeal's words, as he gave her a sign for her to be quiet as they made their way to what had once been a city according to the map he was working off of. Along the way, Xeal smiled at the fights they ended up partaking in, as they slew one demonic animal after another. None of these were a real challenge for Xeal as they were well below his level, though they were decent experience for Austru, who had yet to even reach tier-6, as she stuck close to Xeal and used her racial abilities to manipulate the wind into blades to attack. This was just one more way that this world differed from the main ED world, as it lacked any class system and only had skill books, so you could either learn the skill, or not. It was this fact that made scribes so valuable here, though they still needed the right materials to work with to create the books. It was the time it took to gather and prepare these that took the most time and with the world being in the state it was, such things were in short supply.

Six hours after they had entered the demon lands, Xeal finally saw his goal for this trip as the city came into view. With it, Xeal saw thousands of twisted forms of both demons and demonic creatures moving about its exterior. While Xeal had read Vento's scouting reports on this and the other cities his expeditions had explored, he had still wished to see it for himself. After all, he intended to venture into the true demonic realm one day and was sure such nests would be normal from what little had been made known about them in Xeal's last life. Like all things meant for those above tier-7 in ED, almost nothing was known to the general population of players, but due to him working with Frozen Sky, Xeal had learned some of it. These were mainly things like how it seemed that the dungeon at the center of the continent seemed impossible to ever beat, or that there were even ways to travel to different planes and not just other worlds. Though as Xeal thought about it, the demonic plane had likely just been a world like this one that had fallen to them. What it had been before Xeal didn't wish to dwell on, as he doubted it had been just a barren rock in the middle of space before it became one of the closest things to hell in all of ED.

All Xeal could think of was how this world seemed to have been given a similar treatment, only with himself and the other champions offering a resistance to the demons to complete their quest. Still, Xeal felt like the system had gone too far in its actions to set this stage for them to clash over, as he saw no need for what had been a city of thousands of humans to become such a mess. As he thought about this, he couldn't help but wonder if any of the women that had been in the cages when he attacked the slave market and killed the noble idiot had survived. As unlikely as that was, Xeal couldn't help hoping that his actions that day had saved someone, as he looked at Austru who had a look of horror on her face and spoke.

"Well, this is what I wanted to see on this trip. Any requests before you head back?"

"Is that what the reports mean by a nest?"

"It seems so, and that is what Mauvers, or Tumond, could become if they fall to the demons' hands. If you noticed, the closer we got to this point the stronger the demons became. They are growing to offer those like myself a challenge and possibly more. Honestly, clearing them out before they get out of hand is more important than actually defeating the others like myself."

"How are we supposed to even resist those things?"

"You're not, that is my job. All I can say is that we should just be grateful only tier-6 demons currently exist in this world, at least to our knowledge. If tier-7 demons become normal, I doubt that most of my kind will be much help in holding them back anymore."

"What do you mean?"

"Your world only knows tier-6 dangers and unless a path

to tier-7 opens up for this world, all those who call it home will be helpless against them. It's why I need to get in there to see what we are up against. You have a few return scrolls on you, right?"

"If you mean one of the ones that your followers have started to produce recently then yes, though I would rather not waste one as they are still rare here."

"Ha, if I could only bring items into this world for others to use, they would be so common by now that they would be taken for granted. Anyhow, while I have enjoyed getting some time with you at long last, I am going in there and I doubt that I will have the luxury of keeping you safe while I do."

"Are you insane?"

"A bit, but right now I feel like letting loose and that nest looks like the perfect outlet for me to work out some frustrations. That said, I am well aware that I will need to escape from it and my way out isn't something that I can do if you are here."

"Why even bring me then?"

"I did so on a whim. Really, you may understand more when you read the letters waiting for you. If not, well, I will return once I am done here."

Austru looked at Xeal worriedly, before sighing and pulling out her return scroll and leaving him by himself. At this Xeal smiled as he took stock of what was in front of him, as well as what items he had to work with and quickly got to work. Once Xeal had spent a few hours making his preparations and ensuring that everything was ready and his stats were full, he ran straight at the city that had become a demon's nest. As he did so, it wasn't long before he attracted the attention of the mass outside what had once been the city gates. All of these ranged from level 120 to 150 and were practically worthless to the level 186 Xeal, experience-wise. Still, with a few thousand of them, he could easily be overwhelmed if he wasn't careful, as he used his level 4 fighting spirit skill to release his aura. Doing this caused the skill to switch from a passive to an active state, as it cost one SP point from his pool every second that he used it like this. Though his pool was large enough that he could last over 16 hours like this if he didn't use any other skills.

As Xeal unleashed his aura, the demons who had been charging at him shifted to running away, as there was a three percent chance for every level he was above an unintelligent monster he was facing, that it would flee. This meant that anything level 152 or below had a 100% chance of fleeing from him regardless of the number of monsters involved. Xeal just smiled as he entered the city and found the demonic creatures all fleeing from him, until he finally was confronted by a level 162 shadow demon that resisted its urge to flee. Still, Xeal just smiled as he used his elemental blades to pick it apart in a matter of minutes, before delving deeper into the ruins of the city. As he did so, he was at least happy that most demons didn't leave much behind due to their never-ending hunger. Still, Xeal was disappointed as he continued on facing off against the occasional demon that resisted running, but he had yet to see anything reach level 170 as of yet.

With most top-tier pro players currently around level 178, Xeal had expected to find plenty of demons around the same level, but it seemed that they were lagging behind. Still, Xeal hadn't yet entered the old keep, where he would expect to find any demons that could be considered intelligent inside this nest. Though with only around half of the demons running from Xeal at this point, he wasn't sure if he would even be able to reach the keep. All the same, Xeal just smiled as he managed his MP, SP and stamina, while using his outrageous stats to overwhelm the five to six demons he found himself facing off against at any one time. He was just happy that the stronger a demon was, the less it would tolerate even a demon of equal strength being around it. This was why the weaker ones had been pushed out of the nest and many of the ones who had fled from him ended up fighting another of their kind. The domino effect that this created was a pleasant surprise to Xeal, as he had expected them to exchange a few attacks before separating. However, with them being in such close quarters already, it had led to more demons getting involved in each fight and even multiple demons being killed and eaten.

That was until a massive form, that seemed to be made of darkness, landed in front of Xeal and made him frown. At ten feet tall and five feet wide, the level 200 humanoid demon that held a club looked at Xeal as it let out a roar. Instantly all of the surrounding demons cowered and hid, as Xeal felt his own aura struggling against that of the new arrival. However, he held firm as the demon smiled broadly before speaking to Xeal.

"Perhaps you will actually provide this one with some entertainment today!"

"If you beg for mercy and tell me what I wish to know, I may give you a painless death."

"Ha, hahahahahha, wonderful. You think it will be I who needs to beg."

"I don't think," stated Xeal as he adjusted his stance. "I know!"

With that Xeal charged straight at the demon without a care for what type of monster it was, or its abilities. Now all Xeal cared for was that he had an outlet to focus his frustrations on. As the first clash ended, he smiled at the demon's surprise, before it licked its lips and charged right at Xeal. With each clash, Xeal couldn't help but smile at how easy this fight was compared to what he had faced in the Vault of Ucnuc at the end. However, the demon was a demon after all and its abilities were such that it was designed to be a challenge for a party of level 200 players. If Xeal were to guess, it was on the level of an area boss and he wasn't sure if he had the stamina to defeat it and escape afterwards. Still, one blow after another was exchanged until they were both below 80% health as the demon spoke once more.

"Good, good, I have longed for a decent fight, though it is a shame you have no way to win even if you kill me."

"Ha, I could say the same to you. My kind can never die. Besides, I didn't come here to kill you today."

"It matters not, as you have come and now you will never leave. Hmm, if you can never die, does that mean I can eat you over and over again?"

"Ha, hahaha, ah that is good. Let me just say that if you managed to swallow me, it would give you the worst indigestion you have ever had if I actually died and revived inside of you."

"Ah, so you think you are spicy. Good, good. You make good meal as you never leave my belly!"

With that the demon charged at Xeal while brandishing its club wildly, as Xeal unleashed a blast of dragon's breath into its face. Xeal smiled as he charged at the stunned demon as he activated his double upward and downward slash combo. With each hit, Xeal smiled at seeing the damage accumulation as he continued to channel his frustrations until the demon's club caught him and sent him flying into a wall. Contorting his body midair, Xeal was able to have his feet hit the wall first, before almost spring boarding back at the demon. Despite all of this, the demon continued to laugh as they fought like that as Xeal slowly gained the advantage to the point of having 50% health to the demon's 30%. However, with only ten percent of his stamina left, Xeal knew it was time to leave, or risk running out of it before he could escape, as he broke contact and started running back the way he came.

As Xeal ran, the demon seemed to be confused for a second, before roaring in rage and giving chase. To make matters worse, the path that Xeal had taken was now blocked by many of the monsters who had fled earlier. This forced Xeal to dodge any that didn't flee from him and he unleashed a dragon's breath behind him as he did so to delay the demon, who was a lot faster than its frame would suggest. As Xeal did this, he would catch a taunt here or there, and had to laugh at the demon's attempts to get under his skin. Though Xeal had to frown as he realized his stamina was dropping faster than he had expected, as he got through the gates and into the open field and only had five percent of it left. This was still within what he considered a safe range, but it was also what he had expected to be at once he was done escaping. Xeal wondered if this was a side effect of being in the demon lands for an extended period of time, or something about the demon who was following him even now.

Regardless of the why, Xeal knew that he needed to reach his escape point and let everything else play out as he ran at full speed, now that no demons, walls or structures, were hindering his progress. That said, they were also not hindering the demon's progress and it seemed that they had been more of an issue for it, as it started to gain on Xeal. Sighing at this, Xeal started to use his piercing thrust skill to give him sudden bursts of speed at key seconds, as he put his all into escaping. Unfortunately, executing such a maneuver was draining to both his SP pool and his stamina, and Xeal knew that he was going to end up cutting it close in more than one way.

Finally, as the point Xeal needed to reach came into view, the demon caught up to Xeal, who was now at two percent stamina and it brought its club down in an overhand swing. Xeal was able to dodge this, but it caused him to stop and deal with the follow-up in the form of a baseball bat-like swing. Rather than avoid this blow, Xeal jumped into it such that he connected with the club at the same point that a ball being hit to center field would and was launched into the sky towards his goal. This action also served to further enrage the demon, as it started to charge straight forward while Xeal smiled as he soared right over the point he needed to reach. As Xcal landed and went into a controlled roll to lessen the damage that he took, he was just in time to hear the demon roar in pure frustration as it discovered the traps Xeal had set up. These included spell mines and hidden snares that would drag their victims over more spell mines, before having them end up hanging upside down. Still, even if the demon was hit by most of what Xeal had set up, while this bought him the time he needed to escape he doubted it would be enough to kill it as he activated a return scroll.

With the demon left behind to deal with the traps, Xeal found himself back in Mauvers and wasted no time in heading for Austru's room. As he entered, Xeal found her turning to look at him before frowning and picking up the stack of letters and speaking.

"Alright, from the sounds of things I should write a letter to this Bula to express my thoughts on her actions and where I stand on the matter, but I fail to see what that has to do with you bringing me along earlier."

"Ah, they must not have mentioned about how they decided to overload me with attention and by seeking my affection since Bula acted. As for a letter to Bula, I would say that unless you wish to acknowledge her and help her in getting closer to me, a letter to the others stating your stance will be enough."

"Overload you with attention? Why would that make you want my company over being alone?"

"It didn't, but I figured that there was no better time in seeing if you and I were really compatible as if I could stand to be around you even then, well, you get the idea and you were wonderful."

"I am not sure how to take that, as it makes me feel like the other woman that you go to when you are tired of your wives and not part of the whole."

"Ah, but you see, you are both of those in a way right now. Though all you need do is know that I have set things up so that you can be with me regardless of if I succeed in my quest here, know that I have no intention of you staying as the other woman."

Austru gave Xeal a hard look as she thought about his words before responding to him.

"Yet I am the only one who is not being pushed to raise my level and tier."

"That day may come, but for now you are trapped in this world, at the center of what I plan to make my stronghold. One unfortunate side effect of the demons invading was the loss of all weaker foes for you to level with and while Vento could aid you in power leveling, it would hinder other efforts. Sadly, I have too few of my kind to devote to this world and will need to see to it that they all are ready to attempt to reach tier-7 sooner rather than later. After all, I confirmed that a tier-7 demon was present when I was in the nest just now."

Xeal watched as Austru froze at hearing the news, before frowning and responding.

"If it's there, why hasn't it attacked us?"

"I have my theories, but I think it is, just not physically. When I was near, it drained my stamina more than it should have and if I had to bet, it was corrupting its surroundings with its power."

"So, it won't invade our lands?"

"I don't know, but it is creating a horde of demons that could storm past our defense rather easily. If I had to guess, it has to deal with my dominion bordering the other one, or it is possible that there is another dominion on the far side of that one which I don't know about."

"What will happen if the demons start attacking the other dominion and it falls?"

"Other than the other champion losing their shards to the other player, I expect a new nest will be created."

"No, hasn't this world suffered enough? You have to be able to do something."

"All I can do is keep accepting those who flee into my dominion and try to collect more information from the influx of residents."

"Why not send some of those who fled here back to see if there is a second dominion?"

"Simple, we are pretty sure that the other kingdom has closed its borders to any wishing to leave at this point. The trade caravan that has been delivering food has only been able to interact with soldiers near the border and what little we have learned from those interactions is that they are cautious of me. Apparently my actions in Tumond didn't sit well with the current rulers and neither did my open border policy. King Silas and Earl Altman have sent diplomatic messages to them several times now and have yet to receive a reply beyond essentially a thank you, but no thank you, to any talks."

"Why have I not been kept in the loop about that?" asked Austru, sounding upset. "Is it not my job to be the interface between you and this world?"

"It is, only Vento is handling this one and he reports to Kate, who reports to me. For better or worse, you have become in charge of only non-time-sensitive events that happen within my dominion. When Vento can message me or Kate directly, it just makes more sense for him to do so."

Xeal could tell that Austru wasn't satisfied with this answer, as she looked at him with a slight pout on her face as he smiled at her. This standoff lasted a good minute before Austru sighed and shifted the topic slightly.

"Am I even needed here, or am I just a jewel for you to see every time you visit this world?"

"Never underestimate the power of me looking forward to the first thing I see every time I come to this world. I was ready to simply head straight to the demon lands and vent my frustrations when I arrived here and saw you. The fact that it caused my mood to improve surprised even myself at the time, as I thought that I simply wished to be alone before that moment."

"While that makes me happy to know, I still wish to be more than the prize you are aiming for when this is all done."

"Austru, if I saw you as nothing but that you would know. No, if nothing else, you are the one my wives trust to let them know if you have any concerns about me while I am here."

"Hmm, it seems that I need to write a letter then. After all, everything you have said to me since you arrived has been cause for concern."

"Ha, right, have fun with that."

As Xeal joked with Austru, he realized where she fit for him as he felt free with her, something that he had honestly not even thought of needing before this latest break from everyone. While he kept this to himself as he wasn't quite ready to share it with her as his feelings were only starting to form for her, the fact that he could see her in his life so easily was telling to him. Still, it was early in the relationship, all things considered, and it was time for him to leave as this trip had already cost him a month and a half of accumulated time.

"I will leave you to write your letters as I see to taking care of the others who I hold dear. Thank you for helping me clear my head."

"It was my pleasure, though I wish it wasn't so costly for you to snuggle with me like we did last night."

"As do I, though once I take the next step, I should be able to spend one out of every 16 days here. I think at that point, it will only be fair to spend a night beside you each month if I can. Even if one of the others accompanies me as well for those visits."

"I think I would like that."

Xeal just smiled as he gave her one more kiss, before returning to the main ED world and making his way to Anelqua and Queen Aila Lorafir's palace, with his feelings still slightly out of sorts. When he arrived, he found that like the rest of ED, the elven city was in the midst of celebrating the gods and sighed knowing that he had likely caused them nothing but issues due to his absence so far. Still, when he reached the palace, it wasn't long before he found himself sitting with Queen Aila Lorafir as she smiled at him while waiting for him to speak first.

"So why didn't you stop them as I can clearly tell that you knew that it was a bad idea from the start?"

"Xeal, I love you. Even now I would like nothing more to have you to myself, yet I know that I need to share you with them. As such, I refuse to be in the lead among them as were I to do so, I would overwhelm them to the point that I would become your de facto first wife one day. That path is not one that will make you happy, so I allow little mistakes like this one to occur and allow them to learn from them."

"Right, so can you get them all here tonight without telling them that I am here?"

"Oh, you aren't going to ignore us all for the next few days while you sort out your thoughts?"

"Aila, I needed to blow off some steam. I have done that and have no desire to prolong things that do none of us any good any longer."

"Very well. I will invite them all to dinner to discuss the situation as a private Triday celebration of a sort."

As Queen Aila left Xeal in the room that they had met in, he sighed as he thought about the fact that once the Triday celebrations were over, war could start at any time. While Xeal expected it to be some time still, he knew that most ceasefires had come during these times and it was common for both sides to decide to wait years before launching another attack. It had also been these times that created the most chaos as players flooded into one country, or another, only for it to lead to that country being the next one to decide it was in a prime position to launch an attack. It had been this mentality that had led to Nium having an inflated population in Xeal's last life, as it had become the only country exempt from these worries before Abysses End started to try to take it over. After that, the pros and cons had shifted enough that many players dealt with the issues surrounding the constant wars between nations over the constant advance of Abysses End. It was this future that Xeal was working to prevent, though he wondered just what things would be like once he did as overcrowding had caused its own set of issues.

As Xeal passed the time thinking over things and

deciding just how he wanted to address the situations, the others started to arrive. As they did so, it was clear to all that saw them, that things were tense as they entered the private dining room that was being set up for the event. As they waited for the others to arrive and Queen Aila Lorafir to join them, Xeal found himself being led by Queen Aila Lorafir to a room from which he could listen in from. As he went to protest, she cut him off as she spoke.

"Xeal, I am well aware that you never want to hear the divides that exist between your wives, but in this case I believe you need to. Worry not, I will ensure that things don't get out of hand, not that they ever have since I have been a part of these meetings. Though things have never been this tense before either."

"You want me to know just how deep my actions hurt those I love."

All Xeal received in response was a smile as she asked him to wait for her to send for him to enter and left him alone as he heard Eira start talking to Kate in an annoyed tone.

"Are you happy yet?"

"Eira, we need to remain calm. Xeal-"

"I am calm. My claws aren't in you, after all. That doesn't mean that I am not upset that I let you convince me to go along with this idea for so long."

"Eira, Kate wasn't the only one pushing for her idea," interjected Aalin. "I did as well and we don't need you to tell us we were wrong, as we have been telling ourselves that for the past two days."

"You are all overreacting," commented Mari. "Xeal is simply ensuring that he avoids saying anything that he will regret later. Yes, it was poor timing, but I for one appreciate his consideration for the long-term health of our relationship, as words can be hard to take back while his current actions can be justified."

"Yes," added Lingxin. "Sometimes space is best for all, especially when feelings are involved."

"I still say that we need to learn from this and not always let logic sway us," retorted Eira. "In particularly when we all are fresh off of being annoyed at something that wasn't even Xeal's fault."

"Eira has a point," mentioned Dyllis. "We all over reacted and worse yet, we decided to punish Xeal by rewarding ourselves when we did."

At Dyllis's words the others went quiet as the door opened and Queen Aila Lorafir walked in and spoke.

"It is good to see you all. It looks like we are just waiting on Gale, Luna, Selene and Enye to get started."

"Gale says she is ten minutes out and the other three are stuck in a meeting with Victor," replied Kate.

"You did tell them all that this is an important meeting, right?"

"Aila, I did and they will be here. They are just dealing with the mess Xeal not being here the last two days has been causing."

"Yes, well, send them a message that if they are not here in ten minutes, they will be left out of this discussion."

"Excuse me, that is-"

"No!" shouted Queen Aila Lorafir, cutting Kate off. "I expect them to place this meeting above even the good of Nium, or I will feel they are taking the commitment they have made to making this work too lightly. Today I am not simply letting things flow the way you all want for the most part and yes, I do place being included in this group as being more important than ruling my nation, save for defending it. As we know that no war will be waged this day, there is no reason for them to not already be here as I gave plenty of time when I contacted you, Kate!"

Xeal could feel the tension that Queen Aila Lorafir had created with her words, even from the room he was hidden in. Finally, after a long pause, Kate spoke.

"Victor is pissed, but they are moving as fast as they can," stated Kate.

"I will deal with Victor. Now I want us all to really think about how we feel about the current situation while we wait. Only once we are all present can anything that is said be effective in ensuring that we all learn from this experience."

Xeal began to worry just what Queen Aila Lorafir's intent was, as he resisted the urge to join them and avoid hearing any further contention between them. He knew that things weren't perfect between all of them, but he had simply assumed that they were able to handle things after a bit of discussion. While they had been just talking earlier, he could tell that the tension between them was far more than he had expected, especially between Kate and Eira. Finally, the doors opened once more and Enye, Gale, Luna and Selene walked in together as Queen Aila spoke once more.

"Good, now that we are all present, we can begin. Who would like to speak first?"

"I would," answered Enye. "What is going on that you feel the need to be so forceful in calling us here?"

"What is going on is that I am questioning whether you truly place Xeal second only to your children? I will give any of you who have been blessed with a child from him that caveat, but when I am removing myself from the passive role I normally take by calling a meeting like this, I expect it to be taken seriously. So much so that unless you are defending your nation from something, I expect you to drop all else and come here. Perhaps the fact that this seems to have not been ingrained in most of you, is my own fault for never initiating a meeting before today. Now, who wishes to address the reason we are all here first."

"I take it that it is safe to say that this is about Xeal needing some space right now, right?" checked Gale as Queen Aila Lorafir gave her a nod. "Well, I should add that Freya made me have him visit her when he dropped by his mansion in the capital earlier."

"What was he doing there?" questioned Aalin. "And how did you know to be there?"

"Really," retorted Eira. "Freya has eyes on Xeal obviously and she wanted something."

"Eira, I can talk for myself and yes, she does seem to keep a close eye on Xeal, though all I can figure is that he decided to mark Austru and was adding her blood to the revival point there. However, whatever Freya wanted is beyond me, but she seems annoyed at him right now for leaving before she was done talking to him."

"Great, even a goddess is after our man," interjected Luna.

"Yeah, though that does mean that even a goddess is jealous of us," quipped Selene.

"Now all we need to do is avoid her smiting us over it."

"Though we don't think we should share with her either way."

"How can you both be joking right now?" asked Dyllis, sounding concerned.

"Dear, we know Xeal."

"Yeah, he would never leave us."

"Any of us."

"He also will never let any of us go without a fight."

"Did we screw up?"

"Big time!"

"Will he forgive us?"

"Once he has enough time to cool off."

"He will."

"Without us even asking."

"So, we just need to appreciate that he cares."

"And be sure to give him the time that he needs!"

Xeal found himself smiling at how Luna and Selene took control of the room with their rant as the room went quiet with contemplation. Finally, Eira broke the silence as she sighed and spoke to Kate from what Xeal could tell.

"Sorry for blaming you earlier. I just feel insecure as I don't even have a kitten to comfort me right now."

"You are always welcome to hold Xin, or any of the others," comforted Lingxin. "You are one of their mothers as well now and Xeal would be upset if any of us treated them as anything else besides our own child."

"That he would," agreed Dyllis. "Honestly, it is wonderful to see them all growing together."

"I just wish they would slow down," commented Gale. "I mean, by the time our kids in our reality are old enough to meet them, they will be almost 50."

"Or over 50 for ours," added Luna.

"Yeah, it sucks," agreed Selene.

"Alright, are there any more words on how we treated Xeal after Bula's declaration that need to be shared?" asked Queen Aila Lorafir in a much gentler tone than she had used earlier.

"It's going to be hard to return to not seeking the extra affection and time that I have been enjoying," responded Dyllis. "I know the why, but there never seems to be enough time for us to simply be together."

"Yes, it has been nice to be a bit more demanding," agreed Lingxin. "Though, we all knew that it was temporary…"

Xeal listened to each of the ladies agree as they shifted to chatting about the little moments that they had enjoyed the most. The fact that several of these moments had been, by their own admission, intrusive to his work had annoyed him a bit, but what they all loved about the moments was how he had put them first. Finally, Queen Aila Lorafir cleared her throat and ended the chatter as she spoke once more.

"Anything else?"

After a long pause, she continued to speak.

"Alright, Xeal, if you would be so kind as to join us."

At this Xeal could hear them all take in a breath as Kate was the first to respond while Xeal made his way into the room with them.

"Aila, these meetings are meant to never be shared with him!"

"I didn't call you all here, he did and I never said that it was a private meeting."

"You-"

Kate's rebuttal fell silent as Xeal came into view and he spoke before any of them could.

"To be clear, Aila set you all up as she insisted that I listen in. That said, she did promise to keep things from getting too heated as well. I love you all and while I am still annoyed at the purposeful overloading of me that you all were doing, I forgive all of you. Just please don't ever make me think that you are feeling insecure like that when you aren't. I seriously thought that Bula had you all feeling like you needed to exert your claim to me and ensure that you are all still my world."

"Oh, honey," started Luna.

"All we need to do is smile at you to know that," continued Selene.

"Yeah, the look you give us is just perfect."

"It says that you will hold us gently."

"While defending us fiercely from any that would harm

us."

"All while making us feel truly seen."

"While they aren't wrong," commented Aalin, "sometimes, it is still nice to hear it and I am sorry for weighing you down lately."

"No, none of you could weigh me down. It is all the things I have to do that keeps me from being with any of you that weigh me down. Especially when you're right there with me and I need to focus on it. That said, I do need at least sometimes just to work through my own thoughts at times. On that note, Gale is right, I was at my mansion to add Austru's blood to the revival point there as I spent the last day and a half with her."

"So does that mean she is officially one of us?" asked Enye, sounding slightly frustrated.

"I have kissed, marked and spent a night snuggling with her. If that is all it takes, sure. If I need to be in love with her, then not yet. That said, unless one of you has a real issue with her besides the indirectness of communications currently, she will likely solidify herself in my heart rather easily after this last trip."

"Even if we did have a reason, it would do little good to fight it and it can be said that this is, at least in part, our fault either way," replied Enye.

"Agreed, but no more before the end of the war," added Kate.

"No," interjected Eira. "No more once the war comes to a close. Bula, Daisy, Violet and Dafasli deserve to have a chance to gain his affection while fighting alongside him."

"No," replied Xeal. "I am done with any timelines on falling in love, beyond Aila being the last I marry."

"Ha," interrupted Gale. "Better be careful about any absolutes. You might find yourself dealing with Freya getting in the way. Or did you forget about how she all but said that she would likely come to see what you had to offer once you reached the peak of this world?"

"Is there no end to them?" asked Eira, sounding exasperated.

"There is and I expect that Freya will never make such a move on me, as it would require more of a commitment than she wishes for. Still, Gale, let her know that I am sorry for how I walked out on her after she sought me out for a meeting and I have an idea in relation to our prior discussion."

"Okay, you know that she can't keep using my body to open portals all the time, right? It has a cooldown of 60 days and even then, it sucks to use for me."

"I know and I have no issue with you passing along the message later, but for now let's enjoy the meal Aila is providing for us."

"Sure, just don't blame me when she wants her pound of flesh for what you did."

Xeal just smiled as the chatter shifted back to happier topics as the food arrived and they enjoyed a night before returning to Hardt Burgh to rest before the last day of the Triday events. During this day, Xeal found himself being dragged around as Enye worked to get him to make up for all the appearances he had missed. While Xeal found this annoying, he didn't say much as he knew that it came with the job of being nobility and if he wasn't seen it would cause issues. It had been this that Enye had been meeting with King Victor about when she was running late to the event and thankfully Xeal turning up directly after that had been enough to mitigate the issues. Apparently, a story was already being circulated about him needing to handle guild business to explain his absence. Still, Xeal had just been happy when the day had ended and it was once more time to log out.

(*****)

Morning March 1 to Morning March 4, 2268 & ED Year 5 Days 321-330.

With the air finally cleared, Alex enjoyed his time while logged off as he basically spent all of it focused on his daughters and prepping for the upcoming meeting he had with Eternal Dominion, Inc. This included looking over the plans that had been approved and the concepts for expansion once the city hit certain milestones. Alex knew that he was going to have an uphill battle to secure the quantum-entangled server that could interface with one of theirs, that was networked directly to their main server. It would be this more than anything that would play into FAE's ability to truly expand the city, from a place for a hundred thousand or so people, into one for over a million, if not several million people. So it was that by the time Alex logged in for the last time before the meeting on the morning of the fourth, he had made sure everything was ready.

Day 321 saw Xeal return to his normal grinding, reaching level 187 as he did so, while he focused on the climb to tier-7 that he hoped to complete, before summer in reality arrived once again. At the same time, Xeal had Enye send invitations out to all those whom he had any positive relations with, for a gathering on day 364 of this year. Still, it was on days 325 and 328 that Xeal had his most significant moments during this time, as he had his last required visits with Princesses Lorena and Bianca.

As Xeal arrived at Queen Aila Lorafir's palace on day 325, he was greeted with a kiss from her as she presented Princess Lorena to him. The past five months and change had done wonders for the young princess of Paidhia as she regained a fair bit of her regalness, along with a few inches of her blonde hair. She still had a hardened and resigned look of finality about her as she greeted Xeal once his kiss with Queen Aila Lorafir came to an end.

"I suppose today marks the end of these, at least for a while. I thank you for at least honoring your word in visiting me as promised, Duke Bluefire."

"Alright, since when did you decide to go fully formal on me, Princess Lorena?"

Xeal caught the slight smile on Princess Lorena's face as she responded to his words.

"I have still never gotten you to simply call me Lorena this whole time, so it seems that I failed to even move past formalities with you. Now, if you wish for me to simply call you by your first name, I would ask that you do the same for me moving forward."

"Alright, Princess Lorena and Duke Bluefire it is then," retorted Xeal. "Now, as you know, this will be the last time I visit you like this. In fact, I expect the next 100 hours I owe you to be completed in ten ten-hour blocks once you are in Cielo city."

"By then you will be working to remove my father's head from his shoulders, won't you."

"Yes, Princess Lorena."

"At least you're honest. Is that why you can't move past pitying us?"

"It definitely is playing a role, but I can't say that is all of it, Princess Lorena."

"Please don't treat me, or Bianca, as if we are women to be pitied. We both were raised knowing that our marriages would be for the kingdom's good. Honestly, we are both happy to have avoided being used to secure reinforcements from the highest bidder once the war began."

"No, instead you are simply the hostages that I am holding in case either of them steps over the line and I need to make an example out of you, Princess Lorena."

"Duke Bluefire, you may be a lot of things, but I don't believe you would even make an example out of me. Master might, but you would sooner cut off your own arm than purposely harm me, or Bianca, in any way, physically at least. You have gone out of your way to cause us a bit of mental harm with how you have treated us during these visits after all."

"If that is how you wish to see it, I am fine with it. Now we have a walk to do, unless you have a suitable request for our activity today, Princess Lorena."

"Hmm, would you let me simply lean my back against your chest as we sit under a tree and talk?"

"I am sorry, but that feels too intimate for me to approve of. Perhaps I can allow you to sit beside me as you lean slightly on me, but that is as far as I see as appropriate, Princess Lorena."

"Very well, I suppose I can agree to that if you allow me to hold onto your arm while we do so."

"Alright, but no holding my hand, Princess Lorena."

"Fine, now let us be on our way."

Xeal could tell that his constant emphasis on addressing her by the proper etiquette surrounding one of her station had annoyed her. As while he had never used just her name when addressing her, he had at least not acted like any other noble who was unfamiliar with her would have. Still, she held her tongue as they made their way over to a nice large tree that looked out over the lake and sat together. Once seated, she wasted no time in claiming Xeal's arm with hers and his shoulder with her head as she started to talk.

"Is this really so bad? I mean just sitting here while

allowing me to show you a bit of affection?"

"Isolated by itself, no, but it isn't isolated, Princess Lorena. It is tainted by a contract that requires I spend time with you, a war that looms over us all, the fact that I am involved with so many others and much more."

"Yes, well, I hope you don't dawdle in removing my father's head from his shoulders so you can see that I won't hold it against you. Duke Bluefire, I wish to become just Lorena and for you to see me as such. I know that I am not perfect, nor am I what you are looking for in your next wife, but it is what I want, despite everything you have done to convince me otherwise until now."

"Princess Lorena, I wish you the best of luck in moving past those feelings as I do not see you succeeding in your endeavor to secure a place in my heart."

"Perhaps, but until the last second of my time with you has ended, I will hold out hope that I will find a way in."

Xeal just smiled as he let the topic die there as they continued to idly chat, until it was time for him to return to his daily grind after giving Queen Aila Lorafir one last kiss. Though he once more found himself kissing Queen Aila Lorafir in greeting when he returned on day 328 for his last visit with Princess Bianca. Like Princess Lorena, Princess Bianca had regained a bit of her regalness since her return, but she still had kept her hair shaven on the sides with a single ponytail and her eyes had only become fiercer. As she greeted Xeal, she did so with confidence and a smile that made him wonder if she knew something that he didn't.

"It is good to see you, Duke Bluefire. I trust that you will allow me to make a minor request for today as it will be the last time I get you to myself for a while."

"Princess Bianca, you don't even know what I have planned for today. Are you sure you wish to make a request?"

"Yes."

"Very well, go ahead and ask, Princess Bianca."

"My request is that you allow me to kiss your lips once, in any manner that I desire while you hold me tightly. Do this and I won't care how the rest of the time is spent. You can tie me up and hang me from a tree for all I care."

"I am sorry, but as entertaining as making you frolic around town while wearing a jester's outfit would be, a kiss is something I will not cheapen by not meaning it, Princess Bianca."

"That is why all you need to do is hold me as I kiss you."

"Simply allowing you to kiss me is the same as me kissing you and that is something I can't allow, Princess Bianca."

"So stubborn, but that is part of what attracts me to you. Very well, I suppose I will hear what you have in mind for our day. Oh and I am enjoying you calling me princess every time you speak."

Xeal couldn't help but smile at being called out for doing so in response to being called Duke Bluefire once more. Though just like in combat, it seemed that Princess Bianca was better at adjusting to the situation in the moment than Princess Lorena. However, just because she was better didn't mean that Xeal would simply admit defeat either.

"Just a simple walk with me through the gardens as we pass the time chatting, Princess Bianca."

"What is the most intimate that you will allow me to be with you while we walk?"

"I will allow you to have my arm as we walk, Princess Bianca."

"Hmm, no, your arm holding me to you as you reach across my back and place your hand on my waist, or shoulder, with me being free to let my hand caress your back, or hold your waist."

"We could just sit in a room quietly for old times' sake, Princess Bianca."

"Duke Bluefire, is that really asking too much?"

Xeal frowned as while it was more intimate than he wanted, he couldn't call it too much, just too long. He sighed.

"I will allow it whenever we are stopped and enjoying the view of something in the gardens, Princess Bianca."

"Wonderful. Well, shall we be on our way then?"

With that Xeal found himself walking alongside of Princess Bianca as they made their way to Queen Aila Lorafir's gardens. Once there, Xeal was surprised by how content Princess Bianca seemed to be to simply enjoy the short moments when they paused and he held her for all of ten or so seconds at a time. This continued for the first two hours until Princess Bianca finally brought up a topic other than liking a particular flower.

"You should open yourself up to Bula's affections."

"Excuse me?"

"What happened to calling me princess?"

"What happened to you worrying about my affections for you?"

"There is nothing to worry about there. I will either sway Enye and your other wives to my side, or never know the taste of your lips. Bula, on the other hand, needs you to embrace her if she is to have any hope of long-term happiness."

"No, it is not I who needs to be open to it, it is my wives and loves who need to forgive her for how she approached courting me. Just as you need to overcome your family trying to delay the treaty until I was attracted to you enough to marry you."

"As I said then, I will become what you need me to be.

Whether or not I ever earn your affection, I am married to you in my mind. It is why should you refuse me entirely, I will simply seek out a noble who will marry me for a year and have a single child, if I must fulfil the duty of preserving my house."

"You can do as you like, but it will not cause me to accept you into my life."

"I know, it is just the only way I know how to resolve the conflicts in my mind and heart. Perhaps I will move past it one day, but I need to embrace your will and ignore my family's will. I do not know how else to take a step forward as their will is that I marry you, and your will is that I find another path and decide for myself. By believing that I am your wife in my heart, I can actually feel as if I am allowed to move forward in some way. However, for Bula not having your affection will destroy her one day, from what little I know about the situation."

Xeal gave Princess Bianca a hard look as he tried to figure out why she was once more bringing up Bula's situation that she should have only the vaguest of ideas about. The more he considered this and what else he knew, the less he wanted to dive into the topic as he responded.

"Your opinion is noted, but like with you and I, things are never so simple."

"I know. Still, I will enjoy that I got you to stop calling me princess every time you spoke. Now, if only you would call me Bianca, I could believe that it will only be a matter of time before you fall for me."

"Keep telling yourself that."

"I will, just like I tell myself that you will happily keep my belly filled with your children once I reach tier-8 and prove that I am worthy to be at your side."

Xeal once more found himself being surprised by Princess Bianca's words, as she smiled confidently at him as she continued speaking to him.

"That is right. If I must, I will reach tier-8, just to show you that I will become anything you wish me to be. If you still refuse me then, all I can say is that you better be ready to deal with what I will have become by then."

"You plan to kill yourself to have me if you must."

"No, I plan to force you to recognize my commitment to you."

"Well, we will see, won't we."

"Yes, and it will end with far more than just your lips on mine when I succeed."

As much as Xeal wanted to dismiss her words as overconfidence, he couldn't as he looked at the determination in her eyes. What he saw was the same look that he saw every time he had looked in the mirror in the latter days of his last life, when all he cared about was the fall of Abysses End. While he no longer had the same look at all times, he could still recognize it and knew that if needed, she would kill herself to reach him. Though, with her having a pseudo mark, he also knew that she could kill herself once and be fine, yet he hesitated to challenge her on that fact as he responded to her.

"Just never hesitate to request a feather should you lose the mark I placed upon you."

The smile he received at this was such that he could feel the joy from it infecting even him, as Princess Bianca's only response was to take Xeal by the arm once more as she walked with a new bounce in her step for the remainder of the visit. Even Queen Aila Lorafir took notice as they returned and she spoke with skepticism.

"You seem exceedingly happy. Don't tell me that Xeal actually accepted your feelings."

"No, at least not directly. He just simply let me know that he cares if I live or die, beyond what he is obligated to by the treaty he signed with my family."

"Xeal?"

"All I said was to ask for a feather if she loses the mark I placed on her."

"I see, very well."

With that Xeal felt his lips sealed by Queen Aila Lorafir's as Princess Bianca was escorted away. This kiss held far more passion in it than what was normal for these visits and when it ended Queen Aila Lorafir spoke once more.

"I am going to miss you being here so often."

"I just freed up around six hours every week. Perhaps I should devote some of that time to courting you."

"No, not until Alea is approaching tier-8 and I can crown her queen. Until them, you coming to stay a night every week or so and the occasional family gathering is enough for me. Were you to spoil me any more than you currently do, I might decide to indulge in you before the time is right."

Xeal just gave Queen Aila Lorafir a deep and loving kiss as he held her to him, before looking her in her golden eyes and smiling as he responded to her.

"Aila, I love you and you have a place in my heart as my restraint. For better or worse, I know that you will stop me from becoming that which I hate."

"Xeal, I may be that today, but the day will come where I intend to become your passion. With that and the fact that I know that the day will come where no mortal can stand against you. You need to find your restraint from within, or perhaps accepting Freya as a wife may not be the worst option."

"Gale was exaggerating Freya's interest. At most she wishes for a night of passion from me. I highly doubt, with what form of worship her faith has embraced, that I can make an honest goddess out of her."

"Not today, but once you claim the world you are fighting over, you may stand at the same height as her."

Xeal frowned as he didn't like to think of such possibilities while dealing with Freya demanding that he wait to discuss whatever he had to say the next time Gale could open a portal to her realm. The fact that Gale had even warned Xeal not to push things gave him a bad feeling surrounding the mess he had made by walking out like he did. Still, he bid Queen Aila Lorafir farewell and returned to the grind once more as life continued regardless of what anyone did about it.

(*****)

Afternoon March 4 to Evening March 11, 2268 & ED Year 5 Days 331-351.

Alex logged off in the early afternoon and made his way down to the conference room, with Kate and Tara accompanying him. Gaute would be joining them to complete the FAE ownership group, while only Daryu and Eternal Dominion's lead developer and executive vice president, Ellayina Walsh, would be representing Eternal Dominion, Inc. While Kate had been concerned about the lack of those who handled the financial side of the equation being present, Alex had been fine with it as he was just happy that any meeting was happening at this point. In his last life, it had taken the establishment of several guild cities before one managed to secure the right to host a server for the game. Though once it had happened, it wasn't long before several others secured one as they had an example to follow and the only real issue became geographic separation from the next nearest server. With Denver being the nearest active server, Alex figured that as long as he could convince Eternal Dominion, Inc. that he could create a city for over a million people in the next decade, he would have a chance. Additionally, it would be able to serve all those who currently were at the edge of the latency rates who lived closer to the new city than Denver and even fill one of the holes in the network partially. Though only around 100,000 people would be added to those able to play ED from the numbers that Kate had supplied, as it was a sparsely populated area.

All of these thoughts and more were going through Alex's mind as he entered the conference room, where they found Jacob getting ready to connect the call. With a few minutes to spare before the meeting, Alex double-checked everything once more as he made sure all of it was fresh as Jacob dialed in. As the call connected, Alex saw the image of Ellayina Walsh appear on the holo screen and saw that Gaute was on the call as he started to speak.

"Greetings and thank you for agreeing to meet with us with how busy I know your schedule is, Ms. Walsh."

"Yeah, yeah drop the formalities. This isn't going to be anything more than me taking advantage of the situation to get to know my game's top player and how the hell you seem to figure things out that you shouldn't."

"I am sorry, but I am not sure that I can give you a satisfactory answer and while I am sure your schedule is full, let me assure you that so are all of those who are attending on my side as well. So, if you could at least hear us out before attempting to satisfy your curiosity it would be greatly appreciated and I can even free up time at your convenience for any questions you have if you like."

"Hmm, fine, but unless I call on them, everyone but you needs to stay quiet unless I ask them something."

"Is there a reason that you are hindering our ability to present the best form of our vision to you?"

"Yes, I want to see what you can do, and none of those who will actually need to be involved during such a presentation are with us currently. So, convince me on your own and I will push for you to present to the rest of those who have a say in whether you will be allowed to host a quantum-entangled server in your new city, but it better be good."

Alex wanted to frown as he stood to better project his voice and get into the right mindset as he started to speak.

"Very well. As you know, FAE is looking to do what no other guild has before and build a city around playing

Eternal Dominion. While phase one is designed to be a test with only 15,000 bedrooms being built, concepts for phase two and beyond are already in the works and we have enough land secured to easily house over a million residents."

"Yet you won't even have a tenth of that when you complete phase one. That is unless you plan to cram seven people into each bedroom. So, why should we allow you to house a server before you prove that your city can work? Especially when there are already rumors of our company already being the real power behind you, quiet as they may currently be."

"My city will take 20 years to reach a million residents if I fail to secure a server from you, while if I do, it will allow my city to fill rooms as fast as I can build them. Besides, once it is added to your existing network, the reports I have say it will instantly add around 100,000 people to your possible player base. So, I will be past a tenth of the way to a million, if not closer to 12.5%, or more."

"Oh, so which guilds will be joining your city and in what numbers?"

"The plan is to have 18% of everything that we build be non-FAE facilities and while we don't have any firm agreements in place, Kate has assured me that once the space is available it will fill up. As for the funding to build phase 2, we have it secured, though that is assuming that the wars on the horizon don't cause us to relocate funds in the short term."

"Really, this is your plan to convince me that I should allow you to pitch your plan to the others?"

Alex just smiled as he responded to Ellayina's question.

"Not in the slightest. That is just the reasons why the location shouldn't disqualify us. Kate, if you would send her a copy of the blueprints for our home."

"Your home?"

"Yes, if you would open the file, please."

Alex smiled as he watched Ellayina frown as she looked at the details, until it was clear that she had reached the basement as her eyes widened.

"Hold on, how do you know these specs?"

"Some things are better left unsaid, but that will be the housing for the server as well as the facilities needed for the personnel who will be maintaining it. The first floor will also be set up to act as an office space for both FAE and Eternal Dominion, Inc. If needed, I can even reserve the whole floor for you."

"You actually plan to build this?"

"It will be the first building that is completed and the server can be networked before the building is even completed, if Eternal Dominion, Inc. wishes to take the risk."

"Just how much are you planning to dump into this city?"

"As much as I can afford to, plus what I can convince others to for the next decade, or so. 20 years from now it could be the size of Denver with a metro area starting to grow outside of it. Though and this needs to be kept off the record, but as Eternal Dominion is your baby, I believe you should know that I intend on it being used to keep the game alive, even after the next big game comes along."

"Are you saying that you think anyone can replace Eternal Dominion in your lifetime?"

"Yes, you."

"Fair, but why would I?"

"Because, to not do so would be to run the risk of a competitor coming out of nowhere to replace you one day when, for one reason, or another, Eternal Dominion starts to decline. To be clear, I see that as being another 20 to 30 years down the road at the very least and I hope it is never to come to pass, as paying the bills needed to keep it running will be expensive. Which is why I expect Eternal Dominion, Inc. to help cover those costs until Eternal Dominion only is running out of my city. At which point I will attempt to buy it completely from you and hopefully be able to keep it online well past my lifetime."

"Did the system AI find a way to offer you a reward for doing this?"

"You mean beyond ensuring that those I love aren't murdered one day, simply because they were no longer profitable?"

"That's a bit dark, but I see what you mean and it may be my fault for programing all system AIs to focus on the survivability of Eternal Dominion as a whole. Which is why you cause me so many headaches when you make it seem like no others can stand against you."

"You and I both know that isn't true. The day will come that even the largest guilds need fear the hidden tier-8s, be they a player, or an NPC."

"Unless half of them end up being in your guild."

"Is that really what the current models show? If they do, I can promise you that they need to be ignored until at least after the wars start."

"Oh, are you saying that you know more than we do?"

"Only when it comes to my members, as I only feel sure that Takeshi will reach that point if he doesn't die and quit before then."

"Really, you think that it may be beyond you?"

"500 to 1,000. That is the rough range of NPCs who have reached that level and it will actually be harder for players to ascend. After all, unlike Takeshi, most don't treat a single death as the end of their account. Even I am unsure if the fruit of life, or a drop of phoenix blood, will allow a player to create their own legacy."

"Alright, full stop, which NPC… Queen Aila, of course. Your tactical nuke that has every guild demanding that we ban you, or remove her from the board somehow."

"How many of those guilds are backed by Abysses End and if they only knew just how under my thumb all of Cielo City is. Either way, I believe that you know that while I will use her to hedge my bets in places like the Vault of Ucnuc, I will never drag her into a purely guild on guild conflict."

"Is such a conflict even possible in Nium at this point?"

"No, but that is by design as my guild is almost solely focused on there, even if I have plans to hold a few other key locations."

"So, once you have Nium secured, you won't expand your guild's focus?"

"We will claim islands and strengthen our trade network while sending out mercenary forces, but at least 80% of our activity will be in Nium."

"So long as no other guild pisses you off. I know, promise to allow Abysses End at least two percent of the room in your city and I will push for you to get the server."

"Absolutely not. I am sorry, but that is beyond what I am open to. I am fine hearing out any other guild, but Abysses End will never be allowed to have a presence wherever FAE is the main power."

"You do realize that with Jingong almost collapsing, that if Abysses End followed suit it would be a major blow to Eternal Dominion. Both in legitimacy and financially as they would likely sue us over the fact that you seem to be favored so much and your targeting of them."

"You needn't worry about my intentions regarding Abysses End. I am well aware that them collapsing would cause others to withhold investments as they wait to see if doing so is safe. Especially as Abysses End is one of the few that can be considered a public company, even if 51% of all shares are in five people's hands."

"Yes, we have only just started to truly secure the market while avoiding being called a monopoly. The last thing we need is more government regulation from any country."

"Unless it is in your favor, of course. Don't act like you wouldn't happily see regulations that you can deal with, but make it harder for a new company to challenge your market share."

"Alex, I thought you were here to convince me that allowing a server to be hosted in your city is a good idea, not point out the hypocrisy of those at the top like you and I."

"I don't believe I am a hypocrite. I have Kate to handle anything that requires that as I just focus on the meat and potatoes, so to speak. That said, I am willing to have six percent of the space that is made available in my city for non-FAE players, open to any gaming independent workshops that are just getting their feet beneath them. I will even do so at cost so long as they have no connections to Abysses End and aren't simply a group of rich kids playing around."

"Hmm, what do you think this announcement will do for the price of Abysses End's shares and FAE's evaluation?"

"Simple. It will start what I can only say will be a long and slow decline of Abysses End as FAE rises the longer my city remains on track. Investors will start to flee as new ones rush in thinking that they are getting a bargain, only to wonder just where the bottom is as the price keeps going down. At some point, even the five who hold the majority of the shares will try to offload them and at that point is where everything will enter freefall."

"Oh, and how can you be so sure?"

"Because, when those five schedule their shares to be sold is when I will truly declare war on them."

"You plan to buy them," retorted Ellayina with a broad smile as she looked at Alex in a new light. "Towards what aim I am unsure, but if you can manage to secure 51% of their workshop right as the price tanks, you could reap a massive reward."

"I could, but no. They will collapse completely as I have no need of the toxicity that would result from me or any others buying them as anything but the pieces that are left behind in the aftermath."

"Sure. We will see when the choice is before you, just how you will act. Alex, I get it, you can't tell me what your real plan is else I might use that information to create a bidding war to own them. I mean all the players who would be under contract still and the time it took to develop them is worth something. Now, are you done trying to convince me to support your bid to host a server?"

"That depends on if I have talked you into it yet."

"Oh, just how much more do you have to say on the subject?"

Alex just smiled as he looked to Kate as she shook her head and brought up the slide show that Alex had had prepared as he responded.

"I have only just finished the introduction. As you can see, I have a hundred slides to go over if you would like. Through them I really drill down to the specifics of why this is a mutually beneficial arrangement and finally, if that is still not enough, I have some documents ready to go over on the subject as well."

"Alright, I give. I will get you two hours with all those who matter for this kind of thing, though I expect it will take a few months to do so. Just don't you dare make me sit through more than a dozen slides, or read more than two pages of anything that isn't a technical specifications document."

Alex had to hold in a laugh that Gaute failed to, as he couldn't help but letting out a chuckle as he spoke.

"I take it that means the rest of us can share a thought before we lose this opportunity."

"I suppose," replied Ellayina.

"Alright, perhaps Eternal Dominion, Inc. should remember that it is the small player who sells his iron ore for a few credits that matters. Yes, workshops like Abysses End are an important part of the equation, but if they are gone another will fill the void left. It is when you lose the casual player, or watcher, that Eternal Dominion needs to worry about being overtaken by the next game."

"Gaute is absolutely right," commented Alex. "Abysses End, FAE, Fire Oath and every other organization out there that is focused on contending for dominance in Eternal Dominion are reliant on the casual players to exist. As for the casual player, all I can say is that my intent is to ensure that my actions don't hurt their bottom lines, at least as much as possible. Anyone who tells you that they know just how the market will react to anything is lying, as even the smallest of changes can send ripples through the whole system."

"Noted and known, but it is still Abysses End, FAE, Fire Oath and the rest of the major guilds who buys iron ore and causes the price to rise to a point that makes it worth it for players to even gather it. As such, we as a company need to care about the health that our environment creates for both to survive. Now if there is nothing else, I will send you more info later and I think I might just pop in the next time you are chatting with the main system AI for some fun."

Alex just sighed at how she said fun, as it would be quite

the opposite for him as the meeting came to an end and Kate spoke.

"That was a mess. Honestly, the two of you got off topic far too much and she only really cared about the blueprints I sent her."

"Yes, but I needed to appease her desire to probe my intentions and knowledge. That said, I will not be the one to present when it is the real deal. Kate, that will be all you and Tara as I simply respond to a few questions."

"Alex, how can you be sure she won't pull you into another tangent like she did today?" asked Tara.

"Simple, she doesn't want others, who will need to be present from Eternal Dominion, Inc., to know what she does either. She is working to become the sole owner of Eternal Dominion and will be focused on the possibility of having it housed in our city, which aligns with her goals. Especially as the specifications we are building to has the ability to house a redundancy server for the main ED server, though the billion credits to create it would need to be spent by them."

"Tara, by the time we meet with them again it will just be about closing the deal," added Kate. "You and I will have already created the framework for the deal by working with the finance and legal divisions at Eternal Dominion, Inc. Unless someone at the top wants more, we should be able to know if it is approved within a week of presenting it and be able to adjust accordingly."

"What if they say no?" asked Tara. "I mean, we are about to have billions of credits tied up in this project and we don't even know if it will succeed. Can FAE survive this failing?"

"First, accepting no isn't an option," replied Kate. "Second, while it will hurt FAE, we can weather it."

Alex just smiled at Kate's confidence in his plan as the

discussion tapered off, and Alex and Kate made their way to the nursery to spend some time with Ahsa and Moyra. Alex still couldn't help but smile as he saw Kate interacting with his daughters as they attacked her hair while giggling. Kate was more than used to this at this point, and didn't lose a step in giving them affection as she played with them and Alex until it was time to join the others upstairs.

The next seven days were spent mostly on more work to make sure FAE city could be realized, according to what the plans currently portrayed. In between this was lots of hugs, kisses and other forms of affection, especially when Ava and Mia had returned from their 33-week appointments on the 6th. That night had been nonstop talking about the pair of squashes in their bellies, that they couldn't wait to meet and not have in their bellies anymore. Sadly, while Dr. Avery was sure that they wouldn't reach 40 weeks at the current pace, she was also sure that it would be at least three more weeks unless something was very wrong. Alex had also learned that Ava and Mia had come just after their mom had reached week 37 and how they figured it would be the same. Still, it was clear by the end of that night that if they didn't have to, Ava and Mia didn't want to deal with going downstairs and being active at this point. Luckily, Mrs. Bell didn't care and had taken to making them do pregnancy exercises in their room every day to make sure that they didn't get too lazy, or let their bodies atrophy too much. She also didn't care when they insisted that the maternity pod took care of that for them, as Alex just kept his mouth shut on the matter.

Though Alex's favorite part of his time offline was the first night of what was being called Alex time. As the schedule became four nights where he focused on one of his ladies, or both Ava and Mia in their case, a night where the five of them did something together, one that had them hanging out with the rest of the house and one that was all Alex's. This didn't mean that Alex would spend it all by himself and in fact he ended up spending it with Ava and Mia, but he had done what he wanted as he just enjoyed cuddling with them as they got as comfortable as could be. What had followed was over an hour of him feeling his little ones moving as he smiled as Ava and Mia simply catered to the odd request, while making sure not to smother him with love, too much that is.

Xeal's time in ED was anything but quiet, as he had one event after another to take care of as they had the celebration of Nium's founding on day 333. It, like everything else, had been pushed back by three days due to the Triday celebration that added three days to the year. Following this, Xeal celebrated his third anniversaries with Enye, Mari and Lingxin, just before things got complicated once more in the quest world. It seemed that the demon he had fought ended up attacking the dominion of the player that he had been bordering. According to Vento's report, most of the NPCs had been able to flee into Xeal's dominion while the players and soldiers had held the demons off, but the city had fallen and the entire dominion had vanished. This had come with a request for Taya, Lucida and Arnhylde to spend some time in the world, to ensure that the nests could be cleared as Xeal expanded his dominion. While Xeal could have cleared the nests simply by having his dominion cover the area where they were, the other nests had yielded exceptional loot from killing the demons.

So it was that Xeal found himself spending a significant portion of his downtime expanding his dominion once more, as the others cleared the pair of nests that they could reach. First came the one that Xeal had explored, as he worked to bring the one inside of the fallen dominion into reach. As Xeal watched his time dwindle continually while pressing forward, he sighed wondering just how things had played out and what had happened to the dominion that had gained the extra shard of divinity. At the same time, Xeal knew that the moment that he found that dominion, it would mean a massive fight and find it he did on day 346. With the second nest being cleared out by day 340, after what the report had described as an intense battle with the same demon he had faced off against. Once more, without Lucida's abilities keeping the horde of demons away, Vento had said it would have been impossible to win.

This just left dealing with the rulers of the city that had been transformed into a ruin in a matter of hours. While Xeal knew that they had been in a difficult position and had made a few bad choices, he also knew that they had at least led their people into his lands when it became clear that they were doomed. Still, the sentiments surrounding those who had lost everything and loved ones during the demon's invasion demanded justice be served. The general consensus was for at least a few heads to roll, but Xeal shot this down and instead declared that they all would be sentenced to farming for the rest of their lives. To be clear, they would essentially be prisoners on a farm that they would own, operate and if they succeeded, passed on to their descendants.

At first many had cried that such a thing was too good for them. However, that changed a week into it when the state of all of them were seen by others. Few, if any of them, had ever done a day of manual labor in their lives and none of them knew the first thing about farming or housework, and it showed. Their hair that had likely never felt dirt was coated in mud and their clothing could hardly be seen beneath the dirt that covered it. Xeal had ordered that so long as they worked, that they would get enough food to live, but no training on any of the things that needed to be done, which most simply took for granted as being common sense. Like that, the rage the commoners felt at their former rulers was shifting to a mix of humor and pity.

During this time, Xeal also reached level 188 and took time to enjoy his anniversary with Aalin and Gale. While plans for the assault were well underway, as Xeal recovered a bit of the time he had lost while expanding his dominion. In the end, Xeal only had just over 12 hours of accumulated time for the quest world left when he logged off on day 351.

(*****)

ED Year 5 Days 352-353.

When Xeal logged in on day 352, he was greeted by the sight of all his wives sleeping as he, Aalin and Gale returned to ED. The addition of Eira had finally caused a shift in the order of how they all slept, as the same pairs no longer found themselves always together. Xeal hadn't even realized what the sudden variety that he enjoyed from having 21 different pairings to wake up next to would bring. The simple spice in seeing how each lady interacted together as they snuggled into Xeal and how they greeted Xeal first thing in the morning. So far, Xeal had found that the combination of Eira and Gale had been the most enthusiastic wake-up greeting that he had enjoyed. Today, however, it was Mari and Aalin who he found himself between and after a moment of cuddling and a few kisses, it was time to start the day, which Xeal enjoyed, if for nothing else than it fit who they were.

When they sat down for breakfast, they were joined by the rest of the NPCs in Xeal's party and they enjoyed their morning meal as Midnight claimed a piece of bacon from Xeal's plate. As Xeal looked around at all of them, he couldn't help but think of what the future held for him and the others at the table. For many of them if they had their way, they would still be sitting with him as they enjoyed their breakfast for many years, as only Rina and Alea had removed themselves from pursuing him romantically. Daisy and Violet were always smiling at him when he looked their way as while no steps had been taken as of yet, they hadn't lost the bit of attention that they had gained from him. Dafasli had continued to focus on being able to stay by his side ever since they had leveled with each other, but from what he heard through his wives, she was as determined as ever to catch his eye as a woman. Then there was Bula, who he didn't know what to do with as he had thought that she had come to terms with the fact that he wasn't interested, only for recent events to throw that in his face. It was with this thought that Xeal spoke after swallowing a rather delicious piece of fresh melon.

"Bula, have you grown used to having the sight come from Freya yet?"

"No, it still is focused on love and war far too often, though the image of the deaths of many in battle is growing clearer with each day."

"Yet no way to tell if it is in this year, or the next."

"No, and I am finding it hard to handle the images that the sight keeps showing me."

"Are they that morbid?"

"I mean the ones of passion, particularly involving myself and well, you."

Xeal wanted to curse Freya for what he saw as her purposeful flooding of Bula's mind with images of him embracing her, as a way for Freya to punish Xeal for walking away from her. Still, he remained calm as he responded to Bula.

"Is being near me creating any problems for you?"

"No, it is only when you are around that I am relieved from such scenes coming almost unbidden to me. Were I to be left to such a fate for too long, I fear that I may lose sight of the reality of our situation and be swept up in the moment once more."

At that there was a sudden clatter as Dyllis brought her hand down hard on the table as she looked frustrated at Bula's words. After a second, she realized everyone but Midnight was looking at her as she blushed before sighing and speaking.

"I am sorry, Bula. It is not you that was directed at, but Freya as I can see the issues she is causing and as much as I want to not blame you, I can't. I say that fully knowing that I could see myself doing the same as you have were our situations reversed and it has been bothering me ever since."

"Well, there's one," commented Aalin. "Honestly, I expect all of us, save for probably myself, Gale, Kate, Luna and Selene would have. It is just part of who you all are. Dyllis, had you been in Bula's position and her in yours, the reactions would have been the same as they were and it would be bothering Bula like I am sure it is the rest of you who are native to this world."

"Are you saying that simply because we are from this world, we are sure to feel that way?" asked Eira in an accusatory tone.

"Eira, you know what Aalin is saying," interjected Enye. "Also, now is not the time to continue this topic. That said, I am secure enough to admit that I share the same feelings that Dyllis has. Only I push them aside when thinking about what is best for this family and Bula is currently behind Daisy, Violet and Dafasli in my list of who I am willing to accept currently. As for just how far behind she is, well, it isn't Lorena and Bianca bad, but I might allow Lumikkei or Lughrai to court him first."

Xeal could tell that while honest, Enye's words were not what Bula needed to hear at the moment as he spoke up.

"I believe that this topic is doing none of us any good and I actually do not place the blame on Bula for her words. I put it on Freya. The moment when it all occurred, Bula was on a high from feeling Freya's power surging inside her and it hasn't helped that I pissed Freya off and she seems to want to take it out on Bula right now."

"Xeal is right," added Gale. "Even I have been avoiding

talking to her as of late and I honestly don't think Xeal should meet with her like he plans."

"Gale, I have to. Even if she decides to make things difficult on me, she needs us and we need her at this point. Else you might as well restart."

"Ha, she says that at least you recognize that you need her, though she contends that she doesn't need you."

"Right," retorted Xeal as he returned his focus to his breakfast as the chatter shifted to lighter topics until it was time for him to leave.

With a sigh, Xeal stood as he bid them all farewell and found himself inside the quest world one more time as Austru greeted him.

"So today is the day. I look forward to you returning victorious. Now here are that latest batch of letters and I expect you to deliver them and return with their replies."

"Ha, no problem, though I expect that I will see you again before I can deliver them and certainly before they are done writing whatever they have to say."

As Xeal paused, he pulled Austru into a hug as he gave her a quick kiss and continued talking.

"Just promise me that you didn't ask them to allow you to carry my child."

"Oh no, that needs to wait until either I am in the other world, or you have secured this one."

"Good. Now, sadly, others are waiting for me."

With that, Austru stole one more kiss and Xeal used his fast travel ability to transfer to the location that Lucida had just sent him. Like last time, she was standing by at the edge of his dominion with three steeds and Arnhylde, as they prepared to cross the final roughly 50 miles and charge straight into the other dominion. The plan this time was an exact copy of what had been done when invading Joliette's dominion and Xeal saw no reason to change things up as they started their charge. This was followed by the same four warnings that Xeal had received the last time as he entered the other dominion and found himself looking at two dozen players who were spread out as they awaited him. Though the surprise they showed at seeing him riding the demonic horses was enough to allow him to dart past them. However, when roughly another 150 showed up, it became clear that this group was far better organized than Joliette's forces had been as Xeal shouted out orders.

"Turn right and as soon as I am past their flank, you both need to leave me."

"Xeal, you won't be able to keep riding then," replied Lucida as they turned and ranged attacks started to come at them.

"I'll be fine. Just get out of here and stay alive!"

With that Xeal started to separate from the pair as he unleashed his fighting spirit and his mount started to freak out as it ran like the gates of hell were behind it. At the same time, Lucida's and Arnhylde's mounts broke away back towards the boundary between the dominions. Xeal smiled as all the ranged attacks started to focus on him as he started to take damage alongside his mount. However, he managed to turn the corner and force the demonic horse to turn and head deeper into the enemy dominion. At the same time, another dozen players arrived and stood 20 feet in front of him with spears braced as he ran right into them. Xeal had known that getting around them wasn't possible at the speed he had been going, so instead he leaped off his mount as it slammed into the first spear. This had launched Xeal a good 30 feet past the spear wall as he rolled into a dead sprint that ignored any thought of conserving stamina.

With his health already down to 65% and still needing to cover three miles to trigger the forced battle, all Xeal cared about was opening up more distance between him and his pursuers while dodging attacks. As he did this, he found himself having to get around three more groups of four players, who all basically appeared on top of him. Thankfully, none of the players present had any business facing off with Xeal and he was able to push right through them as he received the notification, with around 60% of his health and about 50% of his stamina left.

(Notice: player Xeal Bluefire has successfully invaded player Frozen Sky's dominion. Player Frozen Sky has been notified and the match will start in ten minutes. All players other than the two combatants will return to the dominion that they are associated with in the meantime.)

(Notice: prepare to be transported to an arena to face off against Frozen Sky. Transporting in 30 seconds.)

Xeal blinked a few times as he realized the name of his opponent and couldn't help but start laughing his head off while smiling brightly. Oh, how he was looking forward to the fight before him. It didn't matter that he knew it would set off a chain of events that he would have rather waited for, or that he wasn't in top condition, this was perfect! He was about to get to work out some of his deepest frustrations and feelings of betrayal, and the best part is there was no way for another to interfere.

As Xeal disappeared, the roughly 200 players that had been trying to catch him looked concerned over how he had been acting as he did so. They could tell that he was way out of their league as he easily outran even their quickest members and had fought through the groups of four like they weren't even there, but still, they had dealt plenty of damage to him. If anything, he should have been concerned about what he was about to face as while they had realized by now that they were facing the recognized top player of ED, Frozen Sky wasn't a pushover either. It was why the 200 present were happy to follow him as he secretly built up his own force while acting as the shadow leader of their guild in ED. All of them had never seen a player stand their own against Frozen Sky and believed that if he had entered any of the arena leagues, that even Djimon Oya and Amser Sojourner would be no match for him.

At the same time the 200 were thinking this, Frozen Sky was getting ready to head to face off against Xeal after seeing the report on how his invasion had gone. Over all, Frozen Sky was happy with what his followers had been able to do with their crippled stats and the limited skills in that world, though he still felt that they could have done better. Still, Frozen Sky was looking forward to removing Xeal from the quest world after the brief, but humiliating exchange that they had had. He still couldn't stand the tone of superiority mixed with disdain that Xeal had towards him and his plans for a mutually beneficial arrangement. Still, even if Frozen Sky knew that Xeal had a leg up on him, it didn't mean that the fight would go Xeal's way. No, even with the level advantage that would be present, Frozen Sky was confident in his skills.

The smile on Xeal's face as the minute-long countdown started caused Frozen Sky to frown as he assessed the situation. From what he could tell, Xeal didn't even put him in his eyes and was looking at him like a conman would look at a little kid who had a wad of cash and no idea of its value. Still, Frozen Sky figured that this was just Xeal's form of smack talk and started speaking.

"Do you really think that smiling like that is going to affect me?"

Xeal just started chuckling softly at Frozen Sky's words while offering no response.

"Fine, I will just let my blade do the talking. Forgive me

for having no remorse about removing you from this world!"

Xeal found it hard not to return to laughing like he did when he learned who his opponent was, at the stupidity of his former guild leader. The poor fool thought that he even had the slightest chance of winning this fight. It was a notion so absurd that Xeal almost retorted that a random tier-5 player had a better chance of defeating him, but he held it in. As the timer continued to drop, Xeal just smiled more and more as Frozen Sky tried to get him to respond, only he might as well have been talking to the wind.

Finally, as the timer reached zero, Frozen Sky charged in with his two-handed great sword that he knew Xeal would need to use both of his blades to stop, if he didn't dodge. Frozen Sky had been expecting Xeal to dodge and try to counter attack, and he had been ready to activate his momentum shift skill to allow his downward slash to instantly become a slash to the left, or right. However, Xeal hadn't even drawn his blades yet as the blade started to descend upon him and the next thing Frozen Sky knew, his blade hit Xeal's left shoulder as Xeal's right fist hit him. What followed made Frozen Sky's brain malfunction for a second, as he was forced back a few steps and Xeal stood still. Thankfully, Xeal had clearly taken more damage in the exchange, but he had little time to appreciate that as Xeal started to assault him using only his bare hands. Once more Frozen Sky seemed to be unable to even start to understand what was going on, as he couldn't even begin to defend himself from the speed at which the attacks came. While each attack did little damage, it was like death by bee stings as they came one after another, and he found himself having to curl his body in and simply try to guard his vitals while weathering the storm.

As Xeal landed one blow after another, he lamented that

his stamina wasn't full as if it were, he would have truly been able to enjoy punching and kicking Frozen Sky to death. However, it was not to be, so as Frozen Sky curled into a defensive stance, Xeal let out a roar as he unleashed a point-blank dragon's breath that sent Frozen Sky tumbling back. When he finally stopped, Xeal was already on top of him as he landed from a jump while planting both feet on Frozen Sky's face. The pure satisfaction that Xeal got from this could have only been better if Frozen Sky knew just why Xeal was doing this. While Xeal had sent Lori Lunaflower and her guild Night Oath off to handle many of those he had grudges against from his last life, he had left Frozen Sky and several others off the list. This wasn't because he was taking pity on them. No, it was simply because he intended to have no mercy on them as he handled things personally. Xeal had thought that he would need to wait until the start of the wars to have a chance to handle any of these, but today he was more than happy to start with the one at the top of the list.

All Frozen Sky felt was fury as he felt the bottom of Xeal's boots on his face. He was an elite player and even if Xeal was above him, he still deserved some respect. This felt like Xeal saw him as nothing but dirt. No, even lower. He wasn't even that to Xeal. He was more like a pile of dung. This thought caused Frozen Sky to abandon all civility as he went to grab Xeal's legs, only to swipe at the air as Xeal hopped up and landed right back on Frozen Sky's face, before jumping off his face. For a moment Frozen Sky readied to grab his ankles when he came back down, only for Xeal to land on one foot in Frozen Sky's groin. Even in ED that area was sensitive to attack and while it was also protected by armor, the way Xeal had landed just caused the armor to make the situation even worse. This wasn't a battle, this was a private humiliation that was designed to do one thing, break Frozen Sky's will and it was this thought that made him resist giving up as he shouted out.

"Bastard! You think that humiliating me here will make me run when war comes!"

"Oh no," responded Xeal. "I need you to fight with everything you have when the war starts. After all, I intend to kill you many more times. This is just a teaser."

Frozen Sky found himself frozen once more at the fact that Xeal had actually responded, though the pure disdain that was contained within sent a shiver down his back. Every sense that Frozen Sky had was telling him that he wasn't facing another player, but a monster that was on a whole other level. How could any player hope to win the struggle to control this world with Xeal participating in it? As this thought was about to take root, Frozen Sky recovered and with a roar of frustration got to his feet as he eyed his weapon that was a few feet from Xeal now. Seeing this, Xeal smiled as he continued to talk.

"Good. This won't be any fun if you don't struggle, so go ahead, retrieve your blade and give me everything you have!"

With that Xeal charged in and kicked Frozen Sky's blade in the air, before sending it flying right at Frozen Sky, who mistimed his catch as the blade hit his face. Once more frustration threatened to overwhelm his better judgment as he fought to keep a clear head against Xeal. He knew that while Xeal may be toying with him, that he was still at the advantage in this fight and if he could just outlast Xeal, he could win. Xeal seemingly didn't care as he unleashed another dragon's breath and gripped his sheathed blades while charging in. Seeing this, Frozen Sky got ready to deal with a slash, or quick draw skill, only it never came as Xeal head butted Frozen Sky right in the nose. As Frozen Sky recovered, he started to swing his blade at Xeal in a pattern that had served him well in multiple fights across multiple VRMMOs, only to see it effortlessly avoided. Had he known that Xeal knew this pattern better than even Frozen Sky did at this point, from the thousands of times he had trained against it in his last life, he would have never even started using it. However, he didn't, nor did he know about the slight opening that allowed Xeal to grab him by the throat at about 25 seconds after he had started using it. Frozen Sky was confused as to why Xeal hadn't drawn his blades for all of a moment, when he felt the electricity start coursing through him.

When the pain finally ended, Frozen Sky had dropped his blade once more and had finally lost the battle of having any hope, as he quickly realized that Xeal's intent was to utterly destroy him. The simple act of Xeal standing over him made him freeze up as he waited for the next form of humiliation to begin. When a kick to his stomach sent him flying, he realized that if he stayed, that Xeal wouldn't stop until he was absolutely destroyed. With this thought, Frozen Sky didn't hesitate any longer as he selected the option to forfeit this fight to avoid ever suffering a death of any kind. As the system announced his defeat and he started to fade, the smile that Xeal gave him spoke of pure satisfaction at this outcome and he realized that he had been broken. Xeal had made him run like a coward and the feeling it gave him made him sick as he was expelled from the quest world, or any space associated with it for the last time.

Xeal couldn't have asked for a more satisfying conclusion to the match between him and Frozen Sky, as it told him that his old guild leader truly feared him. This went beyond just knowing that he wasn't a match for Xeal, as he would have still struggled until his health had dropped below five percent. No, his health had still been above 90% and Xeal hadn't even done more than inflict pain upon him as he focused on that over damage. It didn't matter that both Xeal and Frozen Sky knew that the decision to flee had been the right one. The fact that Frozen Sky had given in after only a short ten minutes of struggling would never be forgotten by either. As Xeal thought on this, the system notifications started to come in.

(Notice: you have been implanted with four shards of divinity. Collect the other 60 to increase your control of this world.

Current control: 1/16

Current time allowed in this world: 37,800 seconds every 7 days in this world.

Time here passes the same as in the main Eternal Dominion world.

Time can be stockpiled and will increase continuously.

Current accumulation: 1 second every 16 seconds.)

(Notice: you can bring up to 400 players with you to this world.

Dominion: You can claim a portion of the quest world as your own and in doing so, keep it safe from demons. Current max 3% of world's land.)

(Notice: You have defeated another champion and claimed their dominion as your own.

Adding 37,800 seconds to your current balance of time allowed in the quest world.

All players associated with them will be removed from the quest world.

You will be unable to conquer another dominion until you encounter one that is controlled by a champion with four shards of divinity.

To signify this, your dominion will gain a copper border that must be crossed to enter it, while all enemies will have a red border unless they have the appropriate number of shards of divinity.)

(Notice: you have two irregularly attached dominions. Would you like to attach them in the optimal configuration? Warning: if not done in the next five minutes, you will not be able to in the future.)

(Notice: you may transfer to the defeated champion's starting location with up to ten others once in the next 24 hours. Warning: NPCs in captured dominion may perceive you as hostile. Exercise caution when approaching them.)

(Notice: transferring you to your designated entry point for quest world.)

As Xeal reappeared in Austru's room, he found the sylph smiling at seeing him, as he selected to combine the dominions and watched as the total area he controlled skyrocketed to over 800,000 square miles as the farthest edges of Frozen Sky's Dominion were connected to his own. While this was only about 1.38% of the total land in the quest world, it was still an area larger than Mexico and was approaching an area that would place it in the top ten countries by size in reality.

"Xeal, is everything alright?" asked Austru. "You have been standing there smiling eerily."

Xeal shook his head as he realized that he still had a smug smile from getting Frozen Sky to surrender as he refocused on Austru and spoke.

"I'm sorry. My opponent this time was someone that I knew and I may have taken a bit too much delight in defeating them. Now, however, I will need to prepare for the fallout that will likely follow as he will likely expose this quest and my involvement to others that I would rather not know. It may also move the timeline for other events that will keep me occupied forward significantly."

"I see. Does that mean that I shouldn't expect to see you

spending a night with me at least once a month moving forward?"

"No, but they may be spread out such that there are several months between each visit and you get me for two nights in a row. I may even have to make up missing three or four months in a row, but I will make sure to not shortchange you on the time that I promised you."

"I never said that you would. I know that you will win the next four fights that you need to for you to be able to call this world yours and ensure that I know your feelings towards me either before, or after that point."

"I will, but for now I need to retrieve a few individuals from the other world. While I do so, if you could have Vento, Bretislaus and Wisnor made ready to come with me in two hours, that would be great."

"Understood and I look forward to your return."

Xeal smiled as he gave Austru a quick kiss, before leaving and finding himself back in Nium. Once there, he sent out several messages for those who he wished to accompany him to assemble, before sighing and making his way to the royal palace. As he arrived, he informed the guards that he needed to speak with King Victor and that it was an urgent manner, and 15 minutes later he was seated across from him. King Victor was looking at Xeal while frowning as he first spoke.

"I sure hope that this is important enough for me to have pissed off Marquesses Mercer and Rais over."

"If it is only those two, I could just want to tell you about a fish I caught and it would be worth it, but no, it is important enough for me to interrupt you, regardless of the circumstances."

"And yet you aren't coming right out with it. So tell me, Xeal, just what have you, or your guild, done this time?"

"My special quest that is beyond top secret had me face

off against a player who I couldn't even begin to bargain with to keep my involvement quiet. Even if I could have, I wouldn't as his price would likely be something beyond what I would be willing to pay."

"This sounds like a FAE issue, not a Nium issue, so what makes it something that affects my kingdom?"

"He is to Prince Ulrich as I am to you."

"Shit. Why, just why did you have to face off against him?"

"Fate can be cruel. The question is, what would your reaction be if you were Habia's ruler?"

"How easy did you beat him?"

"I likely shattered his confidence."

"Why would you do that, Xeal! Never mind, what's done is done. If I were to receive that information and looked at him the same way I look at you, I would only have one choice and that is war. First, I would assault the dwarves while being on guard against us and Paidhia to secure my rear. I may even try to secure a treaty with Paidhia to attack the dwarves together. Ha, that's something I thought I would never say, Habia and Paidhia joining together to take care of the dwarves and us before turning on each other. Xeal, you are a blessing and a curse and you need to handle the last quest as soon as they start their assault on the dwarves."

"I already have everything in place thanks to my members who are living with the dwarves."

"Good, it won't be long now. A few weeks into the new year at best and I will need you to deploy your full force at that time so-"

"No, we will focus on holding the border and raids until FAE's core reaches tier-7. We will call upon all adventurers in Nium to fill in the gaps in the meanwhile."

"Xeal, you are asking for me to fight a losing battle if

you don't take part."

"Victor, all those who join the war will be doing so at a great cost to them. This strategy will cost us for the first six months of the war, but it will pay dividends after that. That said, I will need to set many more things into motion and even need to offer a carrot to all the other guilds who will need to step up."

"Oh, why is the carrot coming from you and not me?"

"Because, you can offer them gold and renown. I can offer to get some of their players to tier-7 faster and more reliably, to offset the loss in power that the early fighting will inflict on their guilds. That said, you will need to still empty your treasury to secure their support for the entirety of the war. Also, every noble house needs to be scrutinized and watched for any betrayal of the kingdom."

"I understand. I will ensure that all are ready to do their part, or die trying and I will be recalling the council from Hardt Burgh until further notice and upping the royal guards there. It will be the staging point for those who will be sent to Cielo city and I will make sure the island that we captured from the pirates is ready to protect the rest."

"I will make sure that the support staff from my guild is ready, as we need to be sure that if its location is compromised…"

Xeal and Victor continued to go over the different things that would need to happen, both in the coming weeks, and after the dwarves were attacked and Nium declared the alliance that was in place. No matter how Xeal thought of it, the coming weeks would be full of insanity as it would be clear to all that Nium was on high alert. Finally, Xeal needed to put a pause in the meeting as it was time for him to meet up with those who would be accompanying him to visit the city in his new dominion.

When Xeal arrived, he found Kate, Joliette, Lucy and

Takeshi waiting for him as he greeted them and wasted no time in returning to the quest world. As he arrived, he found Austru, Vento, Bretislaus and Wisnor all waiting for him as well. This brought his total to eight of the ten that he could bring. As he looked the group over and thought about if there were two more that were available and made sense for him to include, Joliette was the first to speak.

"Alright, why am I back in this world again? I thought only five would be able to go with you to this new city, or whatever. I mean, I was in the middle of working with the others to improve our cold alchemy techniques and it is hard for all of us to find time to swap notes with the pace you have us all working."

"Ten is what I can bring this time," replied Xeal without even thinking. "It doubled, just like everything else. The question is if I should add anyone else to this group."

"Xeal, should Austru and Bretislaus even be joining us?" asked Lucy. "I mean, they are under leveled should things go the same way they did last time."

"Bretislaus needs to come as he is one that they should know of and his words should hold weight," replied Kate. "As for Austru, her life is guarded and if nothing else, Xeal and Takeshi will be able to open a path for her to escape rather easily."

"Still, I need to not be a burden," commented Austru. "Xeal, can you have some of those who have come to this world focus on aiding me in reaching tier-6 after this trip?"

"Vento, make sure it's done," replied Xeal. "Now let's go."

Just like that they all found themselves in a throne room once more, as Xeal looked around as he found it empty and frowned. Sighing, Xeal led his group to the doors and opened them to find a pair of guards looking startled as they lowered their spears at him, only for him and Takeshi to disarm them within a moment. While Takeshi had lost access to his skills and a good chunk of his stats upon entering this world, he was still beyond the ability of any guard that wasn't at least five levels above him. If anything, Xeal could tell that he was enjoying the handicap to his abilities as Xeal spoke to the pair of guards.

"Where is the ruler of this city?"

"Um," stammered the guard that Xeal was looking at while letting his fighting spirit influence him slightly. "Well, we aren't sure. Lord Frozen Sky hasn't returned after he and his forces went to face off against an intruder."

"Ha, that bastard actually had the gall to declare himself king," interjected Joliette. "Looks like there was no point in me even returning to this world."

"Just be quiet," retorted Kate. "Where is the prior ruler, or the highest noble or aristocrat, that still holds power."

Xeal didn't like the looks of uncertainty that the guards had as they looked between each other, so he spoke before they could.

"Frozen Sky and all his followers are never returning to this world. I defeated him and banished him. Now, you can all cooperate and tell me what I want to know, or I can show you just how weak he was compared to me."

"Dead, or hiding. Frozen Sky killed all the major ones and the rest renounced their status to stay alive. There are a couple who are in the dungeon, but they are just some daughters of the last king."

"Just what has been done to them?" asked Lucy, sounding like she might kill someone.

"Nothing!" responded the guard like he was pleading for his life. "Lord Frozen Sky was just holding on to them until one of them accepted him as their husband."

"He was trying to solidify his rule," commented Xeal. "Needless to say, Princess Tsega would have been on his list as well if I had lost. After he killed King Silas, of course, and let's not talk about the fate of the rest of the nobility. So, who rules you now that Frozen Sky and his men are gone?"

Both guards looked like they were at a loss before the one that Xeal was next to spoke again.

"I suppose you do, or we have no ruler at all."

"Wrong, those princesses do. Now, you are going to take me to them while the rest of my friends wait here. Just know that there is none in this world who can face me and win. Also, I have no issue with killing everyone who aided Frozen Sky in his rule should they resist the princesses in carrying out my will."

Xeal could tell that both guards wished that they could escape as he forced the one nearest him to guide him, while letting his fighting spirit skill influence the atmosphere more than normal. For a skill that Xeal had ignored when thinking about how he wanted to set up his build, he now understood why so many players who had it in his last life had sworn by it. Though it was mainly effective on monsters and NPCs as players had a whole other layer to resist the mental persuasion or fear effects of the skill that Xeal was finding so useful. Still, it worked wonders as he walked behind the guard and asked him to explain the current situation in the city of Oserith, as Xeal learned that it was called. Especially when they passed other guards who looked confused at what they were seeing, until Xeal let them feel a bit of what his guide was enduring. Of course, he had his guide tell them that all guards were to assemble in the main courtyard for an address from the new rulers of Oserith and that any looting or desertion would mean death.

Finally, Xeal smiled as they arrived at the dungeons as the guards on duty seemed reluctant to let them through.

Xeal could tell that these were among the more senior of the palace guards as they were all above level 190 and acted like the throne room guard was worthless for leading Xeal to them. The fact that they had resisted his fighting spirit at first reminded Xeal of how hard it was to even intimidate anything above one's own level. Still, a few minutes later, when two of them found themselves disarmed and being held up by their necks, it caused them to quickly change their tune. This included the pair that were still holding blades warily at Xeal as he spoke to them all.

"I am not one to waste resources that can be used, but I am one to dispose of dead weight, or worse, rather quickly. Now, I expect both princesses brought before me in the next two minutes and for a list of all other prisoners and the reason they are here brought to me."

It took a second but finally the man held in his right hand spoke in a hoarse voice.

"Move…you…idiots!"

At that the other two got moving as Xeal let the two men down and it wasn't long before two malnourished ladies, dressed in plain clothes, were standing in front of him. Both ladies looked confused as Xeal gave them the same appraising look they had given him as he took them in. Each looked like a shower was a rare occurrence for them and the smell that accompanied them was overpowering while their hair was an absolute mess. Xeal expected it had lice and other possible infestations living in it. This sight made Xeal frown deepen as he could tell that both had once been beauties, only now they were starving and filthy. As things were, he expected that neither would have lived another six months without some form of intervention.

"Alright, this is horrendous," stated Xeal menacingly while looking at the guards. "I don't care if they were imprisoned here or not, it is clear that they were treated as less than human. Is that how all prisoners are cared for here?"

None of the guards wished to speak as they hoped another one would volunteer an answer as the elder of the two sisters spoke up.

"They are hoping that by denying us anything but a bucket for our waste and stale bread and thin broth to eat, that we will break and accept that monster as a husband."

"I see, and your name would be?"

"Belinda and this is my sister Phoebe. May I ask who you are and what your intentions are with us?"

"It is a pleasure to meet both of you and I am Xeal. Though I do lament the state that you have both found yourself in, I am glad you are at least alive as it will save me a fair bit of trouble. You see, I am assuming that the monster you were speaking of was Frozen Sky and if so, you needn't worry as he will never return to this world, at least not the same way as he did before. I am like him in the fact that I am part of the same quest and can never truly die in this world, but unlike him, I have no desire to sit upon a throne. That is where you two come in, though I would ask you to bow to King Silas of Mauvers. I expect you both to rule your city as countesses, or whatever role is seen as fitting by King Silas."

"And just who do we need to marry first?" retorted Princess Belinda.

"No one if you don't want to. All I care about is that the city and surrounding area are tended to and that my subordinates are free to come and go from the city as they handle their tasks. Beyond that, I expect you to cooperate fully with my efforts to destroy the demons and return this world to a state that people can reestablish themselves in."

"You can't be serious," piped up Princess Phoebe. "No

one would ever see us as anything but your puppets. Even if we aren't, none will accept the rule of two women, especially ones that are little more than girls in their eyes."

"That will be their folly," replied Xeal seriously, while looking at the five guards who were present. "After all, while you will be no puppets of mine, I am the one who is putting you on the throne, so to refuse to abide by your rule is to offend me. I expect that if you need me to make an example, those who were your jailers would make an excellent first choice to display your power. As such, I know these four will do everything they can to support your rule, so long as you don't punish them beyond what I have in mind for their actions while Frozen Sky ruled."

"Oh, and how do you know that you can trust us?" asked Princess Belinda.

"I don't. I just know that if you are unworthy to rule, it will be clear to me rather quickly and I will have to find a replacement. Don't worry, I will not leave you without a leash and observer of a kind. They will simply be here to ensure that events aren't distorted by you, or let's say, the guards."

Xeal could see the sisters considering things as if nothing else, the experience that they had been through had taught them to be wary of everything. Rather than wait for them to decide, Xeal continued to speak as he turned his attention to the guards once more.

"Bring servants to care for these two and see to it that they are given a small and plain meal to start the process of recovering from being malnourished. As for the list you are making, simply give all the prisoners the same bland meal if they are in a similar state, and I will trust Belinda and Phoebe to determine what to do with them once they are healthy. Lastly, you two make sure that every guard is made aware that any of them who fail to fall in line will be the first I use to display my displeasure with. They should be assembling in the main courtyard. Now move!"

At Xeal's words, the guard who guided him to the dungeon practically ran to find a few maidservants and the pair he had held by their throats left to make sure their fellow guards got the message. The final two looked worried as they waited for the maidservants to arrive as Xeal returned to talking to the princesses.

"I will let you both get cleaned up and taken care of before I worry about your responses to my words here, as I am sure that you both have much to consider."

"You really have no plans to force us to become your brides and bear your children?" questioned Princess Phoebe, sounding unsure of herself.

"Phoebe, I already have seven wives, four more who are but a step away from being so, one who is well on her way to joining them and more than I like trying to find a way to join them. The last thing I want is to add two more ladies to those I need to keep happy and if you don't believe me, you will be meeting two of them shortly and feel free to ask them."

Xeal had to hold back a smile at seeing both princesses blink a few times at his response, as they tried to figure out if he was simply a womanizer seeking to lower their guard, or being truthful. As they continued to do this for a long moment, two maidservants arrived and bowed to the princesses while holding in their reactions to the state they were in as best they could. Still, Xeal could tell the shock both of the new arrivals had at seeing Princesses Belinda and Phoebe in this state, as Princess Belinda spoke before they were led out.

"Xeal, was it? My sister and I will think upon your words and let you know our answer when we have had time to recover slightly. Until then, farewell."

"Take your time, though I must let you know that I will be taking care of a few things to ensure a smooth transition of power, whether that is for you, or whoever I place on the throne here."

"Very well, I will trust you for the moment as I see no other option and I thank you for at least allowing us to feel what it will be like to be clean once more."

With that, Xeal turned and smiled at seeing the guard, who had guided him, half hiding in the hall as he instructed him to guide him through the city. The first stop was to a decent spot on the exterior wall of the city to set up one of the two transference points that Xeal had access to currently. As they made their way there, Xeal sent an update to Kate while taking in the shape of the city. While it was clear that food was in short supply and the overall mood was melancholic, Xeal could see that at the very least shops were open and the people were going about their daily lives. From the observations that he made, it was clear that with time and food, the territory would be able to thrive once more. Only it would take generations due to the severe lack in population caused by the demons' invasion. If Xeal's estimates were even close to being right, inside of all his dominions were only around 300,000 NPCs. If it was to be compared to Mexico, Xeal didn't think there was a time in recorded history that it had such a sparse population and he also knew that once the land was healed, it would be even more fertile.

Three hours and an inspection of the guards later, Xeal found himself in the throne room once more, with two women who looked nothing like the ones he had met in the dungeon. Part of this had been due to Lucy demanding to be shown to them and using the abilities her connection with Aceso granted her to aid in their recovery. The effects were astonishing, despite having no access to her normal skills and only the most basic healing skill from this world to work with. This had also forged a connection between Lucy and the two princesses, as Xeal could tell that they had let their guard down towards her, while they still looked at Xeal with caution. Even so, he had to smile at seeing their auburn hair free of the dirt and grime that had made it look like a muddy brown, and a bit of hope in their golden brown eyes that had been so dull before. As much as Xeal didn't wish to rush things, he knew that he was losing time in this world with every moment that he was present and so he interrupted the idle chatter as he cleared his throat before speaking.

"It is good to see that any damage done, physically at least, is well on its way to being undone. Have you both had a chance to think over if you wish to share the throne here and serve under King Silas yet?"

"We have," replied Princess Belinda. "We are still not sure if we will be found capable by your standards, but at the very least we feel it is our duty to try. That said, we wish for our title to remain as princess and for our descendants to retain the same level of peerage."

"You are intending to set the stage for Oserith to declare itself an independent kingdom once more," commented Kate. "You do realize that you are sowing the seeds of disaster, right?"

"We do," answered Princess Phoebe. "But our hope is to have a daughter each marry the next ruler of Mauvers and join the lines once and for all."

"So, if Princess Tsega was a prince, you two would want to marry him?" asked Xeal with a raised eyebrow.

"No," stated Princess Belinda. "At least not yet. We know that it is hypocritical, but after what we went through, we doubt that we will be able to be beholden to any man. While we know that we must marry and have an heir in the next few years, the last year and a half has made us-"

"You needn't say any more," interrupted Xeal. "That said, I hope that my plan of leaving Bretislaus here won't cause an issue. He, like you, found himself in a difficult position when the chaos of the demon lands began. While I will leave the details to him to share, he is the renounced and exiled prince of Tumond and can at the very least offer advice if you ask him for it."

"I see," replied Princess Belinda. "I suppose it was too much to hope for Lucy to be the one that you intended to leave with us."

"I must apologize," commented Lucy. "But even if he was willing to leave me with you, I am not willing to stay. My goals and drive would end if I were to remain in this world. That said, I am sure Xeal will bring me with him once in a while and I will still be able to visit from time to time."

"Letters," interjected Austru. "It is how I communicate with those in the other world that I need to. All you need do is have one of Xeal's kind deliver it to me and I will ensure that they are passed along."

"And you are?" asked Princess Phoebe, sounding unsure about how to respond to Austru's suggestion.

"I am Austru. I am a close friend of Princess Tsega and Xeal's main interface for this world."

"And the one who is well on her way to joining Xeal's wives," replied Princess Belinda.

"That is my hope and the intent from him seems to be genuine. That said, we are proceeding with caution currently due to the issues that his quest presents."

"I see and would the elf over there be the other of his ladies that he brought with him?"

"That I would," replied Kate. "Though I don't know

what that has to do with anything we are currently discussing."

"I simply wish to know as he spoke of many more. Are they all long-lived races like yourselves?"

"Hahahaha, alright, this was worth being dragged here for," commented Joliette. "Xeal, do you ever get tired of beating the women off, and are you sure your stick is big enough?"

"Excuse me and who are you!?" retorted Princess Belinda at having her questioning derailed like that. "I am not sure I like your tone."

"Really, can't say that I care, and all you need to know is that I am one of those who was defeated by Xeal, like Frozen Sky. The difference is, I accepted a deal to keep this whole quest quiet and I expect that it is only a matter of time before that ends now, from the fact that it seems a similar deal wasn't reached with Frozen Sky."

"And it won't be," retorted Xeal. "Joliette, at least show some decorum. As for my other ladies, Kate is one of my kind, so despite what she looks like, she is a human from my reality. Austru is the only sylph, six of my seven official wives are human, and one is a tiger-woman. Past that there is an elf, dwarf, orc, a few dragonoids, a pair of fox-women and a few more humans, unless I am forgetting anyone."

"Dragonoids? I can't say that I have ever heard of such a race, but even an orc and beast-women, are your tastes so broad and hard to satisfy?" inquired Princess Phoebe.

Xeal was about to respond when he saw Takeshi smile as he started to speak.

"Xeal-san certainly has a wide range of taste, though some might just say that he is a man of culture. However, I simply believe that his tastes have more to do with what is on the inside than the exterior. After all, none of those whom Xeal-san has allowed into his life should ever be seen as simply a jewel to be placed by his side. As Kate-san will clearly prove if you get to know her."

"Thank you, Takeshi-san," replied Xeal. "As for if I agree, or disagree, with any of that, I believe in simply allowing others to come to their own decisions. After all, I don't have the time to blow on every windmill that I come across. Now, if there is nothing else, I will leave Bretislaus, Vento, Kate and Austru here to get you up to speed and have Wisnor take charge of organizing the rest of my kind that should be arriving shortly."

"Wait, before you leave, do you have any solutions to our food issues?" asked Princess Belinda.

"Yes, and that will be covered by the others as my time here is too limited for me to explain every detail to you myself. Lucy, Takeshi-san, Joliette, I think it is time that we return to the other world and see to the headaches that await us there."

After a final check to make sure everyone was ready, Xeal gave Kate and Austru kisses before leaving and finding himself back in Nium once more. The last little bit of day 352 was spent making sure everything was in order, as he tasked Taya with reviving at least a few of the farms surrounding Oserith. Even so, he found himself lying awake next to his wives late that night as he thought over the likely course of events that was likely to play out at this point. Still, he just hoped it would be at least a few months before war became the battle cry across all of Nium.

Day 353 saw Xeal return to grinding as he worked to craft a plan whenever they were resting to recover their stats. This included exchanging many messages with Kate, as they figured out what the plays from all of the major powers would be and who they could trust. Though, even with all the plots and the plans that Xeal was making, he knew that they were all next to worthless as war never played out according to how one wanted. No, idiots would do something stupid and turn a victory into a defeat, or grasp a victory that seemed beyond comprehension. Events like these would upend everything time and time again, as the wars consumed more land, more weapons, more gold, more lives. Despite whatever country surviving it being called the winners, it was only the arms dealers who ever really won. The fact that FAE could be considered as one of said arms dealers was not lost on Xeal as he looked at things.

(*****)

Morning March 12 to Evening March 18, 2268 & ED Year 5 Day 354 to ED Year 6 Day 6.

Alex's time in reality seemed surreal to him when compared to the issues he had to constantly deal with in ED, as every session seemed to have another meeting for him to attend, or read a summary of. To say that he was able to relax during this time would have been a lie, especially as Xeal played with Ahsa and Moyra as it made him think of his other children. All four of them were two and his time with them was even more limited than what he had to give to his two daughters in reality. Alex was just grateful for the clerics of Eileithyia that were constantly acting as their caregivers while he and their mothers were busy, even if he wished it wasn't necessary.

Still, Alex made sure to keep up with his time in aikido, kendo and swing dancing as they had become almost meditative to him. During the morning lessons, he could simply focus on the motions of the discipline while letting nothing else enter his mind as he let the rest of the world fall away. Thankfully, all those around Alex had taken notice of this change in his mentality and understood the why. So, other than Sam, Nicole and Kate accompanying him, Ava and Mia to their week 34 OB-GYN appointment on Friday the 13th, they gave him his space. Beyond that, they simply enjoyed having their hour each that week where his attention was focused on them as they chose relaxing activities like soaking in a tub, or just cuddling.

Alex didn't even pay attention to the details of the sixth presentation at his old high school, or the fact that Kate had worked out the details for Nicole's younger sister Alyssa to come to live with them. Though it seemed that finding a few friends to do the same was causing issues and instead, Kate had shifted to looking at any extended family who would make sense to invite out to help care for the new babies. Alex's grandparents had been easy to convince to come out for the first few months, but they were also at the point in life where they didn't like bending over too much. Add in that they were likely to have issues keeping up with them once they became more mobile and it was clear that they would not be a good long-term solution. Though they were all due to fly in on the 20th to be on hand for the last bit of Ava's and Mia's pregnancies, as Doctors Avery and Lunt had warned that the way things were looking, that they would be surprised if they made it to week 38. This also prompted them to move the baby shower up to the 22nd, as Ava and Mia were ecstatic to hear that they would soon have their bodies back to themselves.

In ED, Xeal continued to keep up with his routine as he attended meeting after meeting during his breaks from grinding, as he used advanced return scrolls like candy to do so. While this was rather annoying for both him and those involved in the meetings, he had been insistent on it as he made it clear that his leveling was an absolute top priority. Though Xeal still took the time to spend a day with Dyllis for their anniversary, as he enjoyed the calming day of her singing for him as they focused on each other.

During this time, Xeal had also smiled as Aalin and Kate both complained from the new intensity that Queen Aila Lorafir had begun putting them through during training. This had especially been true for Kate as after missing a few days while she was working in the quest world, Aila had expected her to make up the time that had been missed. This had led to Kate skipping a few logouts as rather than having leniency towards her due to being involved with Xeal, Aila only held her to a higher standard. As much as Xeal could tell that the process that they and most of the others who were marked by the phoenixes were going through was just short of torture, it was also incredibly effective. If he were to try and quantify the difference it was only a five percent increase in their economy of actions, but when speaking about the skills of experts, such increases may as well be 50% with the ripple effects that they had. When a battle was normally decided in milliseconds, the second and a half improvement every 30 seconds they were gaining was just insane.

When day 364 arrived, it was finally time for the party that Xeal had arranged for those who he had made a connection with to attend. This was mainly focused on the NPC acquaintances that he had made along his journey, but he had invited other players as well. This included Lori Lunaflower of Night Oath, Segur Woodlight of Hope of Rejects, Mittie Alabaster and Ferne Acheron of Salty Dogs, Nuthi Draig and Qilong Draig of Dragon Legion and Kenneth Serment of Fire Oath. The fact that they all had come had been surprising to Xeal, as he figured that Nuthi was still holding some kind of grudge and Kenneth had had his career upended due to FAE. Still, Kate had assured Xeal that Kenneth wouldn't cause issues and while things were such that it would be in poor form to invite any of the current leadership of Fire Oath, inviting him would show a bit of goodwill.

However, Xeal's focus was on Baron Ulric, Marshal Sanford, Sheriff Aldway, the Weawens, Earl Smythe and Johanna Smythe, who were in attendance with Casmir and Nada (Jessica), the marquesses of Nium and the other

NPCs in attendance. Many of these were at best casual acquaintances, like Rupert Beckett, who Xeal had met when the airship captain had taken Enye and him up for a ride as part of their courtship announcement. Then there were others like the noble youths that had become young men and married beast-women since he had started to train them. Many even had a child already. While Xeal had lacked the time to spend more than a few minutes with any of them, he had still enjoyed the time that he did get. He just wished it hadn't been tainted by the looming war. By this point things were clear as both Habia and Paidhia were making moves that were clearly preparations for an expected conflict. The only question was whether they would work together against the dwarves, or some other plan would be executed to initiate the war.

By the end of the night, Xeal felt as if the only message that had been clearly sent was that he was overworked and wanted to make sure to let them know he still remembered them before the war started. Though from what Kate had reported on her work, that night had been promising as Mittie had actually helped persuade Dragon Legion into a possible resource deal. Still, it would take time and it seemed that they were mainly interested in connecting FAE's trade network with their own for trading specialty resources at fair prices and not becoming a net supplier. While still a valuable exchange, it wouldn't help FAE supply their crafters with more materials to work with at the end of the day.

However, the greatest harvest had come from Kate's conversation with Kenneth, as the ex-guild leader was rather happy to badmouth the Astor family as a whole. If his words were to be trusted, while he was still part of Fire Oath, he had not signed any new contracts that would restrict him in ED. Apparently, he was almost daring them to release him, knowing full well that doing so would allow him to talk even more brazenly about their secrets. While Kate warned that it could be a trick to feed them bad intel mixed with good intel, she seemed to lean towards Kenneth being upset at the current state of things in Fire Oath. Especially with the current power struggle the Astor family was having to figure out who their new head of the family would be.

With the party over, Xeal sighed as he once more was in one rushed meeting after another as the new year came and went with the normal gathering held by King Victor. Only this year it seemed that the atmosphere was a mix of somberness and excitement, as the positions on the impending war clashed. Apparently, information had leaked far and wide through the channels that nobles had, that Xeal was taking part in a special quest and his actions were raising tensions to a breaking point. This had made it certain that while Frozen Sky and his followers hadn't made a public post about the quest for godhood like an idiot, they had started to contact the major and super guilds. Whether it was to try and find slots for the players who had built themselves up in that world, or simply to cause Xeal issues, he wasn't sure but it was clear that the information was spreading quickly.

It was with these thoughts that Xeal looked over the final preparations for the beast-man and noble marriage meetings to occur once more. Xeal found that he was actually enjoying the time he spent focused on the event despite the headache it normally gave him. As he pondered the why, he realized that while marriage had its conflict, it was the opposite of war in that it was about working together and finding a good compromise when issues came up. For Xeal, it felt like he was helping make the world a bit happier in the face of the impending war and to him that helped him on a level that he hadn't known he needed. Still, he hardly spent any time in the grand scheme of things on the marriage meeting planning as it was basically a repeat of the prior years, with a few special events to highlight the new arrivals a bit. Many of these would-be young nobles, or beast-men, had just recently come of age or reached the point that they wouldn't make a fool of themselves. However, still more had come through the efforts of Kate and her team, as they attracted ladies from noble houses abroad to participate as well.

Although these women were really there to take advantage of the post-war era when many commoners would earn titles and be granted land. Normally such a house was likely to take a few generations to get its bearings, but with the sudden influx in noble ladies to become their brides and help guide them, it could happen much quicker. That said, they needed to find a husband among those who stood out in battle that would allow them to essentially run things and play the part of a noble well enough to pass in society. Additionally, many of those who had been sent recently were too young for them to allow them to do more than observe the marriage meetings, as some were only 14. Though Kate said it would be fine as once the war ended, they should all have learned the etiquette of Nium and be old enough, or close to it, to marry by Xeal's standards.

As day four came to an end, Xeal was happy to see that he had reached level 190. Though this meant that he would be trading Lucy for Sylvi in his party on day eight and Xeal had mixed feelings surrounding it. While he knew that Sylvi made more sense for his current plans, Lucy had to be one of the best clerics he had ever seen and he wasn't looking forward to losing her. Still, unless something changed the circumstances, Xeal knew that it didn't make sense to change his plans as they were for the best long term.

When day five arrived, Xeal smiled as he opened the marriage meeting like he had the prior two years and found himself needing to attend several weddings of those who had found their partners the year prior. Enye had commented about how it would likely become a tradition to travel to Hardt Burgh around this time to have the lord of the city witness the marriage of nobles. She had laughed about how with that and the new year celebration of any new children born to the lord, that the first week of any year was set to be a joyous time in his territory. Xeal just smiled as the first day of the event passed, as both Daisy and Violet grumbled about needing to participate yet again. Meanwhile, Eira seemed to flaunt the fact that she had married Xeal in the face of all the other beast-women present. Xeal just frowned at the looks of envy that many of them sent her way as she just smiled and they made a show of congratulating her.

Thankfully, Aziz had warned Xeal in the meetings that had led up to this event that any interest he showed at this point would be seen as an opening for them to try to add themselves to his arm for many. This could be as simple as a lingering look at any of their features that many seemed more than happy to show off to him as they interacted with him. From bending down to display their rears to other just as suggestive and slightly compromising positions, Xeal found himself needing to find other places to look fairly often. He had just wished Eira had said something to him about this side of beast-men culture, though it seemed that it varied from tribe to tribe. For Eira, had she said anything to him it would have meant that she either didn't trust him, or she wished to control him completely, both of which were things Xeal knew she would never do. So, he simply smiled as he evaded all the attempts that seemed to be most prevalent from the snake-women, though the eagle-women and wolf-women weren't exactly shy either.

Day six came and was just as eventful as Xeal had expected, as new pairings started to form and alliances between those who were to be second and below wives developed. There was even a group of four noblemen who seemed to be under the impression that Daisy and Violet were looking to flip the norm and have several consorts, that had attempted to make a move on them. Apparently, something had been distorted over the years since they rejected even giving the noblemen that Xeal trained a chance. Needless to say that they were rejected, and Xeal found himself needing to deal with the fallout from the experience and Daisy and Violet seemed to not handle it too well. This had involved both telling the noblemen to give up on Daisy and Violet and letting the two fox-women vent at him for a good long while. Eira, on the other hand, had chuckled after seeing the four nobles catch the attention of a snake-woman who was more than happy to entertain such an arrangement. Still, this had created a whole new kind of headache as it meant that Xeal would need to discuss allowing matriarchal houses to be established within his lands if the courtship led to a marriage.

Xeal was still thinking over the ramifications of pushing for what would be seen as an upheaval of the established order in Nium when the news came in. Habia and Paidhia had attacked the dwarven lands and Nium had declared that it was coming to the aid and defense of the dwarves. As this news spread through the marriage meeting, there was widespread unease as all those present wondered what would happen, both now and in the future. All teleportation halls had already been shut down, trapping many players abroad, especially as Paidhia and Habia had done the same at Nium's declaration. The forums were filled with chatter as players complained and grew excited over the situation, as they talked utter nonsense from Xeal's point of view. He knew just what this meant as he took control of his city and called several emergency meetings and speeches. With the first of these being to all those who were participating in the marriage meeting.

As Xeal looked out over the crowd of NPCs who didn't have infinite lives and couldn't escape to another world if they wished to, Xeal refused to show any concern. No, he knew that if he, or any of his wives who were all standing next to him as he prepared to speak, were to even look worried, much less panic, that it would be magnified by those present. So in a calm, yet as serious of a tone that Xeal could manage, he began to speak to the silent crowd, who knew even less than he did.

"War has come to our land. To say that there is no reason to worry would be a lie, but for now, all of you need to only worry about interacting with one another. I am hereby extending this event until further notice. A few of those present may be asked to leave to fulfill their duties, but until King Victor orders otherwise, Hardt Burgh will welcome you to stay. I am sure that I will have more to say once I have counseled with others, but rest assured that on this I will not be moved, even if your family demands you return and you wish to stay.

"Now, look to each other for the reassurances you need as you mingle, as the event will shift focus from games and social events to something a bit more productive. Namely learning something that can be put to use to aid the war effort, whether that be creating mundane bandages for when healing potions run out, or prepping the ingredients for said potions to be crafted. The exact tasks and expectations are not yet known and none of you will be forced to do anything, but I expect that you will, as the goal is to limit how many of you find yourselves on the frontlines as much as possible. Leave that to my kind as you have but a single life to give and we have many."

As Xeal stepped back, he could tell a bit of the worry had gone from the crowd, but they were far from calmed as he left with his wives trailing after him. Still, his goal had not been to put them at complete ease by lying to them and saying that everything would be fine. No, he was just giving them a topic that would distract them slightly. Xeal knew being told that he would see to it that they could aid in the war effort by staying right where they were and learning a craft would provoke a few different responses. First, there would be the ones who believed it was beneath them to take part in such things and refuse to do so, or only do so while complaining. Next, there would be the polar opposite that would happily contribute in whatever way they could, while wishing that they could do more. Then there would be the ones who wished to leave and take a more active role in the war in a misguided belief that seeing battle would do them good, or bring them glory. Finally, you would have the ones who used this as an opportunity to hide where they feel is safe as they just keep their heads down and work, and all the ones in between.

Xeal knew that there would be more types than these, but as they were nobles, gold, image, reputation, achievements and self-preservation were what mattered most to them. Balancing these aspects of nobility was part of what each of the nobles present were still learning and that the beast-men had only recently even been introduced to. The question they would all need to answer was how they were going to respond and if they could put such meaningless things aside, while they placed the needs of the nation above their own need. It was with this on Xeal's mind that he entered the conference room, where all the leaders of the tribes had gathered at his order. His speech earlier had been partially to give them time to assemble and come to terms with the order that he was about to give.

"Thank you all for coming today. I know this is almost a full year before we had hoped when I first met with you all, but such is life. It is with a heavy heart that I say what I am about to, but the first wave that is called up needs to be those who your tribes can afford to lose and a few leaders that can handle coming home alone. To be clear none of you, nor any of the tier-7 and up forces, are to leave your lands, as your main role is to guard against an invasion until Nium has dispatched troops to replace you. As for your youths that you can't afford to lose, I expect them all readied and FAE will see that they all are given the best possibility at reaching tier-7 before they have to see combat. And yes, I am well aware that many of them would have better odds of surviving combat than reaching tier-7. I can make no promises surrounding their futures, but I will not carelessly throw away their lives.

"Once I and my guild's elites reach tier-7, we will shift to a true offensive assault. At that point you should all find that Nium has provided border forces to relieve all of you. Many of these will be independent players and those from other guilds besides FAE, as they adventure during their down time. They will have agreed to act as defenders if an invasion occurs, in exchange for something from either Nium, or FAE, possibly even both."

"How can you ask us to trust your kind to guard our lands when it won't even be the members of your guild doing so?" interjected Adolphus, the alpha of the wolf-men. "While I trust your word and see that your guild follows you faithfully, the same cannot be said for the others of your kind that I have witnessed since I came to this city."

"Your concerns are valid and it is why I will never pull all of your tier-7 and up forces from your lands. My kind are just there to make up the loss in strength from me pulling about one in every three tier-7 members of your tribes and 70% of all tier-6s. I am hoping to not need to call up any of your tribes' members who have not reached tier-6 yet as they are needed for the future. Are there any objections to my orders?"

Xeal could see that all of the beast-men present looked frustrated as they held their tongues. While many wished to charge into battle, others were lamenting the death that was soon to come. Either way, they wanted to say that Xeal's plan was a mistake and that they had a better one, but if they had learned one thing since meeting Xeal, it was that he knew what he was doing. So it was that they all agreed and Xeal relaxed slightly as the meeting shifted to what it would take to mobilize and an hour later, he used his guild's teleportation network to reach Anelqua.

There he was greeted with the sight of the elven city in full motion as they mobilized for war and Xeal frowned as he made his way to the palace. Once there, he was greeted by a rushed servant who quickly led him to a room where he found Queen Aila Lorafir speaking to those Xeal knew were her elder children as she gave orders. However, as he entered, she paused before shifting her tone to one a bit softer as she addressed the room.

"That will be all for now, but don't go far. I expect it won't be long before I have more to share with you all."

Just like that the roughly 15 other elves in the room left, with most of them giving Xeal a nod before departing. Once they were alone, Queen Aila Lorafir spoke once more as she looked at Xeal.

"Is this the part where you tell me how to handle my

troop deployments?"

"Not exactly. Aila, this war came too soon. As I am sure you know, a portion of your forces need to be sent to join the coalition forces that will be stationed at the front. All I ask is that it be made up of the ones you are ready to lose like we discussed earlier."

"Xeal, we are elves. As you know, we are never ready to lose any of our lives if we can avoid it. All I will promise is that I will seek volunteers and ensure that a suitable force will be sent forth. The real question is if you can trust the orcs to not betray us in this war, as vengeance for imprisoning Xuk and Durz."

"If they do, they do. I am not worried about it at this point as I believe the goodwill my guild has built up will keep them from risking everything by allying with an unknown power."

"Fine. I take it that you are having them only send a token force at this point as well?"

"I can only hope that they will listen, but Noriko and Aziz are on their way there now as thanks to Bula's words when I return, I must prove myself to be worthy of becoming their chief."

"As annoying as that declaration is, I must admit seeing you become chief of the orcs before bearing your child stirs something in me."

"No, I am no king, or chief. Heck, I can't wait for Xander to be ready to take over so I can escape my current responsibilities."

"Please. Enye, Dyllis, Lingxin and Mari already practically handle everything for you, save for the few responsibilities that you can't escape and I doubt Victor will allow you to simply retire when you want."

"That's the beauty of not needing to ask him. Aila, when I decide I am done, I will simply take you and my other wives and leave. If I need to live in Cielo city to escape, so be it. If I can take you all to the quest world to live, even better, but regardless, I will leave and none will dare attack my house casually."

As Xeal ended his statement in a tone that he could tell was not needed in Queen Aila Lorafir's presence, he frowned as she responded.

"It is strange how protective we can get when tensions are high and we even think about someone harming what we love. I still remember the early days when I helped build the core to this palace and declared these lands as a sanctuary for the elves. The feeling as I held my first daughter and saw a beautiful future for her, only to hold her in my arms 150 years later as I extinguished the same life. Xeal, I am aware that you know better than most what will be needed to win this war and I look forward to standing by your side when it's over, but now is not the time to let emotions rule the day. So, know that I intend to do what must be done to ensure that my people have a future and I expect you to do the same, no matter the pain it may bring you."

"No, I will not allow you, or those I love, to pay with your lives. Aila, if I have to marry you, become king of the elves and fill your womb with a child to save you, I will. Yes, I love you that much, Aila. I am aware of why you had to kill your daughters that allowed the remnant of your curse to consume them, but I choose to believe you acted in love of who they had been when you did so. Just as you will stop me if you ever feel that I am out of control."

"Xeal, even when it felt like I was putting them out of their misery it still was hell!"

"Aila, I know. I didn't say that it was easy. Sometimes doing what must be done for our loved ones is the hardest thing in the world. It is easy to ignore issues and hold them tight as we tell ourselves that the problem will solve itself, or that everything will be all right, but know it won't. Second chances like the one I have been given don't normally exist and yes, I would say that the life I had is not the one that was good for me, or those I cared for. Aila, I will not claim to have felt what you have and likely still do, but I fully intend to remove the one who cursed you from this reality."

Queen Aila Lorafir just smiled as she looked at Xeal, before giving him a kiss and holding him in her arms and speaking in a soft tone.

"I hope that you never feel the pain that I do and only ask that you not add to it. Xeal, I love you in a way that I never thought would be possible for me. Now, I think it would be best if we put this to the side and returned to the topic of the war…"

Just like that, they each caught the other up on what the current situation of the other's forces were. By the point they separated an hour later, Xeal had what he needed as he transferred to his guild's headquarters. Once there, he was met by Kate and Taya as they all headed to the palace where they were guided to the war room. Xeal smiled as he saw the enormous map of the continent in the center and the various military officers that were discussing the situation, as King Victor sat overlooking it all with the captain of the royal knights, Royce Bexley, standing next to him. While only a captain, Royce Bexley was the highest-ranking military officer in the room due to the fact that he led all the royal knights and they were in the presence of the king. Still, if they ended up on the battlefield, Captain Bexley would be seen as an overqualified captain and nothing more, as would most of the royal knights in respect to other soldiers of the same rank. As the room took note of Xeal's group's arrival, the chatter died down and all attention turned to him as King Victor stood and spoke.

"Duke Xeal, it is good that you have made it so quickly. I take it that we can expect reinforcements from the elves, orcs and beast-men, as well as your guild."

"Yes, though you should expect the first wave to contain substandard individuals as the war came a year early and my priority is to ensure that I and the core of each of those forces is not wasted-"

"Ridiculous!" shouted one of the generals, looking like he couldn't believe what he was hearing. "This is war. We need every available resource now, not when you think it is best-"

"Silence!" exclaimed King Victor, letting fury into his voice. "Duke Xeal, continue."

"Thank you, my king. As I was saying, we must not waste the lives of those who can offer the most in actually invading Habia and Paidhia. Once I have 20,000 or so of my guild's members reach tier-7, it will allow us to assault them with a force capable of overwhelming them over time. The goal now should be to simply hold the forts that are on the borders and repel any invasions while conducting a naval campaign to cut them from outside trade as much as possible."

"If we follow your plan, how are we to aid our allies who currently find themselves under siege?" asked King Victor, setting the stage as they had planned.

"FAE has made preparations to establish a garrison portal that will be tied to one of my networks in their lands. Through that we will exchange goods and ensure that they have the means to hold the line for the most part, at least for the next year. However, this connection will not be regularly active and members of my guild will be the ones to maintain it as we coordinate its use."

"It sure sounds like it will be FAE running this war and

not the kingdom," retorted a general, who had similar features to Marquess Mercer. "Tell me, Duke Bluefire, just how much gold is your guild hoping to make from this war?"

"This one, absolutely nothing," replied Xeal with a smile. "Will our involvement cost the kingdom a fair bit? Yes, but it will all have the portion my guild would normally take for itself removed for the most part. Unfortunately, that will only alleviate a small portion of the cost as the crafters and the players who will be sacrificing their levels to act as the kingdom's fodder still need to be compensated for their work. All that will be left after that will be a bit more to cover FAE's operating costs, which King Victor is aware of as we have been over it, but altogether everything will be about 15% below market rate. More if the kingdom can supply the materials for their orders to be filled, as then I will not need to buy them from sources outside my guild."

Xeal simply smiled at the look on the general's face as it was clear to Xeal that there was more than just a coincidental resemblance to the Mercers from his reactions as he replied.

"All of the nobles of the kingdom are expected to put their entire fortunes on the line during this war and yet you see fit to say that you expect us to help yours from dwindling? How dare you call yourself-"

"I hate repeating myself," cautioned King Victor in an authoritative tone. "Duke Xeal is putting his personal finances at risk. However, his guild can't be allowed to fold while he does so! Furthermore, since his arrival he and his guild have invested more into our kingdom than all of the marquess houses combined. So, forgive me if the next one who questions his willingness to suffer a loss for the kingdom finds themselves and their family visited by the finance ministers."

At these words the room grew rather quiet, as more than one general looked nervous about such a possibility as the general backed down and King Victor continued to speak.

"Now, Kate, I believe you and Taya have prepared a presentation for us…"

With that Kate and Taya smiled as they started to hand out what was a complete breakdown of everything FAE had on the current state of things. This included everything from troop placements, to include the player base who was expected to participate for Habia and Paidhia, to food supplies and likely battle locations. Next came a report of which noble houses were expected to only do the bare minimum and which were expected to put their all into the war effort. When a suggestion came to try and flip the lazy houses, Kate shut it down as she pointed to using them as targets for resentment and that it would be better if they were forced to participate. Put simply, the hope was that an unmotivated and disgruntled portion of the enemy would create openings when they fled, or if they were forced to fight with a sword at their back it would aid in propaganda. Either way, Kate made it clear that none but those who volunteer to serve should be allowed to fight in this war, as gold from houses like the Mercers would be just as useful as manpower in winning the war.

This led into her speaking on having Salty Dogs being allowed to still conduct trade with both Habia and Paidhia on a limited basis. To be specific food, as war often ruined fields where crops were grown and it would be easy to create a food shortage in both kingdoms. As it would be the commoners who suffered the most if famine occurred and starving an army out was unlikely to be an issue any time soon. Furthermore, while an angry population could put pressure on both kingdoms and cause them to make mistakes, building goodwill with them now would pay dividends when it came time to rule them. This was why Salty Dogs would be allowed to ship food that originated from a secret network that FAE had created according to what Kate said, but Xeal knew was the quest world. This was only possible due to Taya's work there, as she had gotten the fields in that world to the point that they would be able to produce enough food to feed around a million each year. That meant that while it would still not cover all the needs that the three kingdoms would need, it would go a long way in mitigating the issues that would start occurring as the grain stores emptied. Still, Xeal had even more plans to increase Nium's imports through the access that the gates to all the phoenixes gave FAE to still travel around all of ED.

After speaking on food, Kate shifted to the propaganda that would soon be spreading in both Habia and Paidhia. The focus on this had nothing to do with making Nium seem better. Instead, it would focus on highlighting the worst aspects of every noble house in both kingdoms, from the commoners' perspective. Even something as simple as hosting a banquet during the war would be spun into them not caring about the soldiers, or commoners, who were lucky to have some broth made with meat once in a while. Especially as the food that Salty Dogs would be delivering would be mostly grains and other crops with a long shelf life or that could easily be preserved. Additionally meat would become rarer with cattle starving and adventurers who were focused on the war still consuming it absentmindedly. Most wouldn't even think about how a meal that used to cost five copper was now a full silver, as they could easily earn that and even two silvers would be nothing to them. Kate continued to highlight how any perceived slight or corruption of the nobles would slowly turn a local lord from a target of slight envy into a despicable monster.

By the time the meeting had ended, the room was silent as they looked at Kate like she was a true monster. Xeal could tell that they all had a single thought on their mind and that was thank heavens she wasn't their enemy. Though he was also sure more than one was also thinking that if she had this much information on the enemy, what did she have on them as the real sinisterness of the presentation sunk in. She had just told them how they would be treated if they acted on any plan to take advantage of the war for personal gain and it wouldn't be a week before all noble houses would be marching in lockstep with FAE. Still, it was late and Xeal needed to log off soon, so the meeting came to an end for the day as the generals all left in a bit too much of a hurry as King Victor smiled and asked for a minute more of Xeal's time. At this Xeal kissed Kate, as she and Taya followed after the generals and it became just King Victor, Xeal and Captain Bexley.

"Xeal, tell me just how bad you see things getting?"

"Victor, if we hold the border forts and repel any other invasions for a year, we will only suffer slightly if no betrayal comes from within. If either fort falls, or an enemy stronghold is established, we will be in for a very bloody decade."

"And what do you see playing out?"

"Victor, this is war, not some simulation that can be run over and over again, where I can see the most likely paths forward. The slightest thing could change the nature of the results and the timing surrounding all of this is not ideal. I know that it is partially my own fault, but what is done is done. Now all that matters is ensuring that Nium survives as intact as possible."

"Huhhh, at least we only need to hold for 42 days before

Cielo city will be able to take our wives in."

"Ha, I have a feeling mine might refuse to go until they reach tier-7 at this point. I know, I know, that isn't acceptable, but what am I to do? Though they will be staying with Aila if they refuse to leave and I can have Nora there tomorrow if you like."

"Do that and at least have your children and the clerics of Eileithyia join them up there."

"I will do what I can and just to be sure, you do intend to send a small group of royal knights as well, right?"

"Yes, though they will be made up of tier-6 ones who are close to reaching tier-7, who will be expected to train diligently while they are up there."

"That's fine. I am just concerned about the possibility of a holy war being added to our list of worries and I don't know which side Eileithyia and her followers would end up on right now."

"Why do I feel like you are at the center of even more chaos? Xeal, I am starting to wonder if you were a blessing, or a curse for my kingdom."

"Definitely a fair question. Just once more, I have no control over this situation as it goes above my head in many ways."

Victor sighed as he responded to Xeal's reasons.

"Alright, leave before you tell me that you've opened a portal to the demonic realm and demons are flooding in freely."

"Nope, at least not yet. Give me a few weeks and I will see what I can do… though now that you say that, it gives me an idea."

Xeal just smiled as Victor gave him a look that made it clear that he was not amused as Xeal left. While Xeal walked to his guild headquarters, he took in the sights of the palace grounds that had four times more guards than normal and wondered what the reaction of the common folk was right now. While some would say that they were the least affected as they only had a pittance to give, they would still end up giving a far larger share of that pittance than a noble would give of their fortunes. It was with this thought that Xeal lay in a cot that he had had brought into his office, as Eira arrived and joined him as they snuggled closely as he logged out.

(*****)

Morning March 19 to Evening March 23, 2268 & ED Year 6 Days 7-21.

When Alex stepped out of his VR pod on Thursday the 19th, he was met by Sam giving him a tight hug, while Kate and Nicole helped Ava and Mia out of their VR pods. For a moment Alex just wondered why as he returned that hug, but he realized that sometimes you just needed a good hug and he smiled as he waited for her to be done. As the hug ended and Sam stepped back before the other four got hugs of their own, Alex felt as if they were all saying that they knew he would be leaving them in reality just like he would be in ED. This realization struck him hard as Sam spoke first.

"We know we still have a little bit before we are separated and you start playing close to 22 hours a day, but we don't want to waste what time we do have."

"Sam is right," agreed Kate. "Though we still expect you to prioritize our birthdays, the wedding that I am planning for all of us, Ava's and Mia's deliveries and you get the picture."

"Yeah, a daddy is there for the big stuff," cooed Ava.

"And he makes time for the little stuff," added Mia with a smile while both twins held their bellies.

Alex smiled in response as Nicole started to add her own comment.

"What we are saying is that we know that you will become a ghost to us most of the time and we understand and love you for it. Just don't forget to show up when it matters and when you can."

"I would never dream of forgetting my responsibilities

and that I have five of the most wonderful women in all the world that want my affection. I will just need to make sure that I can take a day, or two, off from the war when needed. Now let's not keep Sensei Burke waiting. Besides, a bit of aikido will help me clear my head."

With that the morning passed like most, except the main topic was the war in Nium and Alex simply enjoyed the brief bit of affection he received and the time he got to spend with his daughters. That evening, on the other hand, was Sam's night to have him to herself. After dinner and some intimate time, they found themselves with around ten minutes before they needed to return to ED as Sam spoke.

"Alex, promise me that you will end this war as quickly as possible."

"Sam, you know that I can't promise that and even if I could, I wouldn't if the price was too high."

"I know, but I can also see you drawing things out to try and take care of things other than ending the war."

"You mean like ensuring that you know I still love and think about you all the time?"

"Exactly, though you can keep doing that one, especially as I won't get any time like this in ED at all until you end the war and give me a child there."

"That is going to make things so complicated," quipped Alex. "Sam, I love you, but you can see just how much time caring for our little one takes here and how quickly my kids in ED are growing."

"I know and don't worry, I will attempt to reach tier-8 with you when the time for that comes, and I know that you would rather wait until Ahsa and Moyra were around ten, but I know what I want."

"What happened to 'miss not wanting to have kids, or even be called a lady'?"

"She got swooped up by a hopeless philanderer that she

can't help but love for some reason. Though she still doesn't want to be called a lady, but she allows said philanderer his delusions."

Alex couldn't help but smile as he kissed Sam deeply before responding.

"Oh, she must also enjoy being an actress as that philanderer hasn't seen her act as anything but a wonderful lady and mother when he's around, in reality at least."

Sam just started to giggle as Alex started to tickle her gently and they enjoyed their last few minutes together before making their way back to the VR pods for the night.

Friday was a busy day as all of Alex's grandparents arrived, happy to start moving into a house that Alex had rented for them to share for at least the next year as he helped them officially retire. To do this, Kate had taken the liberty of paying Alex enough of FAE's earnings to set up a fund that was designed to earn around four percent interest on a bad year. She had also commented that they would need to do the same for Sam's and Nicole's grandparents in the next few years, or risk possible issues. Particularly from Nicole's grandparents who would wonder why they hadn't been allowed to retire in a similar fashion yet. The reason they could even get away with it being just Alex's at the current time, was the fact that they were basically on newborn duty and would likely stay on it for the next several years, as Anna and Kate both intended to be pregnant before the end of the year.

Additionally, it was time for another OB-GYN appointment for Ava and Mia, as they struggled to get in and out of the SUVs as Kate, Sam and Nicole tagged along as well. Unlike with Sam and Nicole, both Ava and Mia were showing signs of dilation and Dr. Avery seemed to believe that it was only a week or two at most before they would go into labor. Finally she did one last ultrasound when Ava and Mia had asked for it and they all just smiled at seeing the four little ones that seemed to be in a hurry to meet all of them. With a copy of the recording stored, they all left Dr. Avery's office and after a short struggle to help Ava and Mia into the SUV, with Alex sitting between them, they were on their way home.

Upon arriving home, they quickly found themselves seated for dinner with the four grandparents, all smiling as they commented on the size of Ava's and Mia's bellies. Surprising to Alex was the presence of the twins' mom, Lydia, who he learned had been invited by Ava and Mia on the account that they figured that they could at least let her be present when they gave birth. Though, they also made it clear that it was on their terms and they were still reserved about the whole situation, but they figured that if they didn't allow her to be there, they would regret it later. Especially if they ever did mend the fence, so to speak and allow her back into their lives in the future. Still, Alex could tell that things were awkward as Nana Quinn worked to lighten the mood as she talked about remembering when Lydia's belly had been that big right before the twins were born. This and other comments meant to help the estranged trio break the ice seemed to only have moderate success before the night was over as Ava and Mia vented to Alex afterward.

"Why is it so hard just to be around her?" complained Ava.

"Yeah, we even knew she was coming this time," added Mia.

"But it is like just seeing her makes us upset."

"We even know that it isn't rational, but it doesn't help!"

"But it is rational," countered Alex. "You both are terrified of becoming like her. It is why despite your nature to want to party and go wild, you play video games. She really hurt you and seeing her forces all of the insecurities you have up to the surface and it makes you worry if you are really ready to be moms."

"Oh, we are ready alright," quipped Ava while pointing to her belly.

"Ready to serve these four their eviction notices and hold them in our arms," clarified Mia, while mirroring Ava's pose.

"We just can't wait to see our feet again."

"Yes, we have missed looking down and seeing them oh so much."

"Even if the price is having to deal with four new poop machines."

"I believe you mean crying poop machines."

Alex had to hold in his laugh as Ava and Mia smiled brightly at him as he responded.

"I know, you both are going to be great moms, possibly at your own detriment if I let you, but that doesn't mean you don't worry when you see your mom and remember the few good years you had with her. She betrayed that trust and I don't expect you to give it back to her easily. It is why I would shut down any plans that involved more than an occasional visit, even if you both begged for it."

"We know."

"And we love you for it."

"Just like how we know that we will be fine."

"Yeah, we may keep other women from approaching you for Sam and Nicole."

"But they give us the sisters we never had."

"And we know they will be there to make sure we don't become like Lydia."

"Yes, how the four of you are able to coexist so well still confuses me, especially with Kate being in the mix like she is."

"What, we love Kate!"

"She makes everything easier!"

"Though we aren't quite ready to call her a sister."

"Yep, that needs to wait until you put a baby in her belly."

Alex just laughed and the twins giggled as they enjoyed a few more moments together before they returned to playing ED.

Saturday passed quickly as the new arrivals settled in and enjoyed more time to visit, as Lydia had found herself being drawn in by Kate's mom, Catherine, as they chatted. While Alex was worried about this pairing due to the issues with the Astor family, he let it be while keeping an extra close eye on Catherine. Especially as despite the fact that Jasper had yet to even call Catherine since he left, she still seemed loyal to him. It was partially this that had kept Alex from letting Catherine even enter FAE's guild facilities in, or out of, ED as she played while under the watchful eye of one of Kate's bodyguards at all times. He had hoped that she would eventually be able to spend time with Jasper in ED when he left, but now that looked like an impossibility as he hadn't even logged in since he had left from what Alex knew.

Still, after dinner, Alex found himself alone with Kate as they talked about anything other than ED, or her ex-family. They spoke about the upcoming wedding and the plans to remodel the nursery to create a quiet nap area that was set to start in a few days and be done just before Dan and Anna's wedding on the 4th of next month. They covered all of this and more and still found their way back to the situation in ED, as Kate started to talk about Kenneth who had been stuck in Nium when the war started.

"You ever think about making a play to help Kenneth seize power back and restore the good relations between our guilds at least?"

"Kate, I thought we were avoiding talking about ED for once."

"I know, but I barely get any time with you in ED right now and I think there is a good plan that could be made if you agree and he gets behind it."

"Oh, and what is that?"

"Train him and level him up so that when the war in Nium is over, he is the best player in Fire Oath. Then with a bit of support from us and my few contacts in Fire Oath that I know want him back-"

"And make ourselves the king maker of not just NPC nations, but the guild leaders of super guilds. Kate, just what would the ramifications be for that?"

"We would only be seen as allowing him to work with our members while he is stuck in Nium," countered Kate with a smile that told Alex all he needed to know about just how many layers were involved in this idea of hers. "I mean if others see that and think that we gave him the ability to retake control of a super guild, well we can't help that now, can we?"

"You could care less about Kenneth taking Fire Oath back over. You just want our methods to be showcased to the point where we can finally fix our expert issue."

"Exactly. While we are fine right now, as you say tier-7 and tier-8 are the two great barriers that will allow all the guilds to catch up to us. While we can survive the tier-7 one by keeping the ones who do get past it ahead of the true experts by ten or so levels, the same can't be said for the tier-8 one."

"Fine, but you better lock him down to the point where he isn't even allowed to ever train another player, let alone share any of our methods beyond mentioning the mirror shards. Speaking of which, do we know what the drop rate for the clones of them are in the dungeons yet?"

"No, it seems to be either completely random, or dependent on variables that we can't identify yet. Thankfully they are rare and it will be a while before others can really start exploiting them as we have. As for Kenneth, you let me worry about getting him to agree and just focus on the main battles that are before us."

Kate quickly sealed Alex's lips with a kiss as he was about to respond, before leading him away to return to ED once more.

Alex found himself relaxing Sunday morning, as he swam lazily in the pool while a few others either joined him, or found some other source of leisure. He knew that he had a 22-hour login before him, as he planned to simply stay online while the rest of them participated in Ava and Mia's baby shower. As such, he had taken the day as his personal time and was just enjoying the feeling of near weightlessness that being in a pool gave him, until it was time to return to ED.

Monday saw Alex return to his logging out twice a day, as he enjoyed aikido in the morning before the evening saw him alone with Nicole. For this she had decided that she wanted to cook for him and he just smiled as she made the same meal she had for their first date, beef bulgogi over rice with sigeumchi namul (seasoned spinach). The smile on her face as Alex savored every bite was one of his favorite sights. When he had finished and she was about to fetch the dessert that she had made, Alex stopped her with a kiss before speaking.

"That was absolutely wonderful, but I have to check that you aren't trying to have a repeat of the last time you fixed that for just us, are you?"

Nicole instantly started to blush as she responded.

"Um, no, I just know that you enjoy it and that you have

been extra stressed and figured it would be a good idea, though I wouldn't say no to a bit of fun in lieu of dessert."

Alex just laughed as he kissed Nicole as they headed back to her room, where they found themselves an hour later as they got ready to return to ED once more as Nicole spoke.

"Everything is going to be fine, right?"

"Nicole, even if things go wrong, I am not going anywhere without you, Sam, Ava, Mia, Kate and our kids. Life isn't always going to be fine, but we will make the best of it and I know that when it is all said and done that will be enough, at least for here in reality. As for in ED, well, I'm not about to sit back and let any outcome I can't live with come to be. I would sooner marry Bianca and Lorena than lose everything we have there."

"Oh, is that your answer to everything, just give in to the woman that solves a particular problem? Not know how to say no to two of your best friends. Just let them share you. Need a connection to the nobility, a viscount's daughter will work. Oh wait, you can add a princess and really solidify things why not. Need to play diplomat, what easier way than adding two more princesses to your life. Need someone to keep more women in reality away, a pair of red-headed troublemakers and a rich heiress can handle that. Shall I go on?"

"Oh, you mean how I needed a connection to my new subjects, marry one of their kind, need someone that none will mess with, a tier-8 queen can do that and need a link to another world, find an adventurous local. Nicole, you sound like you are upset and think that those are my true motivations and not just the latest in the never-ending attempts that Abysses End is making about me. Though, I added the last as they don't know about her yet."

"It is just hard as they have really ramped up their

character assassination efforts since the war began."

"As they say, all is fair in love and war and when it comes to our situation, the two are not exactly separated and I will do everything I can to ensure that we win at both."

"I know. I just worry that you will be so focused on winning that you don't even know what you are risking."

"Nicole, I love you and I will never willingly risk losing you, or any of the others. If I seem to be drifting away from all of you, feel free to slap me in the face and wake me up to what matters most."

"I will hold you to that."

As Nicole finished speaking, she stole one more kiss before they both made their way back to the VR pod room, where they quickly logged into ED as the others had already done so.

Day seven in ED saw Xeal focused on more meetings as he met with representatives of every guild worth enlisting into the program that he was starting. Put simply, it was an opportunity where for every 999 tier-6 players that were sent to the borders to act as part of Nium's defense, FAE would help level and train one player. This included a fair bit of power leveling and other activities that would cost FAE part of the lead it currently had, but not entirely. At best, the players that were trained this way would still be three or so months behind Xeal and FAE's top players in reaching tier-7, but that was still over 100 days before they would have been ready. With only 10,000 slots being offered and the fact that those who were accepted would be treated just like the players who had paid over 2,000,000 credits for a slot in FAE's other training program, Xeal had to hold many smaller guilds back. Many guilds that only had around 1,000 tier-6 members had heard about the offer and had tried to secure their guild leader a slot, only to be almost entirely ignored. No, the first two guilds Xeal found himself meeting with was Red Crushers and Templar Fall.

Xeal could only smile at the sour looks on both Drezar Snaketoe's and Tyelk Rosewalker's faces, as they sat across from him after he had finished explaining the offer to them. It was easy to see that while both had kept their heads down for the most part since the Hugo Mercer mess, they were clearly holding a grudge. That said, Xeal also knew that they would take the deal unless they intended to ruin their accounts as Drezar spoke first.

"Let me get this straight. You want us to each select our top 1,000 members and basically hand them over to FAE, while the rest of our guilds basically play border patrol until the war is over. Meanwhile, all you are giving us is a promise that our members will see greater growth than we could give them and that after the war we will be released from the damn contract we signed that forces us to aid Nium anyways."

"Yes. The moment that peace returns to Nium, you both will be released from any further obligations."

"You know that none of us here are allies, right?" interjected Tyelk. "The major guild truce is over and I would be happy to see Drezar and Templar Fall fail, just as much as I would love to see your head on a pike! Alright, I might like to see your head on a pike more after the headaches you have given me and for the fact that you have almost ignored me completely for so long."

"Oh, so you wanted me to make you feel a need to look over your shoulder at all times. I mean, I could easily do that. It would just take a few messages and you would feel as if you will never know peace again."

"You're too smug about all of this. Aren't you even slightly worried about how this war will go, or do you really have everything that under control?" retorted Tyelk. "No, I think if you did, we wouldn't even be here right now. We would have simply been called on to serve and tossed aside after the war. So, just what has the unshakable Xeal Bluefire under so much duress?"

"The timing. It should have happened just as you were ready to try for tier-7 and I had long since reached it. Make no mistake, the outcome will be the same regardless, but the price in NPC lives has skyrocketed and that is never good."

"Oh, what, you afraid your next NPC lovers will be killed before they grow up to replace your current ones?" mocked Tyelk.

"You're as big of a fool as ever," interjected Drezar. "He is worried about there being enough NPCs to handle all the work that players don't want to do, like, mucking out horse stalls, standing guard and boosting your ego."

"Bastard!"

"That is enough!" shouted Xeal at Tyelk's outburst. "We are not here to start a guild war! Drezar, you are half right, but even that half is enough to make me want to limit their losses. The other half is the effect it will have on future wars, if another country decides to try and take over all of this continent at some point in the future. Players make a terrible defensive force and I doubt having your guilds at the border areas that I am most concerned for will offer much in the means of a deterrent. Really, the goal is to have forces to counterattack nearby, so we can do so before the invaders dig in and create a defensible position."

"Right, just tell me where you need us and make sure there is a decent dungeon for us to level in as well," retorted Tyelk with his fists still clenched.

"There will either be a decent dungeon, or a teleportation network that will take you to one nearby," answered Xeal.

"Right, forgot that King Victor simply rubber stamps any such gates you want to have, but confiscates ours," grumbled Tyelk.

Xeal knew that many guilds had been pissed to be forced to hand over the control of any teleportation network that they had established. While the search for such networks was still ongoing, it wouldn't be long before none of them were left in the cities and only hidden ones in the wilderness would remain. While Xeal knew that while these wouldn't be heavily used, or suitable for armies to invade through, they were perfect for slipping in a few spies, assassins, or kidnaping and smuggling out high-value targets. It would be such an issue and an impossible task to track them all down by the end of the war, that finding one would auto trigger quests for any players that stumbled upon them. It was with this knowledge and the fact that Xeal knew that all of his, save for the ones in Nium and the one in the Huáng empire, would be considered illegal that Xeal responded.

"You may see it as a rubber stamp, but I see it as having to disclose the locations of the whole network and make them available to Nium for use."

"Still, you have things set up to be able to maintain your operations abroad," retorted Tyelk. "Otherwise, you wouldn't be so calm right now."

"No, while I have the ability to reach a few locations outside of Nium, none of them will do me any good in maintaining a significant volume of trade between continents. At best I can secure food to ensure starvation is rare during this conflict."

"A world with magic and they still haven't programmed in a way for the NPCs to not need to farm," commented Drezar. "I suppose they went for full realism when they made that decision."

"Yes, well, we have gotten off topic," stated Xeal. "Are you both fine with the deal as it is offered? If so, I will have it signed and made official by tonight and no, I can't get you a better one, or add anything to it. This is not a negotiation, but a chance for your guilds not to be used as fodder when it comes time for the hard charges into Habia and Paidhia, at least for the most part."

"When you put it like that, what choice do we have?" bemoaned Drezar. "I will take it. Just know that I intend to even the score between us some day and I look forward to seeing you wish that you had just accepted reality."

"Drezar, you may want to look in a mirror when it comes to not accepting reality before you anger me. I go out of my way to give others opportunities to correct themselves. However, if you feel the need to teach me a lesson, just make sure you are ready for the one I will teach you in return."

"You still think that FAE can stand alone," interjected Tyelk. "You have no true allies and the day will come that all the major powers come to collect the dues that any newbie owes before they are allowed to have a seat at the table. With the interest that you are piling up, I might not want to speak so confidently as the bill will come due one day and you may not like what you have to pay."

"Seat at the table?" retorted Xeal before continuing in a tone of disdain. "I can think of nothing that I want less. No, I am building my own table and the day will come that you may wish you had chosen to sit at it when you had the chance. I am well aware that to your organizations that went through decades of pain, or offered a king's ransom to gain the foothold that they have allowed you, my existence is an eyesore. However, that is not my fault. I tried to explore sitting at the table. With Abysses End and

Fire Oath, it was clear that all they offered was to entrap me. The price that will always be demanded of me will be my guild and nothing less. It is why there is no reason for me to even care about all of you so-called major guilds. I can only hope that Abysses End, or any others, think that now is the time to strike out as it will give me targets to take out my anger on. Now, are you accepting the terms, or not?"

As Xeal looked at Tyelk, he could see the guild leader was actually reevaluating him before he finally responded in a tone of pity.

"I will take the deal and you may be right; oil and water don't mix and perhaps you and the established order can never as well."

Xeal just handed them both the contracts to sign and ignored the fact that he knew that Tyelk assumed that nothing but FAE's utter destruction was possible. Xeal didn't blame any who believed that, as he would have as well if it were not for what he knew that the others didn't, though that wasn't to say that it wasn't still possible. It would all come down to the results of a few key things and the first of the ones that remained was the situation FAE found itself in during and after this war.

With contracts signed, Xeal found himself meeting with one guild team after another as he, Kate, Taya, and Geitir all handled working through the applicants, based on how many tier-6 players they had to offer. Like this, the 10,000 slots filled before they got through half the applicants and Takeshi and Amser were placed in charge of developing them. Meanwhile, a report of this had been sent to King Victor and his generals, along with the just over a half million that FAE would be sending. All said, it brought the total players that would be acting as auxiliary border guards to 10.5 million and would likely be far more than Habia, or

Paidhia, could hope to assemble, even if Abysses End went all out.

Days eight to ten were spent with Xeal and his party getting ready to exchange Lucy for Sylvi, now that they were close enough level wise. They would do this by having Lucy act as a second cleric until Sylvi got the hang of things. The cleric of Freya had been training ever since Gale had selected her when Xeal decided that his party needed a dedicated healer. Only Xeal wasn't even remotely convinced that Sylvi would succeed in reaching tier-7 and it almost felt like she was just looking to join her husband in death after failing. While she was clearly able to play the role of healing them for the moment, if she were to be stuck at tier-6 she wouldn't be able to keep up with the workload that lay in front of them. It was with this thought that Xeal had started to go over the logistics of keeping Lucy if it became necessary.

However, before any such decision could be made, it was time for Xeal to once more meet with Freya as he sat across from Gale in his bedroom in the capital, as she mentally prepared for the backlash that would come. He just smiled apologetically as she sighed before the gate was opened and Xeal stepped through it, arriving in Fólkvangr once more. However, before Xeal could so much as appreciate the atmosphere, he found himself pinned flat on his back by an invisible pressure as he heard Freya's voice.

"Where do you get the idea that you are in any position to walk away from me before I am done with you! I am a goddess and you, immortal you may be in this reality, are still just a mortal. It appears that I have been too lax in my dealings with you."

"It's good to see you too. Tell me, is this the part where you tell me that you don't need to work with me as much as I need to work with you?" replied Xeal calmly. "Freya, I was in a piss-poor mood last time we met and that is no excuse for blowing you off like I did, so sorry. I will try to remember ours is a mutually beneficial arrangement, not a one-sided exchange."

"Thank you, but I still need to teach you a lesson before I can feel sated. Now, the question is, just what would have the greatest effect?"

As Freya finished speaking, she entered Xeal's view as she stood such that her toes were next to the top of his head as he looked up on her form as she looked down at his. Xeal could already tell from the smile on her face that he wasn't going to like this if she decided to hold nothing back as he spoke before she could.

"Effects must be balanced as we still need to want to work together and not set the other up for failure in revenge."

"Agreed, it would be easiest to simply force a contract that would bind us like husband and wife on you to mitigate that in the short term, but that would backfire terribly in time. So, what to do? I need you to establish my new pantheon and you need me to ensure Bula and Gale are able to aid you. I could force you to worship me as your only goddess, but that might just cause more issues and I will not rule you through fear, so how am I to ensure your cooperation?"

"Why are you playing this game? Freya, you have had two months to focus on what you are going to do, now just get it over with so we can move on."

"Fine, but you asked for this."

With that Xeal found himself flying up to his feet and turning so that Freya was nose to nose with him as she looked him in the eye and spoke.

"You will court Bula."

"No, the will of myself and my wives is not something

you have any control over."

"Fine, you are forbidden to court her."

"Also unacceptable for the same reason."

"Oh, so you are undecided on if you will, or will not, allow her into your life. Perhaps I should show her a few more visions of you accepting her than I currently am allowing her to see."

"So rather than torture me, you will inflict my punishment on another."

"No, that was simply a test as I knew where you stood on her. This is your punishment!"

With that Freya pressed her forehead to Xeal's as he saw and felt everything that Bula had since she became Freya's oracle. All of this lasted only for around ten minutes, but for Xeal it felt much longer as he tried to untangle his feelings from Bula's.

"There. Now you can live your days knowing just what she feels when she is near you and just be glad that I am not having you experience Gale's feelings as well."

"Right, crap, this sucks! Thanks. Now I am going to have to deal with knowing what I never wanted to," grumbled Xeal.

"I could still let you know how Gale feels."

"No, thank you. I am having a hard enough time compartmentalizing Bula's feelings. I don't want to think about dealing with Gale's as well."

"Good, now onto the main reason that I need to speak with you, as you have already cost me ground on recruiting other deities."

"About that. I am willing to offer any that you can vouch for to have their divine scion attempt to reach tier-7 before I send them to my quest world to establish your pantheon there. To be clear, none of those there will be forced to convert, but I have a feeling that most of them will jump at having something to pray towards."

Freya looked shocked at Xeal's words, as she looked him over a few times before she responded to him.

"Do you even realize what you are saying to me?"

"That I will allow you all to establish yourselves there and thereby gain access to a second world in case the holy war to come goes poorly for you."

"No, you just implied that you intend to marry me, or submit to me when you ascend to godhood. That, or you are setting the stage to be denied such a rise, as the world would no longer be without any gods as it currently is."

"So, no, though once I die in my reality, you can do what you like with it, so long as you don't turn it into nothing but a battlefield. Also, I wouldn't mind you making sure that if I lost, that no players gained divinity, and it being denied to me wouldn't be the worst either."

"You know not what you are even offering to me. It would be as if I offered to allow others to use my realm as they like. Once you and I came to terms, you would be bound to them and could never expel me without forcing me into submission. Also, if you lost, I and the other gods would be expelled the same as you, as you can only offer what you control. I can do nothing without a struggle if you lose control of it."

"So, whose realm was the world that Nium resides in? Watcher's?"

"Originally yes, but as he took each of the phoenixes as brides it became theirs and their children's. That realm encompassed far more than what you currently know, as it has been broken apart into many pieces in the struggles that followed. Even this realm was once part of that one. It is part of what we deities are needed for as if we were to relax for too long it would want to repair itself."

"Is the world that could be my new realm the same?"

"No, but it has been connected to this one through you and the others trying to claim it, to include the demons. When you brought Gale into the world that you hold a partial dominion over, was when I became aware of it. Now that Lucy has been there as well, so is Aceso and we know the true value of it, which is something that I doubt even you do. So, I will ask you again, are you truly fine with surrendering any chance you have to bend it to your will completely one day?"

"When you put it like that, I have just two questions. What will change if I say yes and do you promise to leave it as a realm for mortals to live in?"

"Mortals are always useful as the more followers we have the greater our power, and I believe that it will allow my clerics and champions to retain their abilities and stats within your dominion. I can't do that for those who step past where you control, but in a few generations the whole of the world would become closer to the one your kind has invaded."

"So, you're saying that once I let you in, adventurers could start to actually gain skills, stats and tier-up the same way they do now?"

"Yes, but only in the area you control. They would still not be able to adventure as the monsters of the world have been consumed by demons. With the demons only attacking a player's dominion once they are connected to another that they can conquer, I don't see it being a very good environment for them to train in."

"That is simple. I simply need to reintroduce weak monsters into that world, something I am sure you could easily accomplish with the right alliance."

"You're insane. You are basically asking me to allow what I consider evil and vile into my pantheon."

"Freya, without darkness how can we appreciate the

light? To be clear, they need to be one who can ensure that a few hundred players can have plenty of monsters to fight until they reach tier-7. That is to say, no monster stronger than that world's current cap is to ever be released by us and they are to be limited to selected areas of my dominion only."

"Why would you inflict that blight on your own realm!?"

"It is what I want if I allow you to establish yourself in it. Can you make that happen, or not?"

"I can, but-"

"Freya, I trust you to balance the issues that it will cause, with those you wish to recruit. That world has been almost destroyed and while I can't address the issues with it right now, I intend for it to be transformed completely in the next 40 years. Though I have to gain control of it first to do so."

"Fine, but be ready for every minor deity that has only a cult at best to want to expand in that world, though its population is likely to not be enough for that."

"I am counting on it. After all, it is their divine scions that will be used to bring true change to that world. Just make sure none of them will try to become the only god in town on us."

"Ha, worry not. As I said, you will have three options. They will only have one and that is to place me as their ruler. As for what I expect you to take, well, we will see what you become between now and then."

"I am not marrying you," retorted Xeal.

"We shall see when the time comes to make such a decision. After all, you will want to elevate Gale and your other wives to divinity as well."

Xeal just shook his head as he sighed before the conversation shifted to more of the details of their bargain. By the end of it, Freya had produced a divine contract that could even hold a divine being to its terms, let alone a hopeless mortal. Even a god like Loki would need to find a loophole in the terms to escape from it. Xeal had remembered what it had cost to get his hands on the paper and ink needed to write a semi-divine contract in his last life, and how it was only used for deals between major powers on rare occasions. Xeal knew that as players reached tier-7, skills to escape contracts would become available, if still rare. These were also skills that NPCs didn't have access to until tier-8, as the system had deemed that it would cause too many issues in the early days of ED. Still, they were restricted by class at that point as a spellcaster like Queen Aila Lorafir would almost never have one, while a rogue like Enye's master, Zylah Novy, would almost certainly have one.

Knowing that once he signed this contract that he would be bound to it, even if he restarted his character 1,000 times, Xeal was careful to look over it in great detail. The last thing he wanted was a line to have been slipped in about him marrying anyone, or having to do something that they hadn't agreed to. At the same time, he had sent a copy of the text to Kate with a summary of what was talked about, to see if she was worried about any of it. In the end, Xeal found the contract straightforward and Kate had only asked him if he was sure about it as it matched what he said it should do. The only line that caused him any concern was the part on when he completed the quest and became a god in his own right. It essentially forced him to pick which of the three options he wanted to go with and if he chose to marry Freya, she would still need to agree. If she didn't agree, he could either fight her for control of the realm, or pick one of the other two options, with him becoming her servant if he challenged her and lost.

"What are you hesitating about still?" interrupted Freya.

"I can tell that you have already looked over the contract ten times and I am sure you have had others do so as well."

"Yes, well it would be easier if I wasn't worried about your intentions once I become a god as while it says I have three options, I only have two viable ones."

"Oh?"

"I can either marry you, or refuse to become a god as if I accept being beneath you, you and Watcher will likely never forgive me."

"Yet you can still choose it. You just won't, though don't expect me to take you as a husband just because you wish it."

"Yeah, that is the other rub. You will only accept me as such if you believe that it is possible for me to defeat you as you will never accept my other wives otherwise. So, you are basically saying that I will never rise to the level of being a god in this contract, at least not one that will be free to do as I like."

"I am not going to allow you the option of founding your own pantheon with your wives."

"Why, you will only need to outlast me if I turn hostile to you, and your pantheon."

"Because of what would be created after your death in your reality that I must not allow to exist. Your existence here will never end. Even if you are simply an empty husk destined to never wake again, you would still be technically alive. That empty husk is what Watcher, as you call him, would seize and use to return to the physical world and he would likely create vessels for all of his children as well."

"You and the other gods still fear him, even now."

"Yes, just because we can't die doesn't mean that we don't feel fear. No matter what he says to you, he can never be allowed to return to power. I would sooner let you release and marry all of the phoenixes than allow him to return."

"He let you all destroy him, didn't he?"

"That is not something you need to know. Just know that I fear that we wouldn't be able to do so a second time."

Xeal paused for a second before signing the contract and handing it to a confused Freya as he spoke.

"Fine. I look forward to seeing if you can accept the terms of the deal when the time comes for me to hold you to them as well."

"You don't think that you will actually be able to overwhelm me, do you?"

"I have no idea, but you will either need to step down from being the pinnacle of your pantheon, or face never having me be among it. I will be sure of only one thing when I make my decision and that is my own freedom. Without that, my own power can be used in ways that I would never allow. Also, I promise Watcher will never be able to claim this body as his own."

Freya looked as Xeal for a long second before responding to him.

"We shall see if you can back that up when the time comes for your actions to do the talking. Now it is time for you to leave and unless you wish for me to have you hurtle to the ground without Gale catching you, I would suggest you use your own means to leave."

"You would do that too. Very well, farewell for now. Oh, and make sure that all divine scions are vetted properly and Gale knows where to pick them up from."

With that Xeal made his way to the quest world before returning to Nium once more. As far as outcomes went, he would say that overall, that was about a C-rank if he were to grade it as the quests were. If he wasn't walking around while knowing just how deep Bula's feelings were right now it would have been an A-ranked result. Still not perfect, but completely acceptable, though the joke of Freya being his true last wife seemed to be less of one at this point. Still, life continues and Xeal didn't waste the time he had as he returned to the grind.

Xeal watched as days 12 to 21 passed as he continued to strive to move forward while getting used to Sylvi's work as his party's cleric, as Lucy focused on attacking instead of healing. This made Xeal once more reevaluate just how skilled she was as she seemed to know just when to do so and how best to use her limited offensive capabilities. If all of the divine scions were this powerful, it would create some hard choices for Xeal in the future. Still, Xeal was also having issues with interacting with Bula during the down time due to Freya's meddling, but thankfully Bula seemed fine to ignore it for the time being as they focused on leveling up. During this grind, Xeal reached level 191 as he was now just eight levels from it being time for him to attempt to reach tier-7. FAE had also risen to being a level 48 guild and opened more than 360,000 new slots for recruitment, and for the first time they did so almost completely outside of Nium.

It was shortly after this achievement that Xeal was finally able to meet with Lori Lunaflower on day 16. The guild leader of Night Oath was as composed and confident as ever, as she entered the room with her long silver hair hanging freely down her back and made her way to Xeal to start the meeting he had arranged. However, that faltered upon seeing the look on Xeal's face as she paused before frowning and speaking first.

"Why do you look like you aren't in the mood to play any games today? I mean, sure, we are ten days into the war, but no major battle has happened yet."

"On land at least," retorted Xeal. "Huhhh, FAE lost a

ship just now. While all of the NPCs on board managed to make it to another vessel, the ship couldn't limp home."

"Wait, your guild already took part in a naval conflict?"

"Our ships were in enemy waters when the war broke out. They had managed to escape after a few skirmishes, but it turns out one ship had just suffered too much damage to make it all the way back."

"Alright, does that have any bearing on why you wanted to meet with me? I mean killing NPCs isn't our normal M.O., but I won't say no during a war."

"I want to consume Night Oath as a whole."

"Excuse me? Xeal, I am sorry but we are not for sale."

"No, I am not planning on buying you, I am offering you a vice guild leader position and access to all of FAE's resources to develop your members. You would become a direct subordinate of Takeshi and the rest of your members will make up our covert operations wing."

"Xeal, we are not the kind of players who play well with others, especially in a guild setting. Besides, I thought you liked not having your fingerprints on the hits you have given us."

"Lori, be honest, you have had a hard time holding onto members as they take the offers of one guild after another. I know for a fact that we have recruited 100 of your members just the other day. If Kate's numbers are right, you only have about 5,000 of the 10,000 you used to have."

"They are the better half of the lot," retorted Lori snippily.

"I know you are having problems getting contracts and while you and I both know that you are about to see a spike in demand, it will ruin your guild to try and keep up with it. You have no guild hall, let alone a headquarters as they would be too big of a target, so you have no major investments that would be lost in a merger. What I am offering is for your members to all have an attempt at reaching tier-7 before they take another contract."

"Wait, what?"

"Lori, I am well aware that your members have started to lag behind the pros due to how you all operate. It is the main reason you are losing members. What I am offering you is essentially control of about one percent of FAE. Right now that is around 27,000 players, so yes, I would expect you to recruit and develop talents after you get settled."

"Xeal, you are acting like it is so easy to essentially have two main forces, as that is the level of skill I expect from my members. Can your guild really afford the price that it will take to sustain that?"

"No as the number isn't just for your combat members, but for the crafters and the information network that Kate will be shifting to you. I would expect only about 20 to 40% of your members to be focused on actually carrying out assassination and sabotage operations."

"What part of my disdain for dealing with such players do you not understand? Xeal, Night Oath may pay more for our goods, but we also don't have to worry about developing our own craftsmen."

"Which is why you are never going to reach your full potential as you are now. Lori, you won't be developing any of the craftsmen, they can take care of themselves. Your members will just be working with them to create the best gear suited for them and taking on the task of getting the rarer components that they need to complete said equipment."

"What are you offering us?"

"Base for all of your members, who pass an assessment that should be easy for them, is 400,000 credits with performance bonuses in addition to that. You, hmm, I know credits can't buy you and you do what you do for the fun of it for the most part, so a million credits should be fine and I promise to let you test your skills against the best players out there."

"I am sorry, but I know my limits. You and Takeshi are out of my league. It is the fact that you are putting me under Takeshi and not Kate that has me even hearing your offer at all."

"Let's just put it this way. I am expecting to need to teach many guilds a lesson soon, and guild leader assassinations are such tricky things to pull off."

"You really don't care about common courtesies…"

Xeal just smiled as he continued to weave an image of what life would be like for Lori if she accepted his offer. She seemed to be interested and about to agree on the spot, until she brought it all back to the reality of the situation.

"Ah, as fun as this sounds, it has one major flaw. The contract that you will expect us all to sign and the inability to turn down certain requests."

"Such is the cost for stability."

"That is only if FAE survives and you maintain your position as its owner and guild leader. What happens when you sell, or are defeated. I am sor-"

"Every contract in FAE has the same escape clause for those situations. I can only hand the guild leader position off to a vice guild leader that has been serving in that role for a significant amount of time. Also, were I to sell, or otherwise lose control of the workshop, or guild, all contracts become void. I would have thought you knew that."

"I knew that some of your members had that, but all of them?"

"When you sign up to be part of FAE, you are signing up to follow me. If that changes, it is up to you on if you want to continue on."

"Fine, I will bring this offer to my members, but I make no promises and I want them to have dibs on the private rooms in the city that you are building."

"If they want to move in, that is fine, but private rooms are going to be hard to come by in the first phase of building as they will be focused on families and setups with roommates. Even then, after I house those in my main force that want to move there, I need to prioritize admin and those who I am on the fence about if they can go pro, or not. However, I wouldn't worry too much about that as phases two to four should come quickly after phase one."

"If you can continue to fund it."

"Which is why I am not playing around with this war."

Lori just smiled as she bid Xeal farewell, and he sighed before checking the time and seeing that it was getting late as he opened the gate to the quest world and stepped into Austru's room. As he did so, he was greeted by the sight of the sylph dressed in a thin negligee, sitting on the edge of the bed and looking slightly nervous. Xeal almost laughed as she looked at him before blushing, but he managed to shift it into a cough as he spoke.

"Is that your normal attire when you plan to sleep?"

"Um, no, but this is what Princess Tsega told me would make you happy."

"Honestly, I think she needs to gain some experience before giving others advice. Though it does look nice, it feels more appropriate if we were intending to enjoy other activities."

Austru went completely red at Xeal's words, before she took a quick breath and regained her composure as she replied.

"I wouldn't say no if that was what you wanted."

"Ah, is that what you were hoping for?"

"Maybe just a lot."

"I see. Huhhh, Austru, it is too soon for me to be willing to take that step as once I do, it means that I am fully committed with you and while I may be 90% there, I am not fully there. While I adore you and find you an absolute delight to be with, I am not ready to say that you have secured yourself a permanent position in my heart yet."

"You're lucky that what you just said matches what the others warned me about in their letters. You will resist this final step until I wear down all of the barriers you create in that head of yours, while you worry about if this is right, or if you are enough for me and I am sure much more. However, I only get to have you like this once a month and even that may be difficult with the nature of the situation in the other world right now. So, forgive me for wanting to skip all of the formalities."

"Where did that bit of shyness you had when I arrived go?"

"Xeal, your eyes haven't left mine since we started to really talk. If you think that I am going to have issues if things don't work out, just stop. I can handle it. Besides, even if you have yet to completely fall for me, I have for you and I know that you will come to love me as I love you. Now let's head to bed and what happens, happens."

Xeal just smiled as he kept his response to himself as he hugged and kissed Austru, before getting ready for bed and joining her under the covers. Xeal could tell she was slightly frustrated when morning came as she held to him for a few extra moments as he kissed her deeply. As he got ready for the day, Xeal also shared the update surrounding the deal he had made with Freya with her as he explained the details of it. At first, she seemed annoyed about the situation as she had been looking forward to Xeal controlling this world once he became the god of it. However, that changed once she started to understand what it meant to be worshiped, as most religions in this world had been formed with the forces of nature at their center. Xeal could also tell that talking about the world before wasn't easy for her, but she held back from diving too deep and he decided against pushing her to confront what was clearly a difficult reality. Still, he held her tight for a long moment before he returned to Nium to continue his grind.

(*****)

Morning March 24 to Evening March 27, 2268 & ED Year 6 Days 22-33.

With his grandparents being around all the time, Alex was finding his time offline to be busier with each passing day as they chatted with him and cooed over the giant bellies of Ava and Mia. Kate had already grown tired of them asking when she was going to just give in already, as they had moved past caring about the arrangement and into simply enjoying the great-grandkids. They had also been more than happy to start helping out with the preparations for Dan and Anna's wedding. Though Dan had found himself going through a couple of almost interrogation-like conversations as Alex's grandparents all worked to get to know him better.

Alex had also smiled when they had surprised Gido and Julie with a surprise first birthday party for Evelyn on the 25th, as they had only planned a small family one. Alex, on the other hand, had set things up for the nursery to play host to the event as when Julie arrived to take over for the night, everything had been set up by Jacob and Alex's parents. While it had been clear that none of the babies understood just what was going on, they still all enjoyed the party favors and attention that they got during it. Though the cake that Sophie had made once more stole the show, as Alex made it clear that Evelyn would get the same level of party as Alex planned for his own kids. While Gido and Julie seemed to still have some reservations due to their upbringing and occupation, they accepted it on the basis that he didn't want Evelyn to feel less special than Moyra, Ahsa, or Andy. Let alone the small army that Alex was expecting to arrive in the next ten years as if dealing with being as pregnant as Ava and Mia were, wasn't enough to curb their enthusiasm to be moms, Alex doubted anything would.

Finally, on the 27th was yet another OB-GYN appointment with Doctors Avery and Lunt, who both agreed that it was looking like an any day thing for both Ava and Mia to go into labor. The giddy excitement that Ava and Mia showed at this made Dr. Avery joke that they might go into labor right then if they didn't stop bouncing in their seats. Alex had to hold in a laugh as that only served to increase their bouncing as they held their bellies stable and giggled. By the time they had made it back home, Alex took note of an energy in both of them that had not been there for the last few months. This was made even more apparent after dinner when he helped them scale the stairs to their private area and return to ED.

Day 22 saw Xeal standing on the docks of Anelqua as he watched the three overcrowded ships come into port. It was clear that all of them had seen combat as chunks of wood were missing from places and others seemed to have been repaired with whatever had been on hand. From the reports that Xeal had read, the Siren's Melody had been the one to sink and that was reinforced when Sylmare leaped from the deck of the Siren's Dream when it was still over 100 feet from the shore. The clearly irate ex-pirate captain wasted no time as she brushed her braid of bleach blond hair off her shoulder and made her way straight to Xeal. As she looked into Xeal's eyes with her sky blue ones, she spoke in a tone that while controlled, left no doubt that under different circumstances she would have simply killed him.

"My ship is gone! My fucking ship is gone! Do you have any idea how long I have sailed her and never let her sink!?"

"Likely longer than I have been alive and I am sorry, but she wasn't yours anymore, she was mine and I could blame you for losing her, but I won't as your life and the life of the others is worth more than any ship is. Now suck it up and get ready to help design the Siren's Revenge as you are still one of my fleet's biggest assets and I expect you to hunt down and sink dozens, if not hundreds of ships before the war is over."

Sylmare didn't seem satisfied with Xeal's response as she seemed to be fighting her urge to attack him even more, so he continued to speak.

"Go ahead, I give you permission to hit me as hard as you physically can. Just make sure that it is enough to release all your anger in the one attack as that is all you get."

"To be clear, I can attack you however I want and face no consequences after?"

"So long as it is a physical attack," corrected Xeal as he saw Queen Aila Lorafir who was standing next to him try to say something as Sylmare grabbed both sides of his head and he braced for a headbutt, only to feel his lips smash into Sylmare's. Before Xeal could even react, her tongue was practically shoved down his throat as she continued the assault as Queen Aila Lorafir stood helplessly at their side, looking like she was ready to kill. When the kiss finally ended, Sylmare smiled at seeing the look on Queen Aila Lorafir's face as she spoke.

"He said that I would face no consequences for my assault. You and I both know that includes from you, else he just broke the contract and I am free."

"Free and dead," retorted Queen Aila Lorafir through gritted teeth. "Have you no shame!?"

"Very little and while I know he has no intentions

towards me, I can at least hold the fact that I got a kiss over yours and his head."

"You would face repercussions for that," commented Xeal as he regained his composure. "I will let your interpretation of a physical attack slide, but if you lord it over us, or others, it will be considered a mental attack. So, I will happily let Aila and my other wives remove the offending body parts if they so wish."

"I love how decisive you can seem to be," replied Sylmare with a smile. "But I know that won't happen as they wouldn't be the women you love then, they would be closer to me. That said, I know that my life will be far less pleasant if I were to cross that line, so I will just hold it over my sisters in bondage to you."

"Whatever. Did you get your anger out of your system, or are we still going to have an issue?"

"Oh, I am still irate, just not at you now. I just got compensation with interest just now on what you are going to go through when I am not around. Now I just need to return the favor to Paidhia and I like the name you plan to give my new ship that will be delivering it."

"You mean FAE's new ship. You will just be aiding its captain in making sure it isn't lost as well."

"Sure, whatever you say."

Xeal just shook his head at Sylmare's response as he looked at Queen Aila Lorafir who was still giving Sylmare a death glare and smiled as he spoke to her.

"Aila, it seems that I have a terrible flavor in my mouth. You wouldn't know of any way to help me with that, would you?"

At that Queen Aila Lorafir's attention shifted to Xeal as she smiled before embracing him and giving him a kiss that put the one Sylmare had given him to shame. By the time it had ended, Xeal just smiled at the sour look on Sylmare's face as she spoke.

"You two should just get a room already."

"Absolutely not," retorted Queen Aila Lorafir. "I want to ensure that any who think that they can make a move on Xeal know that they have to deal with me. After all, there still seems to be many who think they can just casually make a move without facing any consequences."

Xeal knew that she was referring to both Princesses Bianca and Lorena as well as Bula when she spoke of consequences, but the implication extended past them. Once more, Xeal found himself remembering the feelings Freya had forced on him and just how intense they were. It honestly made him worry about just how messed up of a situation the group of women had really become as he suddenly felt like as things were, his relationships were just a powder keg waiting to blow. Especially when it came to any of those who were trying to get in beyond Daisy, Violet and Dafasli, who had curried favor with his wives and lovers rather well. Still, Xeal knew that things were set up for a few major issues once he started to have the group trying to get in reduced after the war, if it could wait that long.

With these thoughts on his mind, Xeal watched as the 12th and what would be the last group of dwarves to immigrate this way, arrived. Like all the groups before them, Xeal watched them fall onto the ground as they relished in the feeling of being off the ships, only Xeal could tell this group was far more exhausted than any before it. The way they moved spoke of little sleep and other issues that came from fitting 33% more people than intended on a single ship. The look of the other three captains as they stormed over told Xeal that Sylmare wasn't the only one to have issues with how the last voyage had gone, as Odelia's orangish eyes locked on to Xeal's. The ex-captain of the Siren's Song had been the original pirate that Xeal had discovered and subdued with Queen Aila Lorafir's help. Since then, her and her four fellow ex-pirate captains had been serving out their sentence under his guild's care as they helped develop the players Xeal hoped would become the core of his navy. With the ex-captain of the Siren's Dream, Cremia and the ex-captain of the Siren's Embrace, Itylara, at her sides. Only the ex-captain of the Siren's Call, Saphielle, was absent as she and her ship were still acting as an escort for the naval trade between Nium and Anelqua. As the trio arrived, it was Odelia who spoke first.

"So, where are our kisses for surviving that insanity? Or are you just going to act like you didn't let Sylmare have one?"

"Good point. Sylmare, make sure you put just as much passion in theirs as you did mine."

At Xeal's words, Sylmare looked like a fish out of water as the other three seemed to want to scream their heads off. When none of them moved after a few seconds, Xeal decided to prolong the bit as he continued speaking.

"What, I thought you all wanted a kiss? I mean Sylmare couldn't hold back long enough to wait for you three, but I am sure she can still give you each one to remember. No? Alright, now let's get back to what matters. I am sorry that war broke out before you were clear of Paidhia's waters, but things just happened too quickly. Now, I expect you all to ensure repairs are made and we should see if we can't salvage the Siren's Melody as if we can, it would be a waste to just ignore it with how close to making it back it was. Other than that, I expect you all to play your roles and cooperate with Nium's navy until the war is over. If you all follow orders and make it through the war, I will consider letting you retire at the end of it."

"Right, from pirate ships, to merchant ships, to warships. Before you know it, we will be on sunken ships at the bottom of the sea," retorted Itylara as she closed her sea green eyes while struggling to remain calm. "Our deal was to train and keep our heads down, not fight a war."

"Your deal had no such restrictions in it," interjected Queen Aila Lorafir. "The fact that Xeal is offering you retirement is already more than generous."

"We need to be alive to enjoy retirement," countered Cremia as her yellow eyes stared into Aila's golden ones. "The reason pirates live so long is because we are cowards. When we know we can't absolutely win, we run!"

"Yet you reached tier-7. I dare say that if you all tried to, you could reach tier-8, so why haven't you?" inquired Queen Aila Lorafir. "You all likely could create a rather unique legacy if you tried to."

Xeal was taken aback by this statement as he hadn't considered such a development as he looked at the four illusionists and considered what could be possible. Though as he did so, he couldn't help but think about how much of a pain such a legacy would be to pass down as not only would five illusionists need to undertake it together, but if one failed they all would. That wasn't even mentioning other compatibility issues that would need to be overcome, like being a pirate before being captured and other possible characteristics it would require. Still, Xeal liked the idea as he spoke to the four of them.

"Aila's right. You four and Saphielle are going to attempt to create a new legacy. I will even provide you each a revival item with almost no side effects to do so."

At this the four of them looked at Xeal like he was crazy as he just smiled at them as he knew it was a risk, though he suspected that Queen Aila Lorafir's intent was akin to telling them to go die in a hole. However, Xeal believed that if they were given a chance to reach tier-8 as a group, that they would have at least a five percent chance of success. That said, he also knew that one failing would result in all of them doing so and that would mean that they would all die. While they came to terms with what he had just said, Xeal turned his attention back to the dwarves. As the first few started to recover, Xeal could see the looks of determination set onto more than a few of their faces as they stood. Xeal knew that they were all aware that their homes were likely under siege even now and while it would be a long fight, it was one that wasn't in their favor the longer it went on. Especially in the dwarven cities that had regular dealings with Habia, or Paidhia, as they were the ones most at risk of being conquered in the immediate future.

While Xeal had been focused on this, Queen Aila Lorafir and the four ex-pirate captains had been going back and forth about the insanity and plausibility of the five attempting to reach tier-8. Xeal had been ignoring the exchange, because to him it was an already settled deal that they would be attempting to ascend to tier-8 as with their ships out of service, or destroyed, they would just be sitting around otherwise. So when Odelia spoke to Xeal and he ignored her angry words, she about blew her top as she yelled to get his attention back on her.

"Xeal! At least look at me when I am speaking to you!"

"Huh? Oh, you are still fighting my order of reaching tier-8. Odelia, you five have been sailing for FAE for over three years now. All of you have gained the last 9 levels that you needed to max out during that time as well, so what is the issue when I am going to send you in with a guaranteed way to survive?"

"Oh, I don't know, maybe because if we fail we may be mentally scarred for the rest of our existences! I don't know what you know about forging your own legacy, but it will force us to experience hell or worse and that is not something the five of us wish to do."

"Too bad. I need more war potential and the five of you are perfect candidates to give it a shot. You all are talented, you have a unique aspect to you that can become the seed of your legacy and you have no need to fear death. So, if you are worried about the trauma that doing so may cause you, whether you succeed or not, then suck it up. A whole continent is about to confront the trauma that war brings. Fathers, mothers, daughters and sons will all lose someone, or be lost and if I can lessen that even slightly by ending the war earlier I will and to do that I need power. I expect you all to fail and for me to lose the item that will protect your lives, but you know what, that is something that I am willing to accept as on the off chance that you all do reach tier-8, I can at least rest easier about one side of any naval invasions."

"Wait, you would leave the five of us together after we reached that height?" questioned Odelia. "Would it not be better to split us up?"

"Odelia, my intent is for the five of you to create a shared legacy. I am not about to weaken that by separating you. If anything, I will have you aid in the capture of every port as you circle the continent. Who knows, you may all become the biggest factor in ensuring that the war only lasts a few years."

Xeal could see the four ex-pirate captains thinking hard and had to hold in a laugh at the whispers they shared as they discussed the possibility. Finally, he decided to interrupt them as he didn't like the direction they were going.

"Yes, I will sign a contract that will let you retire once the war ends and no, you can't get anything beyond that as

I value the quality of my life too much. So, take getting it in writing, or don't and still be forced to do it anyways."

"Fine," replied Odelia. "We'll go willingly…"

The next ten minutes were spent figuring out the details of just what would be needed to ensure that they were ready and Queen Aila Lorafir agreed to handle the needed prep as Xeal left with the dwarves. As he arrived at Darefret's mine, he was met by the scene of Dafasli standing over Thatram, who despite being level 192 and Dafasli being a level lower, had clearly lost in a physical altercation. The look on Harrulir's face as Darefret held the other tier-6 dwarf back told Xeal that whatever had happened, had been only between the siblings and it had gone terribly for Thatram. Upon seeing Xeal, Dafasli's expression shifted from being stern as she looked down on her brother, to a confident smile that fit her face much better in Xeal's opinion. The dwarves behind Xeal, on the other hand, were just confused, having witnessed this scene, that went contrary to what they had been told to expect, had been too much for some. Seeing this, Dafasli cleared her throat as she spoke to them.

"What ye all just witnessed was a simple disagreement between I and my brother. Dur not think it means that he is not yer new lord. I am simply not going tur be around tur help keep ye all in line, as I will be fighting in the war alongside Xeal while ye all mine materials tur equip FAE and Nium tur win said war. That will be all."

As she finished, Xeal heard one of the dwarves behind him mutter "glory hound" to himself and it hadn't gone unnoticed by Dafasli as she had her hand on his throat a second later as she continued.

"Don't be mistaken. I could care less about the glory of war as I agree with Xeal that such things are pointless next tur the horror that it brings. What I am after is him and if I am not next tur him now, I will never have a chance tur be ever again!"

"Hahaha, ye are in trouble, Xeal," chuckled Darefret. "Now that she done said that, ye might as well marry her now as she ain't going to give up."

"Right, that doesn't mean that I have to make it easy. Besides, even if I like her, my wives need to accept her fully as well," retorted Xeal lightheartedly. "Now, Thatram, are you going to cause any issues over this?"

"Ye can go tur hell. There be no point in me even trying tur keep this quiet now. My own sister has shamed me."

At this Xeal sighed as he turned to Darefret and spoke.

"Right. Darefret, sorry to ask this of you, but can you take over governing the dwarves in the mines until after the war is over?"

"I can do that for ye, though I will need to keep these two idiots up here to be safe."

"That's fine. My dad and a few others should be enough to keep them in check if they get any ideas when you're away, or indisposed."

"Good…"

Xeal just smiled at how well things had worked out as he had sent Dafasli ahead to ensure that her brother didn't get any ideas in his head regarding the war. The last thing Xeal needed was a bunch of idiots seeking glory and ruining battle lines as they did so. Still, her little declaration was off script and he could already tell that he was about to find himself dealing with her being far more active in attracting his attention. Especially as Xeal knew that she had toed the line in how she had done it and his wives would have little if any objections to her actions. With that thought in mind, Xeal worked through the details of what needed to be handled to ensure a smooth transition of power, as Darefret ended up heading below with Thatram and all the new arrivals. The plan was simple. Thatram would hand wartime power over to Darefret and it had been sealed with a contract, such that Darefret had to return power to either Thatram or Dafasli after the war ended. The only exception was if a majority of the dwarves in the mine found Thatram unfit to govern at that time, or if there had been an attempt to seize control back before the end of the war by Thatram.

With that taken care of, Xeal once more returned to the grind as he and his party delved deeper into the dungeon beneath the Mist Woods. Though now Xeal was dealing with the annoyance of no longer focusing on monsters that were at least 10 levels above him as his leveling speed plummeted. While he felt like he and Lucy could have handled the level 201 monsters, it was not the same for the others as even Sylvi seemed to struggle against the level 200 monsters that they were facing. The increase in difficulty between tiers was obvious to see and while Xeal normally would have been fine to slow down and take his time to get used to the difficulty, they didn't have that luxury now. He thought about what it would take to overcome the monsters having a 40% increase in the time dilation effect during combat that occurred, or going from experiencing three and a third seconds for every second, to four and two-thirds. This allowed for faster casting, attacks and general reactions to occur, and was the main reason that between tier fighting was so lopsided. Particularly at the higher tiers as every little advantage was magnified many times due to the increase in total stats that players and monsters had to work with. Though Xeal also knew that training against monsters one tier up was the best way to hone your abilities before reaching the next tier.

As Xeal continued to focus on getting his party used to facing tier-7 enemies, he was also keeping tabs on other events in ED. This included the ongoing sieges of the dwarves and the minor skirmishes along the borders of Nium and on the seas, as no major battle had occurred yet. There were even those who thought the war would be called off before it truly began and things would return to normal. However, Xeal knew better as he read the reports on troop movements and insurgent operations that were handled before they could be carried out. Often times it was players that had just happened to be in Nium when the war started, but were based out of Habia, or Paidhia, who were attempting these in Nium. That said, as those involved were sentenced, it became clear that it wasn't worth carrying out any such operation as it would mean 100 days in a mine before they were forced onto one of Salty Dogs' ships to work until they reached a port outside of Nium. That was just for attempting one. Had they succeeded, the punishment would be just short of being worse than restarting for a tier-6 player.

This had created what Xeal knew was just a momentary pause, as many players were just waiting for the right moment now, with there being well over a million stranded players in each country who were based out of one of the other two. That didn't even count the millions that were stuck due to the war and wanted to get back to other continents. A fact that Xeal intended to take advantage of once the war's momentum was clearly in Nium's favor and a single good push could topple either Habia, or Paidhia.

If anything served as an indicator on just how much this war was affecting things, it was the start of the latest arena league. With almost none of those who were based in Nium, Habia, or Paidhia taking part and many others being more interested in the war, or the competition for dragonoid slots, participation was way down in all brackets. Thankfully, Xeal had written the contract to gain the dragonoid slots for Fire Oath, Salty Dogs and Dragon

Legion such that they had to find their way to Dragon's Heart City, and if they failed to arrive that was on them. Mittic had about laughed her head off as she thanked Xeal as her guild's services were requested and had been more than happy to take advantage of the situation to benefit Salty Dogs. Had she not added comments in about how sweet he was being with the war and how he was providing her with easy jobs that paid excellently, he would have been happier. Especially as she seemed to want to continue her game of flirting as he ignored it while talking about how she would be leaving soon. While she had been stuck in Nium since the war started, she would be taking direct control of the fleet that would be delivering the other super guilds' players when it left Nium. That would include delivering the first shipment of food that Xeal had sold her at a cheap rate, before heading off to other continents. The fact that he had gotten all the food for almost free from the quest world was left out as she thought that he was simply giving it to her at cost to make the trading of it worthwhile.

This was the general state that things were in when day 33 ended and Xeal logged out once more shortly after reaching level 192. He was also focused on getting ready to begin the quest that he needed to complete, that would bring an end to the 12 quests that made up the questline King Victor had given him over four and a half years ago. Were he successful, it would cause Habia and Paidhia to end the unofficial truce they seemed to have while assaulting the dwarves and total war would officially break out. Xeal wished that he could have delayed it more, but the reports already had it as a matter of a few weeks before the situation for the dwarves turned ugly.

(*****)

March 28, 2268

As Alex stepped out of his VR pod and stretched out while thinking about the kendo lesson that he was about to have, he smiled as Sam and Nicole helped Ava and Mia out of their VR pods. Kate came up to Alex for her morning kiss as had become the norm and was just about to claim it, when Ava suddenly cried out. At that Alex and Kate both turned to look, only as they did so Alex's chin met Kate's forehead as Ava shouted.

"I think it's time!"

At this Alex went to move to Ava while rubbing his chin as Kate rubbed her forehead while Mia started to bounce excitedly as she spoke.

"It's time, it's time, IT's TIME!"

On that last one Alex looked over to see Mia holding on to Nicole with a pained expression as a wet spot spread from her crotch and time slowed for a long second. They were both likely in labor and Mia had definitely had her water break as both struggled through the pain that was clearly on their faces as Kate spoke.

"Jacob is pulling an SUV around. Gido, yours and Sam's fathers are on their way up to help get them downstairs!"

"Right," responded Alex as he got his mind back in order. "Kate, if you could open the doors. Sam, Nicole, you help Mia and I will help Ava to the stairs."

With that they got to work as they met the other three men at the top of the stairs. From there they carefully carried Ava and Mia down them. Once there, they helped them walk to the elevator and out to the SUV, where Alex found himself between the pair as they each claimed one of his hands. It was clear that things were moving much faster and that both Ava and Mia were in far more pain than Sam or Nicole had been as both of Alex's hands protested from how hard they were being held. Still, Alex went into shut up and deal with it mode as he worked to calm the pair down while Jacob drove and Alex's dad rode shotgun.

"Just breathe. Jacob will get us there as fast as can be done safely."

"Alex!"

"We love you!"

"But not right now!"

"Yeah, just kiss us on our cheeks!"

"And tell us you love us!"

"And that we are amazing!"

"Other than that!"

"We don't want to hear it!"

Alex just caught his father holding in a laugh at Ava's and Mia's words, and grimaced slightly as Ava let out a scream and a wet spot started to spread from her crotch. With that she started to breathe like she had been shown by Dr. Avery, Sam, Nicole and even Julie as Mia joined her in the exercise as Alex spoke.

"You're both amazing and I love you both!"

With that he spent the rest of the car ride kissing them both on their cheeks, hands and foreheads while he repeatedly told them that he loved them, they were awesome, amazing, incredible and much more.

20 minutes later they were met at the hospital by nurses who had two gurneys ready to bring them in. Alex knew that this was a bit overboard as usually those who arrived to deliver were expected to at least make it to the lobby before getting a wheelchair at most. Still, he just chalked it up to the extra that he had paid to ensure that everything was taken care of being put to use, as they quickly got Ava and Mia onto the beds on wheels. Following this, they

wasted no time in pushing them into the hospital as Alex almost had to run to keep up. As they entered a delivery room that had been once more set up for a dual delivery, the nurses wasted no time in prepping everything as Alex checked his messages to see Doctors Avery and Lunt were ten minutes out still. Sighing, Alex returned his attention to Ava and Mia, just in time to hear a nurse comment that the babies weren't waiting as they called for an on-staff doctor just in case. Two minutes later, Alex was gritting his teeth as Ava and Mia tried to hold on while gripping his hands as the on-staff doctor arrived and started to check over everything.

Alex didn't hear much over the following 20 minutes as Ava and Mia were too far into labor for any anesthetic to be safely administered and their reactions to the contractions were extremely loud. Though he did smile when Dr. Avery walked in two minutes after the staff doctor did and Dr. Lunt came in five minutes later. Which was perfect because the first baby for both Ava and Mia was crowning a minute later and ten insane minutes later, all four babies had been delivered. As they worked to regain their bearings after the whirlwind of events, Ava, Mia and Alex found themselves being congratulated by the whole staff who had stuck around for the deliveries.

While his hands were in extreme pain, Alex didn't think anything had been broken, and the smiles on Ava's and Mia's faces as they held their babies was easily worth the bit of pain he was in. Along with the normal tags that the hospital put on babies and patients, was an extra one that was just a plain color. Ava's babies both had red tags and Mia's had yellow ones to ensure that they could tell who was who at a glance. There were other slight differences in facial features, but both girls had gotten their mothers' red hair while the boys had a light brown hair currently. Add in the fact that even a DNA test would fail to determine who the mother was between identical twins and Alex was grateful that they had purchased a custom order footprint reader. As fingerprints took a while to be reliable, the easiest way to identify who was who after bath time, or play time in the coming months, would be their feet. While they didn't intend to need it, as they had also already bought color-coded clothes and other items to tell who was who, it never hurt to have a backup plan.

When Sam, Nicole and Kate finally got to the room, they had all been surprised at the fact that it was already over. Though as Alex would hear many times over the years, the look they got from Dr. Avery over how lucky Ava and Mia were to be done so quick was enough to make them rethink that. Apparently, from what Kate had learned later, four babies in ten minutes was pure insanity and had the staff doctor not stayed in the room, even with Dr. Lunt's help they would have breached contract. That being that all babies would only be handled by qualified doctors until the umbilical cord was cut and the babies were cleaned. While there were provisions should a woman deliver before Dr. Avery had 30 minutes from notice to arrival, Ava and Mia held on just past that point.

Still, it was done and the rest of the day passed with Alex, Ava and Mia all sharing a room while everyone took some time to visit. This had included an emotional visit from Nana Quinn and Lydia, who both had been crying at seeing Ava holding Evan and Nova, and Mia with Aidan and Nadia. The fact that they had continued the tradition of having the last letter in each girl's name be an A was not lost on either woman and neither was the VA in Evan, or AI in Aidan. Alex had just smiled when they had come up with those names as they talked through just how they wished to do so. There had been a bit of a discussion on focusing on the meaning over carrying over parts of their names. They had thought of having each boy's name start with an A, but Alex shut it down. After all, he was expecting to have 15 kids at this point and if they all started with an A it would just be ridiculous. It was bad enough that Enye, Lingxin and Mari intended to have the first two sons they each had have X names, as Alex wasn't sure that there were that many good ones. Still, he understood the reason and traditions for nobility doing so in ED. As for reality, he wasn't about to have five to ten sons all with A names if he could help it.

By the time Ava and Mia had received the nanite-infused stem cell booster that evening, Alex had accepted that they would be staying a full 24 hours due to their being two sets of twins, who were technically premature, if only barely. Still, they were all fine with it as they would rather be safe than sorry, even if the risks had been minimal. So it was that Alex found himself spending the night in the hospital with Ava and Mia and their four new babies.

(*****)

Morning March 29 to Evening March 30, 2268 & ED Year 6 Days 38-42.

When Alex made it home with Ava, Mia, Evan, Nova, Aidan and Nadia in the early afternoon of the 29th, they were greeted with smiles as they spent the day just visiting with everyone until after dinner. This marked the longest Alex could remember being offline since ED had launched, as despite the messages from Kate assuring him that everything was fine in ED, he still felt anxious. So it was that after dinner he found Ava and Mia telling him to hurry up and take care of what he needed to and that they would see him in the morning as he kissed them and returned to ED.

Monday the 30th saw Alex returning to his normal schedule for the most part, though he took a four-hour break in the morning and a three-hour one in the evening. He still couldn't help but smile at the four newborns who were being watched in one of the bedrooms below the area that was just his and his wives'. This would be the case until the nap room, which was currently in the final stages before actual construction started at this point, was completed in the nursery. At the same time, another of the rooms was being used for watching Ahsa, Moyra, Andy and Evelyn during the construction as the house adjusted to its new reality again.

When Xeal finally made it back to ED on day 38, he found himself catching up on the time he had missed with his wives and children who had not yet been evacuated. As Enye had been firm on them not leaving Hardt Burgh until they either reached tier-7, were carrying another child, or the city as a whole was being evacuated. She was of the opinion that if the marriage meeting was to continue, they could not leave without making it seem as if the danger of remaining was greater than Xeal was making it out to be. As much as this frustrated him, he was also happy to still get the kisses and hugs that he was so used to while he looked at his children running around awkwardly as they played. At around 29 months old, it was clear that all of them were the best of friends as they didn't even realize anything was off, besides the fact that Prince Vicenc was gone. He and Queen Nora had been evacuated to Cielo city already, along with Princesses Bianca and Lorena, who had all been accompanied by a small contingent of royal knights and servants.

Still, Xeal wanted to see his wives reach tier-7 and head to Cielo city as soon as possible and was just happy that they were quickly leveling under the care of the four dragonoid women. Even so, they were expected to reach tier-7 after he did at their current pace and that would put them past what Xeal felt was safe. However, all there was to do was to ensure that the guards on his children were increased and place a pseudo mark on each of his children, bringing his stock of phoenix blood down to 22 drops. Though he still had 92 feathers if he included the ones that had been made into medallions, though many of these were being used to ensure the NPCs that FAE was training were safe when tiering up. While none had failed so far, save the five young noblemen that had done so in the first group Xeal had been nurturing, that was also the only group to have attempted to reach tier-6 as of yet.

Still, Xeal felt that the 92 feathers were more than enough for what was needed as he focused on catching up on work all day. Though as night came, he smiled as he received a request to meet up with Lori Lunaflower once more as she told him she might have an answer. As Xeal entered the private room of the tavern that he had been requested to meet her in, he smiled at seeing her waiting for him with a torn expression on her face. As she noticed Xeal, she didn't even try to hide it and as she spoke, she did so cautiously with each word chosen carefully.

"Xeal, thank you for meeting me. I wanted to reach out to you a few days ago, but my information says that congratulations are in order. Four more children in one day. I must say that is something that intimidates even I to think about."

"Yes, well, I have many who are by my side that are willing to help."

"Indeed, now onto the answer to your desire to acquire Night Oath. Our price is 200,000,000 credits and guarantees that we will still be free to take any freelance contracts that we want."

"The credits aren't an issue, but any freelance contracts need to be done such that they comply with a set of guidelines that FAE sets. After all, while I understand the reasons that your members want to do so, FAE needs to protect its reputation."

"You can't just expect us to limit ourselves to those FAE is in conflict with."

"Lori, I am aware, but I can't have Abysses End paying your members to target the guild leader of one of our allies either. All I can promise is that once the war in Nium is over, that if the player is not a member of a directly allied power, or on a do not hit list, that they should be fine taking such jobs."

At Xeal's words, Lori frowned as she thought them over until she sighed and responded.

"That will work for all but about 1,000 of my members,

as they are hardcore about never having any limits on the hits they can do. I suspect that a few would even take a hit on me if the price was right and the rest would take any that wasn't on a guildmate. The rest of us know better than pissing off the wrong players, especially after you proved how easy it is to figure out who we are. Though I am still trying to figure out how you found my real name without help from Eternal Dominion Inc."

"So, secrets are best held closely. As for the 1,000 who will walk under that condition, let them. Heck, hand the guild over to them if you want. As much as I would love to have their skills, they are not worth the headache of dealing with those who will only think of their own gains or motives, and not the consequences of their guild when they act."

"That is fair, but the other 4,000 might have an issue with abandoning them like that and they might decide that FAE is their new favorite target for ruining Night Oath."

Xeal paused as he considered this and thought back to how it had ripped him apart when Twilight Sky was acquired by Abysses End in his last life. While this was a much different situation, Xeal knew that not all of those who were in Night Oath would ever be in that situation. It was with this thought that Xeal formed his response.

"Lori, leave the decision up to the 1,000 who would refuse to join over such a restriction. Tell them that I have no desire to force anyone to join FAE and understand their desire to play ED the way they want. My offer only came as I need talent and I see Night Oath as an instant boost to my guild that if invested in, will return dividends over time and I believe our core values don't clash. That said, also be clear to them about reality as I can honestly say that your guild is in a precarious situation and while I think that you could survive the war, it is not certain either. Do that and let me know by midday tomorrow."

"Do you really think that they will vote for me to accept your deal?"

"No, but if things start to fall apart, it will earn me enough goodwill to recruit you then."

"Fair. Well, I suppose I need to call a meeting. Hopefully it goes well."

Xeal just smiled as they said their goodbyes and he returned to handling everything that needed to be done before turning in for the night.

Days 39 and 40 passed with Xeal grinding and receiving an update from Lori that simply read that it had been close, but at least for the moment Night Oath was going to remain independent. While this disappointed Xeal, it also didn't come as a surprise to him as he adjusted his plans and looked over what resources he had to shift around to maximize their use. At the top of this list was the mirror shards and the new items that functioned like them, only with more restrictions. Instead of matching the level of the user, it maxed out at the level of the dungeon that they had been recovered in, which was great as it relaxed the demand for the mirror shards. This caused Xeal to think about the possibility of at least partially merging the mirror shards once he reached tier-7 and seeing how many it took to be worth still using at level 279. Still, that was a ways away and for now, his party and the other elites of FAE had top priority on all such resources as they focused on reaching tier-7 before summer hit in reality.

When Xeal returned to ED on day 41, he sighed knowing that today was a make or break maneuver, as he would be taking on his quest that had been delayed due to the events of reality. This just put Xeal up against the clock as the most vulnerable dwarven cities were in dire need of relief already and if it didn't come soon, the rest of the war would be much harder to finish. It was with these thoughts that Xeal made his way to the royal palace after spending a bit of time with his children, and retrieved the same teleportation device that King Victor had loaned him on prior occasions. As Xeal held it once more, he sighed as the minor probing about getting one of his own had been met with a stone wall as it was clear that such devices were not going to be sold lightly. It was also through this that Xeal learned that Nium only had two of them and had King Victor not trusted Xeal completely, he would have never even shown the device to him, much less let him borrow it.

Still, Xeal knew that it wasn't something to take for granted as he drank an invisibility potion and activated the teleportation device. With that, Xeal found himself in the bottom of the valley that created the easiest land path between Habia and Paidhia and surrounded on all sides. On two sides were the mountains that made the valley and two sides that were blocked by forts that were manned by Habia and Paidhia respectively. It was at these forts where Xeal's task lay on this quest, as he read the quest notification once more.

(Quest: "Create a breach in the defenses between Habia and Paidhia." Rewards: unknown. Warning: failing the quest will have negative repercussions on your account.)

As he looked over the quest, Xeal knew that a true success would only happen if war actually broke out between the two nations. So, his plans were far more intricate than simply attempting to blow a hole in a wall that would take weeks to repair, or any other normal sabotage attempt. No, Xeal spent the full day drinking one invisibility potion after another as he noted the habits of both sides and completed all of his prep work. Finally, as the sun set, it was time to execute his plan as Xeal set up the teleportation gate in a small cave that was little more than a hollow that was at about the midpoint of the two forts. A message later and Daisy and Violet stepped through, wearing smiles as they joined him and cast an invisibility spell that would keep them all invisible to others, while allowing them to see each other. The only downside to this spell was that it required both fox-women to maintain it as it slowly drained their MP pool.

Still, Xeal just smiled as he guided them by using hand signals, due to talking breaking their spell, as they got a look at the guards at each fort. These forts were essentially just large walls with turrets atop them, roughly two miles apart. Once they had a good point of reference, it was time to get to work as one buff item after another was used to enhance both Daisy's and Violet's illusion magic, as they began conjuring up illusions that would be seen differently from both walls. Though it would essentially be the same scene playing out as the soldiers would see the other side launching an assault and feel the spell mines that Xeal had set up hitting their wall. These mines were a new product that came out of FAE's enchanting department, with them launching projectile spells at 15 to 70-degree angles. They also could be triggered remotely and were practically invisible due to them being made with the skin of a chameleon monster, allowing them to take on the color of the ground beneath them. If Xeal were to estimate how much he had spent to lay out this battlefield, he would say it was well north of 10,000 gold and that was with him not paying the portion that FAE normally took.

Still, Xeal smiled as a fog bank seemed to roll in and the illusionary forces seemed to descend from both walls through the use of ropes, ladders and even magic. It wasn't long before shouts rang out and alarms were raised, while the illusions seemed to charge forward into battle while Xeal used the spell mines to send a mix of spells at both sides. As these slammed into the wall at a pre-determined point, it gave off the appearance of a coordinated effort to destroy a portion of the wall in preparation for a second assault. This in turn led to the forces on both sides actually descending the walls as all ranged attacks were seemingly met with a force shield. Xeal really grew to appreciate just how skilled both Daisy and Violet were, as he watched the details that they were able to maintain. Though doing so came at the cost of them not being able to do more than breathe and maintain their invisibility spell, as they sat cross-legged in front of Xeal while he watched the scene play out.

Once the counter forces on both sides were about to attack, Xeal set off the rest of the spell mines laid in the field, signaling that Daisy and Violet should have it seem like the illusions were retreating. Both forces pursued the illusions, in fear of letting them escape to launch a similar assault in the future without consequences. Daisy and Violet were allowing the pursuers to slowly close the distance with the illusions such that just before the two illusions crossed each other, they made it seem that they had turned to fight just as the real soldiers slammed into each other. While each side only had about a thousand soldiers at the start, the sounds of battle quickly intensified as more and more soldiers joined the battle from both sides and a true mess followed. Xeal knew that each side had over 100,000 soldiers stationed near enough to arrive in eight hours and that as they arrived by the thousands, they would likely create a feedback loop. Were this to be allowed to continue without any intervention, the result would likely be nothing more than massive losses on both sides as they were evenly matched.

However, Xeal had one last spell mine placed at the base of each wall and of all the ones he had placed, it was these ones that were the most costly as they were void mines. Unlike the rest that had to travel through air, these mines would instantly move a certain distance away and teleport anything that was within a ten-foot half dome of that point to a designated location. In this case, Xeal had aimed the target such that it would target the foundations of the wall right below where all the spells had hit and send it directly above the wall at the same point. As Xeal triggered these mines, he watched as a sink hole essentially opened below the walls and a mound of earth and stone fell on top of the wall on both sides. The effect of this was instant as the walls gave out and crumbled at those points, as the men locked in combat continued to fight in the illusionary fog and those on the wall rushed to defend the breaches. Calls for more forces came from both sides and now whichever side won would push forward, neither side able to back out after such an event.

(Quest, Create a breach in the defenses between Habia and Paidhia: Complete. Calculating completion rate… 125% completion, rank SSSS. Rewards: 100,000,000,000,000 XP, 20,000 guild renown points, and 25,000 gold)

Xeal blinked once at the results as they were beyond what he had thought possible, as the XP was worth more than a day of grinding. Next, he had just hoped to break even in this quest, yet he had profited and the guild renown was a nice bonus, though an SSSS-ranked result was beyond anything he had heard of. Still, Xeal didn't linger as he tapped Daisy and Violet to let them know that it was time to go as he drank one last invisibility potion. As they escaped through the teleportation gate, Xeal packed it away and used the teleportation device that King Victor had lent him to arrive in Dhurnrim. Once there, he found himself alone in a room with King Dorrin Dragonaxe who looked and sounded like he was exhausted as he spoke to Xeal.

"Has hell descended upon the surface?"

"It would appear so and while I expect your lands to remain sieged, the pressure should be reduced and if all you do is focus on holding the line, you should outlast this. Though if what I just started is allowed to grow, it will likely cause you to only be sieged by one, or the other, eventually."

"Ye think that ye caused them tur become that committed?"

"When I left, both sides seemed to be emptying their forts and I expect losses to be too high on both sides for either to take a step back now. Though if they gain irrefutable proof that all of this was my doing, it could be bad for me, so don't share too much."

"They will know that it was ye. It will be clear tur them the moment anyone with half a brain looks at things. Now, about how ye're treating my son and daughter. Just what is yer intent in training Dafasli up while leaving Thatram tur languish?"

"Simple, Dafasli has yet to cause me any issues. Your son, on the other hand, seemed to think that he was the one who controlled her future. That and he and I never seemed to be on the same page as far as what powers he has and doesn't have inside the mines and believe me, I tried to let him govern and learn. I even thought that he might have until this latest instance."

"Oh, ye sent my daughter tur make a fool of him and-"

"I sent her to check if he was ready to lead the residents in the mine to support the war effort. Yes, I set him up to fail if he tried to confront her about her absence and didn't accept that she was beyond his reach, but it's his own fault for not holding his temper."

"Right, ye didn't care that during so would let ye hand

power over tur Darefret for the war."

"I did and had you sent me a dwarf with half a brain instead of Harrulir like you did, well, Dafasli would still be training with a few of my wives and wouldn't have been able to do what she did."

"Say what ye will, but I expect that my son will be allowed tur redeem himself."

"That will be up to him. After all, I am not going to ignore his failings. If he wants to gain my respect, it will need to be earned."

"As long as ye don't intend tur refuse to recognize his achievements once he is ready. Now, about ye and my daughter, when is the wedding?"

"Who says I am marrying her? King Dorrin, while she is working towards that being a possibility, I have not made any such commitment to consider her for courtship."

"Sure, sure, ye know that ye are playing with fire then. After all, from what I hear, she be set on ye and tur others it looks like ye tur are involved. I will say this but once. If ye insult my honor, or my daughter's, ye better hide with the dragonoids as it will be I who seeks ye out tur settle things otherwise."

"King Dorrin, it is good to know that she has your blessing, but I will not marry her out of fear of you, nor will I simply accept her because she is chasing me. I will treat her the same as any other who wishes to stand by my side, on and off the battlefield at this point."

"Ha, ye act as if ye durn't know how things will turn out. Ye and I both know how stubborn my daughter can be. So, ye better just be ready to accept her, be that now, or in a decade. She will wear ye down someday."

"If you say so…"

Xeal was happy to shift topics before spending another hour going over the current situation, as he sent the order for the gate between FAE's headquarters and Dhurnrim to be opened. Xeal knew that over the next few days supplies and reinforcements would stream in, before the gate was closed until it was needed once again. The last thing Xeal or King Dorrin Dragonaxe wanted was a path for deserters to escape through, or invaders to reach Dhurnrim through. Once Xeal saw everything was in order, he left another bead with King Dorrin Dragonaxe as he returned to Nium through the newly opened gate. As he came out on the other side, he made his way to his mansion in the capital. Upon entering, he was greeted by Daisy and Violet who were all smiles and dressed in their nightwear as Daisy spoke.

"That was certainly an intense situation."

"Yes, and I will hold up my end of the bargain," replied Xeal halfheartedly.

"If you don't want to, we won't force you," replied Violet. "After all, we want to move closer to you, not farther."

"No, I am not withholding this as it is a rather reasonable request and you obtained permission from everyone else before asking for it. I just worry that I am going to get in over my head."

"You are already there," quipped Daisy. "Letting Violet and I help you fix that will only do you good."

"Yes, we promise to not add to your burden and are willing to take our time," added Violet with a smile.

"Right, because the solution to loving too many women is to add more to that list," retorted Xeal. "Sorry, but I am not following your logic."

"It's not about logic," replied Violet. "It's about balance and we will help bring that to your house, even at our own cost at this point."

"Yes, all your wives know that each lady you add reduces

the time you have with them," commented Daisy. "Especially in terms of the ever precious alone time that they rarely get, but once you accept us, we can boost you such that you will be able to spend less time grinding and more time at home."

Xeal just sighed as they had explained about how their ability worked as it reduced the experience needed by a third and provided a permanent boost to all other stats. Still, Xeal wasn't going to simply accept them to take advantage of such an ability as he responded.

"Everything is a two-way street. Now let's get some rest as I am sure that King Victor will have much to discuss with me in the morning."

At that Daisy and Violet smiled as they walked with Xeal as they made their way to his master bedroom, where they would get to spend the night snuggling with him. This had been the price they had asked for and had been agreed on, a single night of snuggling with him and nothing more. As Xeal fell asleep that night, he couldn't help but smile at them as they slept peacefully while using his arms as pillows.

The following morning, Xeal awoke to Kate clearing her throat as the three of them had shifted greatly during the night. This had caused Xeal to find both Daisy and Violet on top of him such that his head was sandwiched under their chests, a fact that they both only realized after being awake for a long moment. At which point they both seemed to just giggle before rolling away and getting out of bed while Xeal sat up as Kate spoke.

"I am just going to put that one under your bodies shifting in the night. Now, Xeal, are you ready to hear just what you caused?"

"Yes, but I doubt I am going to like the number of dead."

"Xeal, it's war. Losses on at least one side are necessary and inevitable. As for the death toll from last night, it was around 10,000 between both sides. At least according to the preliminary numbers, Paidhia has pushed into Habia and both are shifting forces to wage a full-out war with the other. At the same time, they are drafting any and all able-bodied men and women to fill their ranks. They have even started to pay adventurers to help them level up the new recruits. They definitely had a plan in place before today. Unfortunately this is one of the scenarios that has the potential for the greatest losses over time if allowed to persist."

"At the same time, it will aid in our propaganda once we start getting serious, especially as it will take time for them to train any NPCs from being farm hands to the peak of tier-5," replied Xeal morosely.

"Either way, it just highlights the struggle that is before us."

"Yah, so what are your current estimations showing?"

"A decimation of both nations at the very least, with one in ten NPCs dying before all battles are fought by mostly players. It could reach as bad as a third of all NPCs being killed."

"Xeal, you aren't going to let that happen, right?" inquired Violet, sounding worried. "I mean, you have said all along that your goal is to limit deaths of those native to this world."

"I am not letting anything happen. I am simply going to do what I can to mitigate the losses the best I can. Now, before I make any promises, I need to meet with Victor."

Xeal could tell that Violet wanted to keep speaking, but held back as he gave Kate a kiss as he took the paper copy of the report she had made. Xeal then surprised Violet and Daisy by giving them each a hug and sharing a few reassuring words before heading out. An hour later and he was seated alone with King Victor, as they both looked over the report of Xeal's actions as well as Habia's and Paidhia's as they discussed the options before them.

"Xeal, I don't see how you can expect me not to call upon the citizens to take up arms when both Paidhia and Habia have already."

"Victor, call for them to train, but make it clear it is voluntary and that you would only call upon them to defend their homes should Habia's or Paidhia's invasion reach them. Forced conscripts are never healthy for the morale of a military, or effectiveness of its actions and my hope is that your response will force Habia and Paidhia to alter their plans. After all, the last thing they need to do is train the very masses that will rise up and rebel."

"I hear you, but I can't agree. All established military doctrine says to call up the populace now, lest they fall behind the populace of Habia or Paidhia."

"That is why you need to impress upon them that while it is voluntary, that you highly suggest that they not sit idly while ignoring your words. However, you should plan to throw out established military doctrine as you know it now, in another six months. After all, from the training that you put your commanders through in preparation for this, it should be clear that it will only increase your losses as the war intensifies."

"Yes, well, that is six months that we can't afford to ignore."

"Victor, will a significant amount of conscripts be ready to fight by then?"

"No, but this is war. We need to do everything we can to win it."

"No amount of tier-5 citizens will change anything when you have an endless supply of tier-5 and tier-6 adventurers and that is what you will have in six months."

"Fine, I will trust you, but if the majority of the citizenry fails to put their all into leveling up, I am going to have to begin conscripting them."

"I will have Kate ensure the kingdom is aware of the dangers of doing nothing, as well as the benefits for those who volunteer to fight and distinguish themselves."

"Alright, now before we move on, I suppose I should thank you for completing all the quests that you were assigned, even if you did pass some of them off to your subordinates."

(Quest line, For Nium's prosperity: Complete. Calculating completion rate... 90% completion, rank A. Rewards: 200,000,000,000,000 XP, 30,000 guild renown points, and 50,000 gold)

Xeal simply smiled as he saw the notification as he thought about how it had made up for the extra time that he had been offline recently before responding.

"Yes, well, I must say that it was rather rewarding on its own..."

As Xeal finished accepting King Victor's praise, they shifted to other topics surrounding the war as the morning turned into the afternoon and Xeal left the palace. At level 192, Xeal only needed to gain seven more levels to attempt to reach tier-7 and while he was confident in reaching it, he also knew the rude awakening that many players would receive when they made their attempt. After all, if FAE managed to have 1,000 of the first 10,000 players that it sent through pass, Xeal would be ecstatic. It was with this thought and goal that Xeal spent the rest of the day focused on as he returned to the grind, monotonous as it could be, once again. Still, with Dafasli's declaration, and the night he shared with Daisy and Violet being known, it caused his time with his party to become even more awkward. Not because any of his party members were making it so, but because he intimately knew Bula's true feelings and he couldn't help but think about how all of this was making her feel. Despite the stoic persona that she was currently presenting to them all, Xeal knew that she was in pain and that if a solution wasn't found, it could ruin the cohesion of his whole party if left to fester.

(*****)

Preview.

Xeal found himself dealing with many things, both good and bad, as he handled things in-between his grinding sessions in ED. The first of these was the return of the five ex-pirate captains after Queen Aila Lorafir had taken care of getting them set up to attempt to create their own legacy. While Xeal didn't know the exact details of this process, he did know that it was a unique experience every time. While many legacies could be similar, they could never be identical. That was unless it was a shared legacy like what the five captains had been attempting to create. As Xeal received the summons to come and see the results of their attempt, he laughed at the fact that it had failed to mention if they had succeeded, or failed to ascend to tier-8. Still, he figured that Queen Aila Lorafir was just having a bit of fun as he made his way there on day 44 with Eira in tow.

When he arrived, he was greeted by Queen Aila Lorafir's guards and let in as if he was more of a resident than a guest. This was something that Xeal was still getting used to as while he was no longer escorted out by guards at Nium's royal palace, he was still guided to King Victor each time. Though he knew it was due to the fact that he was in a relationship with Queen Aila Lorafir, even if it was a measured one that wouldn't be consummated until her daughter Alea took over the duties of ruling. Still, as Xeal made his way around on his way to the room that Queen Aila Lorafir had instructed him to head to in her summons, he wondered just what the five illusionists' new legacy would be like. Though as he stepped into the room, he was met with a scene that was not what he expected. Sitting there were the five ex-pirate captains looking exhausted and jittery like you would expect from someone who had been thoroughly traumatized by something, and even after escaping didn't believe they had. Each of them was surrounded by a blue dome made of force magic that Queen Aila Lorafir was maintaining as she looked at Xeal with a frown as she started to speak.

"I am sorry, but it appears that they failed and each of them was essentially scared to death during their attempt at ascending. I wish that my summons had been good news, but it seems that their minds are beyond my ability to recover. As such, I am recommending that we simply put them each out of their misery."

Xeal frowned as he looked at the five women that had once seemed so sure of themselves and defiant, and sighed as he rested his hand on the hilts of his swords.

"It seems that I was mistaken in believing that they could-"

Xeal quickly flung his sword at Odelia who was the closest and watched as the blade bounced off the shield and clattered to the ground. Queen Aila Lorafir was just about to speak when Xeal held out his hand as he recalled the tiny bit of electricity that he had left in the blade after activating his elemental blades skill. Instead of coming from the sword on the ground, it came from off in the distance as he spoke.

"I have to say that you almost got me. Honestly, you should have had one, or two, of you still be sane if you wanted me to believe it. Would have also made a much better scene for you all to act out."

"It seems that they will need to do a bit more work," replied Queen Aila Lorafir from Xeal's right as the scene before him dissolved. "Still, I wish you would have touched something before ruining my fun. Now here, try this apple."

"I order that all illusions being cast by Odelia, Saphielle, Sylmare, Cremia and Itylara are to be dropped right now!"

As Xeal finished speaking, he smiled as Queen Aila Lorafir became Odelia holding a lemon and the other four could be seen in the four corners of the room. Queen Aila Lorafir could be seen seated along the far wall from where Xeal entered looking smug as she spoke.

"You could have at least played along and eaten the apple."

"Aila, I didn't believe the scene, so sorry, but I doubt that it would have tasted like an apple. You would have kissed me before offering me the apple."

"True, now let them turn that lemon back into an apple and see if that is true," replied Queen Aila Lorafir.

"Don't tell me that they can alter reality with their illusions now. That would break more than a few rules of what I understand."

"We don't alter reality, we alter your perception of it," retorted Odelia. "You were the only one who saw anything. I did nothing to shift my voice, yet you heard me as if it was Aila speaking, even after you stopped believing I was."

"While there is still more testing to do, they each have the ability to completely fool one of the five main senses even if you know it's a lie," commented Queen Aila Lorafir. "The only drawback is that it requires all five of them to work together if they wish to fool all five senses."

"Which is why we wish to be placed on the same ship for this war," added Odelia. "That way we can truly rule the seas. Just imagine what will happen when we put an entire fleet under such an illusion."

Xeal instantly thought of sailors seeing a massive fleet of hundreds of ships emerging from a fog and thinking that thousands of attacks were headed for them. Add the results of them believing that their perfectly intact ship was sinking, and the ability to capture vessels with no fight became insane and too easy. Xeal frowned as he thought about this and replied.

"What is the drawback? Anything that broken must be balanced by something."

(*****)

Thanks!

Thank you to all of my patrons on Patreon, especially my knight-tier patrons Ottojanius, Jim Hall, Carl Benge, Alexander Casey Donnell, Timelesschief, Christof Köberlein, Benjamin Grey, Casey, Daniel Sifrit, Michael Jackson, Tim Bartlett, Jeffrey Iverson, JWR, James Vierra, David Peers, Kyle J Smith, Roman Smith, William J Dinwiddie II, Rick White, Ryan Harrington, Michael Mitchell, Stefan Zimmermann, Grantland Case, Francisco Brito, Peter Barton, Peter Hepp, Kore Rahl, Joel Stapleton, Lazai, Richard Schlak, Shard73, Blackpan2, Thomas Watret, Adamantine, William Adams, Matthew, Douglas Sokolowski, Edwin Courser, Sam Ellis, Andrew Eliason, Nick Stockfleth, DAvid Marksz, Fred Rankin, Georg Kranz, William Puryear, AR Schleicher, Angus Christopher, Collateral_ink, Roy Cales, JOHNNY SMILEY, Thomas Corbin, Spencer Ryan Crawford, Outwardwander, David Guilliams, Bern DG, Christopher Gross, Tony Fino, Ciellandros, David French, CannonFodder, Dances with Kobolds, ABritishGuy, PeeM, F0ZYWOLF, Dan Dragonwolf, Marvin Wells, Dominic Q Roddan, Tanner Lovelace, Daniel Diaz, yo dude, Aimee Hebert, James A. Murphy, Mark reilly, Erebus Drakul Zaydow, tawshif tamjid, Kor Vang and nathrielos.

(*****)

Afterword.

Well would you look at that, April has come and gone and it is May! At least for all of you who are reading this. For me it is just barely April. As some of you may be aware, I am currently writing while my wife is away on work and I am handling both of my kids right now. Now, I do have help in the form of my parents and my nephew's fiancée, who is helping me out two of the three days my son has no preschool and the whole of their spring break. Thanks to that, I am at least getting between 50% and 80% of what I normally get done in a day after the first two weeks like this. Though, I think part of that is all the other stuff I have going on surrounding the big push that I made at the start of April. Hopefully it all paid off and my audiobooks will see good growth, as I work to secure the next group of them to be produced. That said, so long as I can get a deal that makes sense done, I will be working to ensure that they all get finished one day, even if I have to eat a loss to do so. After all, I am a completionist when it comes to writing and reading a story, and I will not leave any part of my audience hanging forever.

Speaking of that, I am really enjoying the current part of Eternal Dominion that I am writing, as I am finally to the long-awaited war. Not to mention all of the tier-7 tribulations and oh man, am I having fun with them, though my editor tells me I am evil. Either way, I hope you all are looking forward to this major arc that will have lasting consequences for the remainder of the series, as the build-up to the end. Though, that is still between 10 and 18 books away, depending on how things flow, though I feel like 14 more for a total of 32 books sound right to me. I know I am basically telling you all that you are only around halfway through this story, but on the other hand, that means that you still get to enjoy these monthly releases for a while longer. After all, I think I am going to slow down and just release every other month with my next series.

Now, don't think that I am planning not to write two books a month. I am just going to be focusing on having enough books done that I won't worry about taking time off when I want to. I will admit that I really pushed myself with my current schedule and workload and well, had I kept my books around 60,000 words, I would be fine, but at 75,000-plus words, well, I want to breathe again. Especially as I am going to be looking at possibly going to 90,000-plus words in each book to try and make sure that the audiobook length is better for the algorithmic overlords. Though we will see, as it means that I need to increase the word count of book 1 of my next series by around 10,000 words and I hate fluff that is just there to pad the word count. That isn't to say that I don't leave unnecessary things in, though what is and isn't necessary is something only I will know, at least until I write the words the end for the very first time.

That said, I know that I was hopeful to get the first book of my second series out this spring, or summer, but I just can't see me getting to it until I have the first draft of the last book in Eternal Dominion done. I think it is just part of how I write right now, as I have basically been spending around 40% of all my time focused on the world of Eternal Dominion. The short time that I tried to split it such that I was writing two different stories, it was just too hard to switch between them. What I am hoping to be able to do with my next series is to try to do it again, only while extending the time that each book spends in the hands of others, as they help me refine each of them. So, I will essentially be writing a book in one series before doing one in a different one. I know that this is how several authors out there do it and I want to try it out for a while, so I always have two series going in the future. Put simply, it is a bit of insurance, just in case one of my stories does really poorly and I find myself needing to support me completing it from the other's funds.

After all, I am still holding to my mantra, "Write for yourself, not for someone else, or you'll never love what you write." So, never fear, while the cover art may suffer, I will never lower the standard of what is inside of each of my books as I craft stories that I would want to read and hope others enjoy them as well. Be that just enough to pay the bills to create them, or 500,000,000, I don't care. Once I publish book 1 in any series, so long as I still draw breath, I am committed to finishing it no matter what it takes. Now, I think I will leave you with that and ask that if you know someone who you think would enjoy my story, please introduce it to them. I can run all the ads in the world and go on every podcast in existence, but nothing will move the needle like a friend recommending it to them. After all, one of my favorite things to do is talk about books with those who enjoy the same ones I do.

Now, as always, I hope you all are doing well and staying safe out there. Now take care and read more books!

Now onto the repetitive stuff. Did you know I have a newsletter and that by signing up you can get a free prelude novella for Eternal Dominion? Heck, it is really easy too. Just go to my website below and scroll to the bottom, where you will just need to put in your email address. Or you can go to https://BookHip.com/BAMDFBA, put in your email the single time and confirm it in your inbox to get the prelude and sign up for my newsletter in one go.

If you haven't already, go to https://soundbooththeater.com/team/bern-dean/ and listen to the free shorts that are available there. If you do it through a web browser you don't even need to create an account to do so, just select the listen now option. Zach and Annie have really gone above and beyond with their performances!

As always, if you feel I have forgotten something, feel free to reach out to me on Facebook through my page, or join my group. I am only one person and sending a message to my Facebook author page is the fastest way to get me to see it, as I don't get alerts on my personal page when non-friends message me for the first time. That said, I will not answer personal questions, like where I live, even in a general fashion. Please keep it to my story, or my writing process.

If you would like a weekly extra that focuses on looking at the supporting cast and is not plot necessary but is canon, I publish shorts on my Patreon. The first several of which are currently available to my $1 patrons, who will get another one every four weeks, while my $5 patrons get one each week. If you want to see what these are like, I have put a few up on my Facebook group as well now. I also now have a $5.50 tier for those who want to read the first 5 to 7 thousand words of the next book a week or so early, as that is when I have it back from the copy editor. To be clear, I delete the extended preview just before, or after, the book it is attached to is released. Some may ask why the extra 50 cents and to that I give two reasons. I have had some patrons tell me that they don't want the extended preview and it lets them ignore it. Also, it allows me to see just how much demand there is for extended previews.

https://www.facebook.com/groups/berndean

https://www.facebook.com/Author.Bern.Dean
https://www.patreon.com/berndean
https://www.Bernsbooks.com

Thank you again for reading my story and I hope you return for the next installment of Alex's tale. If you enjoy LitRPG and GameLit books, check out the following Facebook groups. Both are great and have helped me get my stories out to you!

LitRPG:

https://www.facebook.com/groups/LitRPG.books

GameLit:

https://www.facebook.com/groups/LitRPGsociety

Made in the USA
Monee, IL
01 July 2024

61040457R00152